A NEW LEAF

"After I spoke with you on the phone yesterday, I chatted with Amos and Mattie Troyer," Kraybill continued matter-of-factly. "And I asked Marlene how she'd feel about you working here—especially while I was away."

"Wh-what'd they say?" Isaac rasped. If his former neighbors had all expressed their negative sentiments about him, he'd been doomed before he'd arrived. His instant, smoldering attraction to pretty Vera was going nowhere.

"They all echoed Rosetta, Christine, and Deborah," the storekeeper replied. He was still leaning on his elbows, observing Isaac so calmly, yet so intently, that Isaac started to sweat. Why didn't this guy just send him packing and get it over with?

"But I figured you knew what you'd be up against when you applied for this job, Isaac," Kraybill continued. "You anticipated being under everyone's scrutiny, yet you took a chance and answered my ad—surely you realized I'd know about your past."

Truth be told, Isaac had been in such a rush to get out of Coldstream, he hadn't considered his former neighbors' reactions—and on that count, he'd fallen short. He'd also underestimated the man sitting across from him.

"To me, that means you've got moxie—if you're truly looking for a fresh start."

Miracles at PROMISE LODGE

Charlotte Hubbard

ZEBRA BOOKS
Kensington Publishing Corp.
www.kensingtonbooks.com

He hath shewed thee, O man, what is good; and what doth the Lord require of thee, but to do justly, and to love mercy, and to walk humbly with thy God?

—*Micah 6:8*

Acknowledgments

Many thanks go to God for the energy and imagination to complete this story—and to finish this Promise Lodge series!

Many thanks, as well, to my editor, Alicia Condon, for her ideas and enthusiasm for my Amish stories. And special thanks to my agent, Evan Marshall, for advising my career for more than twenty years!

Also, a word of appreciation to Vicki Harding in Jamesport, Missouri, and to the network of Amish friends—especially Verna Graber—who have answered my questions about the Amish faith. Guidance about Mennonite services has come from Mary Ann Hake. If I've gotten things wrong over the years, it's my fault and not theirs!

This book's dedicated to the many friends we've made at Presbyterian Church of the Cross in Omaha, who have welcomed us—and become avid readers of my stories.

Chapter 1

As Isaac Chupp entered the bulk store at Promise Lodge, he was immediately aware of how bright and clean it was—and that all the aisles ran perpendicular to the checkout counter. Compared to Coldstream's tired old market, it was a step into the twenty-first century: the glass-front refrigerator units and overhead lights were electric, and their radiance was reflected in large mirrors that covered the upper walls. The owner, Dale Kraybill, was Mennonite—

And he's savvy. From the checkout counter, he can see everyone in his store.

In the mirrors, Isaac noted that several shoppers, Plain and English alike, were pushing carts along the well-stocked aisles. He stepped away from the front door to browse while the storekeeper helped a young woman in an Amish-style *kapp* set up a display of the most colorful pottery dishes he'd ever seen. He wanted to know something about the store's organization before he introduced himself to Kraybill, who'd recently run an ad for help. The store's owner had spoken at length with Isaac over the phone yesterday before inviting him to come for an interview.

If he got the job, today—July fifth—could be his personal declaration of independence. He'd step into a whole new world, leaving his narrow-minded *dat* behind—

"Vera, your pottery will fly off the shelves!" Kraybill said to the young woman. "I'm glad you've decided to sell your pieces here."

Isaac's eyes widened. If his father, Bishop Obadiah of Coldstream's Amish community, were here, he'd order the girl to pack up her colorful wares and confess before the congregation because she was sinful—too artistically inclined. The way his *dat* saw it, God would never accept her because she'd broken the conservative mold of Amish conformity.

Vera blushed modestly at Kraybill's compliment. When she smiled at Isaac, the nerdy, endearing way she pushed up her glasses made his heart turn a flip-flop.

"*Denki*, Dale, you're very kind," she said in a low voice. "You've given me quite an opportunity to display my work."

Opportunity? Have I got an opportunity for you, Miss Vera!

Isaac sucked in his breath, hoping she couldn't hear his hammering heart.

I have to get this job! I have to convince this beautiful, unique girl that I'm the one for her!

Where had that idea come from? At nineteen, he'd never given a thought to a permanent relationship, yet just one look—and the sound of Vera's voice—had sent him off the deep end.

While Dale and Vera finished the pottery display, Isaac forced himself to focus. He could *not* come across as a lovesick puppy who would moon over Vera. He reminded himself of the experience he'd acquired while clerking for his father's auction company—not to mention his expertise at setting up the sale barn's computer and recordkeeping system. He rehearsed all the positive-sounding reasons he was ready to come to work for Kraybill at Promise Lodge, three hours away from his family in Coldstream.

After smoothing his shirt beneath his suspenders and putting on his best smile, Isaac stepped forward with his hand extended. "Mr. Kraybill? Is this a *gut* time to talk?" he asked enthusiastically. "I'm Isaac Chupp, and we spoke over the phone—"

"Isaac! Happy to meet you, young man," the steely-haired storekeeper said as they pumped hands. "And I admire a potential employee who shows up early to get the lay of the land, so to speak. Let's step back to my office. This young woman coming to run the cash register is Marlene Lehman—"

Isaac held Marlene's wide-eyed gaze, challenging her with his confident smile.

Yeah, it's me—looking for a new life, same as you were when you sold your farm in Coldstream without telling anyone.

He'd known Marlene all his life because she and her brother had recently moved here to escape his father's narrow-mindedness, as had many of the residents of Promise Lodge.

"—and you'll be answering to her while I'm away for a few days, after I marry Irene Wickey," Kraybill continued jovially. "As I told you over the phone, I'm looking for—"

"Is that Isaac Chupp?" a woman behind them asked loudly.

"Lo and behold, it *is* Isaac," another woman replied. "After our last run-in, I didn't figure he'd ever come back."

Isaac hadn't seen the women in the large mirrors, but he recognized their voices. He reminded himself that he'd been *invited* to interview—that he had every right to be in Dale Kraybill's store—yet his confidence sagged. Isaac had no choice but to turn and face two of the three sisters who'd transformed a deserted church camp into the thriving community of Promise Lodge.

Rosetta Wickey and Christine Burkholder stood beside another familiar young woman from his past, Deborah Peterscheim Schwartz. She held his gaze unflinchingly as she bounced a toddler on her hip.

Never one to beat around the bush, Rosetta crossed her arms. "What brings you to Promise Lodge, Isaac? Did I overhear Dale calling you a potential employee?"

"I hope you've left your beer—and your matches—at home," Christine chimed in. "I've just built a new dairy barn, and I don't want to look out some evening and see it engulfed in flames."

From the corner of his eye, Isaac caught Vera's startled expression as she gathered her empty boxes. And he couldn't miss the way Kraybill's face had tightened as he turned toward the three shoppers.

"What are you ladies saying?" he asked carefully. "I'm guessing you knew Isaac when you lived in Coldstream—"

"*Jah*, back when he used to smoke and drink with his English friends in our barns before they burned to the ground," Christine put in sternly.

"And let's not forget that Christine's husband died trying to save his livestock when their barn caught fire," Rosetta said as she slung her arm around her sister's shoulders. "And he shoved Deborah into a ditch out in the country because she'd called the sheriff when she spotted him in my family's burning barn."

"Isaac's behavior was the main reason my family left Coldstream a couple years ago," Deborah remarked quietly. She swayed with her child, a far cry from the frightened, vulnerable teenager who'd suffered Bishop Obadiah's vengeance after she'd reported Isaac's wrongdoing.

"And since we've come here, we've heard stories about money gone missing from his father's auction receipts, and we've caught him red-handed, forging his *mamm*'s handwriting in a letter," Rosetta added as she gazed purposefully at the storekeeper. "Be sure you're satisfied with Isaac's response to these issues, Dale. We hope you'll hold him accountable—and we hope you won't be sorry if you hire him."

Isaac's confidence bottomed out. His throat was so dry it clicked when he swallowed. But he had to defend himself. If Kraybill—and Vera—believed only what his accusers had said, he'd be going back to Coldstream with his tail between his legs. And he refused to do that.

"I came here hoping for a second chance—a fresh start with some of that forgiveness you Promise Lodge folks are known for," he stated in the firmest voice he could muster. "You and your families left Coldstream and moved on. I want to do that, too."

After a few moments of uncomfortable silence, Kraybill gestured for Isaac to follow him through the swinging double doors into the warehouse. They entered a small office with ledgers on the bookshelf and a computer on a side table. The storekeeper nodded toward a straight-back chair and then seated himself behind the modest desk. He looked at Isaac with calm blue-gray eyes that saw everything and gave away nothing about what he was thinking.

"Isaac, have you ever stolen anything from a store like this?"

Isaac's body tensed. Was that a trick question? Or was it a *test*?

He knew better than to drop Kraybill's steady gaze. The longer the silence stretched between them, however, the more the man behind the desk would figure out about him—in addition to what the Bender sisters and Deborah had revealed moments ago.

"Yeah, I have," Isaac admitted softly. "When I was a kid, I took odds and ends from the market in Coldstream—not because I really wanted the stuff, but because I wanted to get away with it. The old guy who owned the place back then was clueless."

"I imagine the store has changed since Raymond Overholt and his new bride, Lizzie, took it over earlier this year. I was sorry to see those kids go—but I'm sure the Overholt family's delighted that they're living in Coldstream."

As he spoke, Dale Kraybill's gaze didn't waver. His voice remained as cool and smooth as a shaded lake.

But still waters run deep. He knows more than he's saying—and he's going to hold it over me.

Isaac looked around the office, grasping for something that might save his bacon. "Look, about what Rosetta and Christine and Deborah were saying—"

"Your reputation has preceded you, Isaac. More than

half the families here came from Coldstream, after all, and they've known you all your life," Kraybill put in as he leaned forward on his desk.

Isaac braced himself. Although the storekeeper's voice and gaze remained unthreatening, he was about to dismiss Isaac without further ado—and Isaac understood why. After all, his older brothers had informed him last week that he wouldn't be clerking any more auctions. Sticky fingers, they'd called it.

And even though Raymond Overholt was hopelessly in love with his ditzy bride, Lizzie, Isaac was pretty sure Raymond wouldn't even *talk* to him about working in Coldstream's bulk store after enduring so many years of teasing and . . . well, *bullying*. Isaac had enjoyed razzing the artsy, red-spectacled Overholt kid because—before he'd joined the church and married Lizzie—he'd worn colorful, mismatched English clothes from the thrift store.

"After I spoke with you on the phone yesterday, I chatted with Amos and Mattie Troyer," Kraybill continued matter-of-factly. "And I asked Marlene how she'd feel about you working here—especially while I was away."

Isaac swallowed hard. Preacher Amos and Mattie—even when she'd been married to her first husband, Marvin Schwartz—had always been on his case, watching him as though they suspected he was up to something. Which had usually been true.

And Marlene was gawking at me in disbelief just now, wondering why Kraybill was even considering me for this interview.

"Wh-what'd they say?" Isaac rasped. If his former neighbors had all expressed their negative sentiments about him, he'd been doomed before he'd arrived. His instant, smoldering attraction to pretty Vera was going nowhere.

"They all echoed Rosetta, Christine, and Deborah," the storekeeper replied. He was still leaning on his elbows, observing Isaac so calmly, yet so intently, that Isaac started to sweat. Why didn't this guy just send him packing and get it over with?

"But I figured you knew what you'd be up against when you applied for this job, Isaac," Kraybill continued. "You anticipated being under everyone's scrutiny, yet you took a chance and answered my ad—surely you realized I'd know about your past."

Truth be told, Isaac had been in such a rush to get out of Coldstream, he hadn't considered his former neighbors' reactions—and on that count, he'd fallen short. He'd also underestimated the man sitting across from him.

"To me, that means you've got moxie—if you're truly looking for a fresh start."

Isaac's eyes widened. The people who'd told him to move on hadn't put any sort of positive spin on his situation. The word *moxie* had never figured into their conversations about his misdeeds. Isaac waited for Kraybill to speak next—waited for the proverbial other shoe to drop. The man had an unnerving knack for manipulating Isaac's responses with silence.

The storekeeper rocked back in his wooden chair. "Were Rosetta, Christine, and Deborah correct, Isaac? Did you burn down the two families' barns and leave Deborah in a ditch to walk home in torn clothing, after she called nine-one-one to report the barn fire at Rosetta's place?"

Isaac sighed. "*Jah*, but the fires weren't intentional. My English friends and I were drunk, and the lanterns must've gotten kicked over—"

"But you did nothing to make up for the damage you caused?"

Isaac glanced down at his lap. "No. I—"

"And your father, the bishop, didn't make reparations to those families, either? And he didn't hold you accountable?"

"Don't ask me to explain my *dat*'s behavior!" Isaac blurted out bitterly. "I have no idea why he didn't punish me or—"

"And the way I understand it, Deborah bore the brunt of her father, Preacher Eli's, judgment as well as the other church leaders' disapproval because she reported the fire?"

"They didn't like it that she got the cops involved. The Amish prefer to handle such matters themselves."

"You haven't yet joined the Amish church, correct?" Kraybill asked. "But being in *rumspringa* does *not* excuse you from acting like a decent human being and apologizing to those you've hurt."

Gripping the sides of his chair seat, Isaac knew better than to smart off—or to storm out, as he'd done when his father had lectured him. How had the storekeeper known that Dat had used *rumspringa* to gloss over his youngest son's errant behavior—even though no one in Coldstream had accepted that excuse any more than Kraybill had? Isaac couldn't explain it, but he felt the steely-haired storekeeper deserved a different level of respect than his father, who had tried—and failed—to demand Isaac's absolute obedience.

"If you're sincerely interested in a fresh start—and

if you're going to work in my store," Kraybill added firmly, "you'll have to *earn* forgiveness from Rosetta, Christine, and Deborah. And you'll have to *ask* them for it, Isaac. You can't expect them to wipe your slate clean just because you say you're starting over. That moxie I mentioned earlier means nothing unless you prove you've become a different, more responsible person."

The tiny office rang with silence. After being lulled by the storekeeper's quiet conversation at the beginning of the interview, Isaac now felt nailed to his chair by Kraybill's sermonette.

He was in a tight spot. Mamm's words still stung, and there was no way around them: *If your brothers no longer want you clerking for them, you'll have to find your own way, Isaac. I won't have a thief hanging around the house.*

The thought of facing Deborah, Rosetta, and Christine—begging them like a whipped dog to forgive the damage he'd done to their barns, their families, and Deborah's reputation—made him queasy.

But he couldn't go home.

He could fake his way onto an unsuspecting boss's payroll under another identity, in another town where they didn't know him. But constantly looking over his shoulder to see if anyone had caught on would be exhausting. It would also mean a life on the run, and that wasn't what he wanted.

Especially now that he'd seen Vera. He didn't know her last name or anything else about her, except that she created outrageously colorful pottery, but Isaac *wanted* to know her. He wanted to believe Vera could save him from himself.

I'm asking for a miracle. What's the chance of that happening when I'm not sure I even believe in God?

With a sigh, Isaac met Kraybill's gaze again. Wasn't it a minor miracle that the storekeeper, knowing what he did, hadn't already shown him to the door? Isaac widened his eyes slightly, putting on an earnest expression as he assumed his most sincere tone of voice.

"So . . . if I ask those ladies for their forgiveness, and they accept my apologies, will you hire me?"

Chapter 2

Dale considered his next words very carefully. Isaac was a good-looking kid—a youngest son who'd played on his parents' favor—and at nineteen, he'd perfected the appearance of penitence and contrition to get what he wanted. Manipulation was a game to him.

There was no way around it: the young man was a catastrophe waiting to happen if he messed with Dale's computer system, or if he created a side business by filching store inventory. And there was no refuting the long list of misdeeds folks from Coldstream would hold against Isaac, either.

But Dale's ad hadn't attracted any other potential employees. His store was out in the country, surrounded by farmland. The men at Promise Lodge all had occupations, and the boys were still in school. Except for Marlene, the other young women didn't show an aptitude for managing a store, or they had their own pursuits—and Marlene, who'd married Lester Lehman in May, would probably start a family soon.

Dale had spoken to his fiancée, Irene Wickey, about wanting to retire in the future, and when he married her on July nineteenth—two weeks from today—he wanted to take her away for a few days. His future wife was a patient, practical woman and she would understand if he couldn't leave his store. But as a middle-aged, self-sufficient bachelor who'd unexpectedly found the love of his life, Dale wanted some time away with Irene before they moved into their new home and resumed their routines. Irene deserved a honeymoon, and he was determined to give it to her.

He'd considered closing the store while they went away, except that Marlene would valiantly insist she could run the place by herself. Dale believed she could—but he didn't want to subject her to the sheer exhaustion of helping customers in one part of the store while other shoppers waited for her at the checkout counter. Not to mention restocking the shelves and checking in the deliveries.

Dale's only alternative was sitting in front of him, trying to pass for the perfect solution to his problem. But did Isaac Chupp, with his checkered past and dubious attitude, pose an even bigger problem?

"You've told me about clerking for your *dat*'s auction company and running the sale barn's computer, Isaac," he said. "How do I know you won't manipulate the entries in my system—or sell some of my items online—and pocket the profits? A little here and a little there could add up to quite a nice sum, over time."

Isaac's blue-eyed gaze didn't waver. "You'd figure that out in a heartbeat, *jah*? You're a savvy business-man, and you know your inventory like the back of your hand," he replied without missing a beat. "You've also installed mirrors and arranged your aisles so you can see to the ends of them from the checkout counter.

Helps you spot shoplifters. I've never seen that in any other country store."

Dale chuckled despite the need to maintain a serious demeanor. No doubt Isaac's astute observation—his compliments—were a way of buttering him up.

"Most customers have no idea about the mirrors or the shelf arrangement—but *you* noticed those details because you like to pocket things you don't pay for," he pointed out. "You impress me as an intelligent young man who's used his God-given smarts to achieve the wrong ends. Do I have your word that you've put such thievery behind you?"

"*Jah,*" Isaac replied smoothly. "And if you have doubts, don't share your passwords. In a store this size, you could keep me busy restocking shelves and helping customers, without allowing me access to your computer system."

"If I can't trust you, I won't hire you."

Isaac's nonchalant shrug suggested that he didn't need this job, yet Dale suspected he was as desperate to get away from home as Dale was to have another employee. Amish children didn't usually leave their communities unless they were forsaking the faith—although younger sons sometimes relocated because the family business was already supporting their older brothers. Given what he'd heard about Bishop Obadiah from the folks who'd moved to Promise Lodge, however, Isaac might have had a serious falling-out with his contentious father.

"Okay, so I have to reconcile with my three accusers, and I can't do any creative accounting," Isaac summarized in a voice edged with impatience. "What else do I need to know about working for you, Mr. Kraybill? And where would I live? The Promise Lodge apartments are only for women, and I've heard that the cabins destroyed by the tornado haven't been rebuilt."

"Excellent questions." Dale glanced at the notes he'd jotted on his desk blotter. "If I offer you the job, you'll be on a two-month probationary period—which should give you plenty of time to reconcile with Rosetta, Christine, and Deborah."

The kid nodded. "September fifth. I'll work on it."

"The construction of my new home—on the land where some of those cabins used to sit—is far enough along that I can move into it while Amos and the other carpenters do the finishing work," Dale continued. "As part of your compensation, you can live in the apartment above the store. If you'd like to eat your meals at the lodge—which I highly recommend, because the Kuhn sisters are fabulous cooks—I'll cover that, as well. If you prefer to cook for yourself, I'll give you a weekly allowance for groceries from the store. And if living in a rebuilt cabin suits you better, I'll pay your rent when the workmen have completed one."

"Seems fair enough."

Isaac still appeared detached rather than needy. Dale allowed him a few moments for further questions, mostly to see if he broached the subject of his pay.

"All right, I'm willing to try this if you are, Isaac," he offered, praying he'd made the right decision. "When can you start?"

"How about right now?"

A muscle spasm in Isaac's jaw revealed his nervousness. Dale had expected the kid to return home for his clothes, probably to start on Monday—which told him that the rift in the Chupp household was deeper than he'd anticipated.

"And—and because you're providing me a place to live and my meals, what if I work the first week without pay?" Isaac blurted out. "After you see what a dedicated employee I am, we can talk about money, all right?"

Dale's mouth dropped open. "Isaac, I would never expect you to work without—"

"Nobody here expects me to be honest or successful either," he pointed out resentfully. As he pushed his collar-length blond hair back, however, his handsome face lit up with relief. "I'm grateful that you're willing to take a chance on me, Mr. Kraybill. A lot of store-keepers wouldn't."

As Dale rose from his chair and extended his hand, he hoped that his new employee was being sincere—because he genuinely wanted Isaac Chupp to turn around and make something of himself.

"Your attitude of gratitude will take you a long way, Isaac—with me, and with everyone at Promise Lodge," Dale said. "Just between us, if a storekeeper in my hometown hadn't looked beyond my, uh, tendency to relieve him of unpaid merchandise, I wouldn't be run-ning this successful business today. He challenged me to be the intelligent, generous man God had created me to be, so I'm doing the same for you, Isaac."

"You won't be sorry, sir!" Isaac promised as he re-leased Dale's hand. "What shall we do first?"

Dale chuckled at his new employee's eagerness. "You're moving into my apartment, so I need to have the shop in Willow Ridge deliver my new furniture to the house. Why not look around the store to see how it's arranged, and I'll join you after I've made my call?"

Chapter 3

As Ezra Overholt and his younger brother, Raymond, joined the other men waiting to file into the lodge for Dale Kraybill and Irene Wickey's wedding, he felt at home already. "Mose, it's been too long!" he exclaimed as he stuck out his hand. "How's married life?"

Mose Fisher stood a burly six-foot-four and his huge hand swallowed Ezra's. "It's all *gut*, Ezra. Glad to hear Christine's hired you to help expand her dairy herd. And how's it going at the Coldstream store, Raymond?"

"Lizzie and I have done some major reorganizing," his brother replied. "I'm hoping everything's finally the way we want it by the time the baby arrives. Lizzie's in the family way, you know!"

"Congratulations!" Mose crowed. "I'm delighted for you two—and I'm excited about having Ezra amongst us at Promise Lodge."

"Happy to be here," Ezra remarked, playfully jostling the slender fellow who'd joined them in line. "We hope Schwartz feels the same way about being my supervisor, ain't so?"

Roman Schwartz—Mattie's son, who'd grown up down the road from the Overholts in Coldstream—let out a laugh. "A bigger barn and more cows mean more stalls to muck out," he teased. "It's the perfect job for a new employee."

Ezra shrugged. "I've been shoveling manure all my life, same as you. Somebody's gotta do it."

When he saw another familiar fellow coming out of the bulk store, he lowered his voice. "How's Isaac doing at his new job? The grapevine back home's buzzing about why he left so suddenly—and he's come *here*, of all places. Nobody in Coldstream knows where he went."

"I haven't heard any complaints from Marlene in the two weeks he's been working there," Mose remarked softly. "She says he's learning fast. Behaving himself."

"We'll see if that changes when Dale and Irene leave town," Roman put in. "Considering his reputation, I'm surprised Kraybill's letting Isaac live above the store. Sort of like inviting the fox into the henhouse."

"Let's hope for the best," Mose murmured, raising his hand in greeting as Isaac approached them. "Hey there, Isaac! How's the new job?"

"I'm on it like a bonnet!" he replied quickly, nodding at Ezra and Raymond. As he smoothed the front of his black vest and adjusted his white shirt collar, Isaac scanned the crowd of young women who were lining up to enter the lodge's meeting room from a different doorway. "Looking forward to the festivities. Weddings are always a *gut* place to meet girls."

"*Jah*, and today they'll be coming in from Cloverdale, right?" Ezra asked. "Isn't that where the Wickeys and Dale go to church, at the Mennonite Fellowship?"

"It is," Isaac replied. "And that's where Dale owned a bulk store before he built the new one here. He says their minister is conducting the ceremony, but he and Irene wanted the Kuhns to cook their meal, so the whole party's being held here."

"Party? Did someone say *party*?" another young man teased as he hurried to take his place in the line that was moving inside.

Ezra quickly stuck out his hand. "It's Ed Brubaker, right? And you live in the blue tiny home at the lake? I'm your new neighbor, Ezra Overholt."

"Hey, it's *gut* to meet you! When Christine and Bishop Monroe pulled that red tiny home into place with his Clydesdales, she told me she had a new dairy guy coming," he replied. "You got here yesterday afternoon, *jah*? By the way, most folks call me Eddie—"

Their chatter ceased as they stepped through the door, taking their places behind the older men who'd filled the pews in front of them. Ezra settled on the backless wooden bench alongside his brother, surveying the crowd. As the aromas of the wedding meal wafted around them, he understood why the folks here liked to hold their services in the lodge's large meeting room rather than in members' homes, as the Amish typically did. When it was his family's turn to host, they held church in the concrete basement—not nearly as cheerful and well-ventilated as this room with its big windows and the morning sunshine slanting in.

When a sparkle caught his eye, Ezra's brows rose. On the wall across from him, a rustic wooden sign sported a large glittery star and the words *Star of wonder . . . Guide us to Thy perfect light.*

He elbowed his brother. "One of your signs—and it's not even December!" he whispered. "These folks must really like you, Raymond."

Raymond's face lit up as he gazed at his handiwork. "Bishop Monroe bought that sign and even preached about it one Sunday," he recalled wistfully. "I miss a lot of things about Promise Lodge, Ezra. I envy your coming here to—"

The crowd sat straighter, silencing their whispers as the bishop, Preacher Marlin Kurtz, and a man in a dark English-style suit and tie strode down the center aisle between the men and the women. Bishop Monroe Burkholder, as tall and almost as broad as Mose Fisher, gazed around the crowded room.

"Welcome to this beautiful day that the Lord hath made," he began in a resonant voice. "We're delighted that you've joined us to celebrate with Dale Kraybill and Irene Wickey as they unite in holy matrimony. We're also honored that the bride and groom are holding their ceremony here, and we welcome our guests from the Mennonite Fellowship in Cloverdale, as well as Zachary Miller, who will conduct the ceremony."

Reverend Miller nodded cordially at the congregation before he took his place on the preachers' bench near the front.

"Our blended service will be different from what we Amish are used to—and shorter," Bishop Monroe added with a sparkle in his brown eyes. "Irene and Dale have asked me to preach a sermon during the church service, and Reverend Miller will preach during the wedding before conducting the ceremony. Let's praise God with our opening hymn."

As the church service progressed—even before Bishop Monroe began to preach—Ezra noticed an immediate difference in its tone. Folks at Promise Lodge sang with joy and conviction. When Preacher Marlin, the district's deacon, opened the large Bible, everyone paid close attention, as though they were eager to know God's word on a personal level.

"Our Scripture is read at weddings so often that most of you can probably say parts of it along with me," Preacher Marlin said. "I challenge you to really *listen* to these words written by the Apostle Paul in his first letter to the Corinthians, chapter thirteen. And if it clarifies matters for you, substitute the word *love* each time you hear *charity* in this ancient King James text."

When he'd found his spot on the large page, the preacher began to read. "'Though I speak with the tongues of men and of angels, and have not charity, I am become as sounding brass, or a tinkling cymbal.'"

Ezra smiled. He hadn't yet met Marlin Kurtz, but he already admired the man who read with such enthusiastic expression—all about how love was patient and kind, and how love could bear, believe, hope, and endure all things. The faces around him radiated peace and goodwill, creating an atmosphere that felt so different from the one in Coldstream.

"'When I was a child, I spake as a child, I understood as a child, I thought as a child: but when I became a man, I put away childish things,'" Preacher Marlin continued. His voice filled the room effortlessly, and after he'd read the final verse about faith, hope, and charity, folks in the congregation nodded their appreciation as he sat down.

Bishop Monroe rose from the preachers' bench, surveying the crowded room with an expression of such benevolence that Ezra felt blessed before the man even opened his mouth.

"One of the best things about the Bible is the way we

can read a passage again and again throughout our lives, yet those verses can take on a different meaning—often depending upon our circumstances," he began, clasping his hands before him. "Today I'm going to delve into one of the verses you've just heard that's not usually associated with weddings. The New King James version modernizes the words for us: 'When I was a child, I spoke as a child, I understood as a child, I thought as a child; but when I became a man, I put away childish things.'"

As was the custom with Amish bishops and preachers, Monroe Burkholder spoke without any notes or preparation. Ezra was amazed that he'd quoted from anything other than the standard King James version, which Bishop Obadiah and the Coldstream preachers never strayed from. They didn't usually explain it or apply it to everyday life, either.

"Even though Dale Kraybill's a bit older than most first-time grooms, we could still say that today he becomes a man and puts away childish things—but we won't!" the bishop teased.

As everyone chuckled, Bishop Monroe strode over to shake Dale's hand. Dale rose from the pew—and rose to the occasion, flushed but laughing as he returned the handshake.

Ezra was again impressed: although Mennonites and Old Order Amish often lived in proximity, Bishop Obadiah spoke as though Mennonites had lost the true faith. At Promise Lodge, the preachers had even agreed that Rosetta Bender, a former member of Coldstream's Amish church, could marry Truman Wickey, a Mennonite. Obadiah Chupp had never condoned their union and had even preached against it as an unholy, unbalanced alliance.

Ezra had lived here less than twenty-four hours, yet it seemed to him that he'd come to a district where God smiled more graciously on His people. Was it any wonder that so many families had moved to Promise Lodge?

"'When I became a man, I put away childish things,'" Bishop Monroe repeated after he'd returned to his place between the two sides of the congregation. "Ladies, don't think for a minute that these words don't apply to you! What I'd like us all to consider is what it means to reach a point—at whatever age—when we not only grow up but also assume the mature responsibility God expects of us.

"And because we've become accountable, we can shed the cocoon of our former habits to take on a whole new life," he continued in a lower, more intense voice. "When we give up the sinful ways that displease God, we change from fat green caterpillars to glorious butterflies who can fly. If we're wise, we'll choose a new life that's more loving. More Christlike."

A hush enveloped the room. Ezra sat spellbound. Folks leaned forward, eagerly awaiting what this man of God would say—

Loud weeping and wailing rang out, coming from the direction of the kitchen. "I've lost everything—my bakery, my car, my sister!" a distraught young woman cried out. "I cannot go on living!"

The wedding attendees sucked in a collective breath. Many of them glanced nervously toward the distracting racket as Bishop Monroe paused.

The young woman continued to cry loudly, while

two other women—older, by the sound of their voices—
hastened to comfort their unexpected guest.

"Dearie, let's step outside—"

"There's a wedding going on. You've got to settle
yourself—"

"I *can't* settle myself!" came the desperate reply.
"Everything that matters to me burned in that fire and—
and I've got nowhere to go—"

"Maria, we can help you, if you'll quiet down. Come
with us—"

"Are you taking me outside? Making me leave,
like before?" the younger woman protested. "But I'm
homeless!"

Beside Ezra, Raymond had stiffened. "Maria," he
whispered. "It's got to be Lizzie's sister from Cloverdale."

Ezra's eyes widened. He'd met Maria Zehr at Raymond and Lizzie's wedding earlier in the year and had
immediately written her off as a high-maintenance
blonde. Because the Zehr sisters had lost their parents
several years ago, the Overholt family had held the
wedding at their own home in Coldstream. Maria had
served as Lizzie's side-sitter, and Ezra had stood up
with Raymond.

Over on the women's side, Lizzie's face had gone
pale. She rose from the pew bench, probably hoping to
quiet her sister's outburst so the church service could
resume.

Bishop Monroe took up where he'd left off, but Ezra
couldn't focus on the rest of the sermon. He kept recalling the way Maria had flirted with him so outrageously
at Raymond's wedding, even though they'd just met.
She was a shapely young woman, probably four or five
years older than he. It still embarrassed him, the way

Maria had gazed into his eyes and grasped his hand as they'd sat together at the *eck* table in front of all the other wedding guests. She'd become such a clingy, suggestive pest that Ezra had excused himself to use the bathroom, then escaped upstairs to his room instead.

And now she'd come to Promise Lodge, apparently because a fire had destroyed her bakery and her car.

Dale and Irene rose to stand together before Reverend Miller. As they exchanged their vows—looking as overjoyed as any couple he'd ever seen—Ezra wished he could share in their excitement. His stomach rumbled as aromas of the wedding dinner became more enticing, yet his enthusiasm for the day's festivities had wilted.

All he wanted was to slip unnoticed through the crowd when folks headed into the dining room, to escape to his tiny home before Maria realized he was here.

Chapter 4

Isaac sat on the pew bench, intrigued by the dramatic interruption of the church service. It gave him a break from feeling that Bishop Monroe was preaching about *him*—implying that he should give up drinking, shoplifting, and his other dubious habits so he could become an accountable adult. Acceptable to God and the others in his life.

When I became a man, I put away childish things.

This message wasn't new to him, of course—his brothers and his parents had nagged him about his English friends and the trouble he constantly got into, until they'd finally kicked him out a couple weeks ago. The real eye-opener, however, was Monroe Burkholder's interpretation of the Scripture:

. . .we can shed the cocoon of our former habits to take on a whole new life. When we give up the sinful ways that displease God, we change from fat green caterpillars to glorious butterflies who can fly.

Isaac's heart had stilled at those stirring words. Instead of threatening him with eternal damnation if he didn't change his ways, the bishop of Promise Lodge was promising a new life that would give him wings. It wouldn't be easy, taking on the life of a butterfly, but the image had captured his imagination.

And hadn't he gotten off to a commendable start by working diligently in the store? Dale had complimented his organizational skills and the way he'd caught on so quickly when the storekeeper had showed him how to use the computerized cash register—and how to manage inventory on the office computer. Marlene was competent while checking out customers, but if she hit the wrong button or something stalled in the program, she was too intimidated by the technology to fix her mistake.

After a couple of such instances this past week, Dale had even confided that he felt better about leaving the store because Isaac knew how to correct computer errors and keep things running smoothly.

Isaac listened as the young woman in the kitchen continued to wail. The Kuhn sisters were doing their best to restore order so the church service and wedding could continue, but Maria—whoever she was—had obviously reached the point of no return.

"I've got nowhere to go—"

Although he could empathize with Maria's situation, he didn't want to get involved in it. As he gazed at the women's side of the meeting room, searching out Vera's pretty face, Isaac's heart beat with a purpose that was giving him a lot to think about when he was alone in his apartment. He'd learned that she and her brother, Eddie Brubaker—seated on the pew behind him—had come from Bloomingdale, Missouri, about a month ago. Vera was helping Minerva Kurtz, Preacher Marlin's daughter-in-law, as she went on bed rest, hoping not to miscarry again.

The baby details didn't interest him, but Vera certainly did! And when she saw that Isaac was watching her, she didn't look away as she had when Rosetta, Christine, and Deborah had announced his past misbehavior in the store.

Maybe she feels safer because she's in church among all these other folks. But I've been working hard, giving reports of my progress time to reach her. Someday she'll trust me.

Isaac smiled at her. Such a timid girl Vera was, hiding behind her big glasses. She glanced down demurely after he'd held her gaze for several precious moments.

Maybe today—while everyone's happy about being at a wedding—I'll strike up a conversation. Let her know that at least five or six pieces of her pottery have sold because I encouraged customers to buy them.

He knew better than to rush her, however. Now his greatest incentive for seeking Deborah Schwartz's forgiveness was the hope that Vera would come to see him as a butterfly rather than a caterpillar still munching on his mistakes.

Maybe it's a gut time to apologize to Rosetta, too, during the day's festivities. She'll tell folks that I'm making amends, turning over a new leaf. Surely that will convince Vera that I'm worthy of her time.

As Dale and Irene stood up to exchange their vows, Isaac watched them with interest. He'd attended dozens of weddings in his lifetime because his parents had insisted on it, yet this ceremony felt different. The minister, Zachary Miller, seemed so much more relaxed than the leaders of his church in Coldstream—genuinely happy for the middle-aged couple standing before him, rather than focused on reminding them of their obligations to God and to their church district.

Dale appeared nervous yet deeply in love as he stood with Irene's hands in his to say his vows. Irene, who'd been widowed for several years, flushed prettily as she repeated the words and gazed into Dale's eyes.

Isaac wasn't usually caught up in weddings, because in his church, each and every ceremony was exactly the same except for the names of the bride and groom. As he took note of the way Irene and Dale stood face-to-face, silently encouraging each other as they repeated the words after the minister, Isaac gained a whole new perspective on what love *looked* like.

A lot of the couples his father married weren't yet twenty, and although they gazed earnestly at each other as they stumbled over the ancient vows, Isaac sensed that they had no idea whether marriage would provide the happily-ever-after they were hoping for. And if it didn't, they were stuck with each other anyway, until one of them died.

Dale and Irene, however, radiated joy and confidence. After spending his days with the storekeeper, watching him deal with female customers, Isaac had no doubt that Kraybill was relatively inexperienced with women. And Isaac had a hard time imagining the physical side of their relationship—especially at Dale and Irene's age.

But it didn't seem to matter. When the bride and groom turned to face the congregation as Mr. and Mrs. Dale Kraybill, Isaac sensed that when one of them died, the other would mourn.

Why am I thinking about death at a wedding? I want to enjoy every moment of this Thursday away from the store. And I need to focus on my strategy—zero in on Rosetta or Deborah to apologize, so I can get better acquainted with Vera someday soon.

Maria stood in the mudroom with Lizzie, hunkered over her heaped plate of food as though she couldn't eat it fast enough. The Kuhn sisters had mercifully filled a plate with ham, potato salad, and slaw before the services let out—mostly to stop her wailing.

But she wasn't ashamed of her outburst. She'd come to the end of her proverbial rope, and she didn't have enough of it left to tie a knot and hang on anymore.

"Didn't you know about Dale and Irene's wedding? Didn't you notice all the cars and buggies parked along the road when you came in? And how'd you get here if your car burned?" After peppering her with questions, Lizzie scowled, lowering her voice. "Everyone in the meeting room could hear you—"

Maria filled her fork with the best potato salad she'd ever eaten. "Hitched a ride. And why would I know anything about Dale and Irene getting married?" she retorted. "In case you've forgotten, I have to run the bakery by myself now—mmm, this potato salad has pieces of dill pickle in it!"

Lizzie let out an exasperated sigh. "Folks were surely talking about their wedding at church. You don't work on Sundays, after all."

"I haven't been to church for a while," she admitted before sticking more potato salad in her mouth. "What's the point? God doesn't listen to me any more than you or anyone else does. Besides, there's no one there for me."

"You think church is just a place to meet guys?" her sister asked in disbelief. "Hey, slow down! You're eating that fabulous food so fast you can't even taste it."

"It's the best meal I've eaten since your wedding. Not much point in cooking when you're not around, Sis," Maria said sadly. "I really wish you and Raymond would move to Cloverdale."

"Well, that's not going to happen, is it?" Lizzie challenged. "Thanks to Dale hiring me and selling Raymond's Christmas signs last fall, we both got enough experience at the bulk store that Raymond was in the right place at the right time when the storekeeper in Coldstream passed on."

"*Jah*, and you have a husband and a baby on the way, Lizzie." Maria was weary of this conversation, in which her little sister was acting more like her mother, so she snatched a chocolate-covered bar from one of the cookie trays the Kuhns had stored in the mudroom for later. "I have *nobody*—and I can't stand being by myself anymore. The fire is a *gut* excuse for me to leave Cloverdale—"

"And how'd it start?"

"I have no idea! I looked out to see flames and smoke coming out from under poor Ruby's hood," she explained, referring to her car. "Then she exploded and the bakery caught fire." Maria shoved the entire bar into her mouth, an excuse not to answer any more of Lizzie's tiresome questions.

"Peanut butter mixed with crunchy stuff," she mumbled with her mouth full. "And fabulous chocolate on top. This is *amazing*." To soothe her frazzled nerves, she grabbed another one.

As guests' voices rang in the dining room, Maria

glanced down at her plate. How had so much food disappeared so quickly? She looked at Lizzie again, totally envious of the happiness on her sister's face and the round bulge beneath her conservative Amish-style cape dress. It was yet one more thorn in her side that her sister had given up her Mennonite freedoms to marry into a conservative Amish family, yet Lizzie's life seemed to be joyful and fulfilling.

"So now I'm out of business and I have *nothing*! And nobody to help me!" Maria continued in a pitiful tone. "Lizzie, you have no idea how lonely I've been since you and Raymond—"

A tall fellow with dark hair burst through the doorway, but at the sight of Maria his eyes widened. "Oops, sorry—wrong door!" he rasped before rushing back into the kitchen.

Maria blinked. "Was that—why didn't you tell me Ezra Overholt was here!" she blurted out. "What's he doing at Promise Lodge?"

Why did she detect a look of reluctance on Lizzie's face, as though her little sister didn't want to answer?

"Never mind!" Maria said, shoving her empty plate into Lizzie's hand. "I'll go ask him myself. Ezra! Ezra, wait up! It's me, Maria Zehr!"

Feeling alive for the first time in days, Maria shot into the kitchen and then down the interior hallway to avoid the crowd lining up at the steam tables. When she heard a door slam, she hurried toward the sound, thankful that because she'd lived in the lodge before, she knew her way around. She nearly crashed into an elderly lady coming out of the bathroom, but moments later she was outside.

"Ezra! I'm so excited to see you!" she called when

she spotted him heading across the side lawn. "You might as well stop, because I won't let you get away!"

Ezra, wearing a black vest and pants with a white shirt, finally slowed to a normal walk. Triumphant, Maria closed the gap between them and whirled around to stop in front of him.

"Oh, it's really you," she murmured, gazing raptly at his face. "It—it must be a sign from God, the way we keep meeting at weddings, ain't so?"

His deep green eyes were all the reminder she needed. She'd seen this handsome, muscular man in her fantasies for weeks after Lizzie had married his youngest brother. She'd cherished every moment she'd spent sitting beside him at the *eck* table during their wedding dinner, making sure Ezra knew that she was interested. Available.

"From what I overheard, you didn't come here for the wedding," he pointed out coolly.

Undaunted, Maria forged ahead. "And what brings *you* here, Ezra? Have you decided your former neighbors were smart to come to Promise Lodge? Are you joining them?"

He paused as though he didn't want to reply. Why was she seeing the same hesitation on Ezra's handsome face that she'd noted on Lizzie's?

"Christine Burkholder hired me to help manage her dairy herd."

Maria widened her eyes playfully. If Ezra was working for the bishop's wife, he was at Promise Lodge for the long haul. Solid. Paid well.

"*Gut* for you!" she crowed. "You have a job! You're set for life!"

When Ezra winced, Maria chided herself for sounding

so predatory—so ready to pounce on this handsome man who'd relocated to where *she* had returned! But what young woman wouldn't be attracted to Ezra Overholt?

Maria tried to think of a less personal topic to keep the conversation going. "I—I noticed that the cabins are gone, and I know the lodge apartments are only for women, so where are you staying, Ezra?"

He pressed his lips into a line, as though he preferred not to answer her. When Ezra crossed his arms, the sleeves of his white shirt pulled against his broad, muscular shoulders. "As part of my wages, Christine provided a tiny home—"

"So you have a *house* now!"

"—but don't be getting any ideas, Maria," Ezra continued firmly. "The place is barely big enough for me to turn around in. And as I told you at Raymond's wedding, I'm not looking for a girlfriend. Excuse me. I have cows to tend."

As he strode toward the big dairy barn across the private road, Maria couldn't help watching the way his backside filled out his pants—just as she couldn't help following him. His take-charge attitude, handsome face, and authoritative voice drew her like a powerful magnet.

But Ezra turned, staring her down. "You can't follow me into the barn, Maria. We don't allow non-employees around the cows—and you wouldn't want to get manure all over your shoes."

At the thought of cow poop squishing between her toes—and ruining her sandals—Maria stopped. "I—I guess you have to milk even on special occasions," she said, sighing as she watched the man of her dreams walk away.

But it was only a matter of time before he'd finish milking, and then Ezra would rejoin the wedding festivities. Maria smiled, filled with fresh hope. She'd come to Promise Lodge a couple of years ago to start a new life, and she could do it again.

And this time, she'd stay here instead of returning to Cloverdale. Her happily-ever-after was right around the corner—she could *feel* it.

Chapter 5

After congratulating Dale and Irene, Isaac watched the crowd enter the dining room behind the newly-weds. The guests' happy chatter filled the room, yet the festive mood didn't carry Isaac along on its current. He was on a mission: how could he receive Rosetta's forgiveness in a way that Vera would observe, and thereby admire? Some time would probably elapse between the cause-and-effect actions he hoped to set into motion, but wouldn't it be great if he impressed both women today?

As he planned his strategy, Isaac gazed at the barn-board poster with the sparkling, garish star—glitter and gold paint that caught the sunlight streaming through the windows. Although dozens of Raymond's pieces had sold in the store last December, Isaac didn't understand why the local church leaders would display it in the room where they worshipped. Sure, it said "Guide us to Thy perfect light," but why would an Amish congregation find such a gaudy, over-the-top signboard inspiring?

Obviously, Lizzie Zehr had been inspired because she'd married Raymond and was carrying his child. The young couple was so lovey-dovey that Isaac could hardly stand to watch them beaming at each other and grasping hands. When Lizzie came in from the kitchen, where she'd been consoling her older sister, Raymond lit up like the summer sun.

As the Overholts blended into the dinner crowd, a movement across the room pulled Isaac from his thoughts. Eddie Brubaker and Fannie Kurtz, Preacher Marlin's teenaged daughter, were emerging from a side door with telltale pink lips and secretive smiles—so caught up in each other that they had no idea Isaac was watching them.

"I thought the wedding would never end," Eddie said, gazing raptly at his girlfriend.

"I couldn't wait another second to kiss you, Eddie," Fannie confessed in a loud whisper. "I wish we didn't have to wait so long for *our* wedding."

There were guests near the dining room doorway, so the lovebirds knew better than to engage in any further smooching. They went in to get their dinner.

Someday soon Vera and I will be that happy together. But I won't be so publicly affectionate with her. She's shy, and she'd be embarrassed if her younger brother—or anyone else—caught her looking so red-lipped and guilty.

The last of the crowd finally moved into the dining room. Isaac still had no exact plan for talking to Rosetta or Vera, but he trusted God to give him the right words at the right time: he'd never been shy or inept around women.

He entered the room where folks sat shoulder to shoulder, eating at long tables draped with white cloths. Others were heaping their plates at the buffet line. A glance at the dessert table in the corner made Isaac's mouth drop open.

Rosetta and Vera were *both* there, helping guests choose plated slices of pie and cookies from platters. Isaac couldn't have arranged their proximity if he'd tried—which suggested that maybe, for once, God was smiling down on him. He reminded himself to remain calm and polite, and above all to sound *sincere* as he apologized to Rosetta. As one of the three Bender sisters who'd founded Promise Lodge, she was the key to his acceptance here. Based on her reaction, folks would either accept him or forever consider him a loser.

Christine Burkholder was at the table in the corner behind Rosetta and Vera, cutting more pies. Isaac had no illusions about pursuing *her* forgiveness today. The fire he and his friends had accidentally started was the reason her husband, Willis, had died—held captive by a burning beam when the barn roof had fallen in on him. It would take some serious preparation before Isaac could face Bishop Monroe's wife, so he kept his aspirations manageable.

He inhaled to fortify himself. He imagined the expression of peace on Rosetta's face as he erased the black mark on his record, settling the contention between them. He could also envision how impressed Vera would be because he'd manned up to ask forgiveness for the careless mistake he and his English friends had made that fateful night on the Bender farm. Surely his apology to Rosetta would also wipe away the doubts Vera must have about him—especially if Deborah had told her about his unfortunate behavior with *her* that same evening.

Rosetta laughed at something Vera said to her. When

she glanced up, she appeared radiant and filled with the joy of the occasion. "Care for some pie, Isaac?" she asked. "We have apple, cherry, coconut cream—"

"I—I've come to apologize," he stammered, continuing before he lost his nerve. "I want to ask your forgiveness, Rosetta, for burning down your family's barn and for leaving this—this emotional wound to fester—"

Rosetta let out a loud cry, dropping her triangular pie server to cradle her midsection. As tears rushed down her cheeks, Vera and Christine hurried to either side of her, appearing as flummoxed by her outburst as Isaac felt.

"Let's go to the kitchen, sweetie," Christine murmured, steering her younger sister away from the dessert table. "We'll get you a cold drink of water—"

Isaac stared helplessly after them. Vera handed pie to a couple of other guests, wide-eyed. She didn't seem inclined to talk to him, as though he'd said something horribly unforgiveable.

A strong hand clasped Isaac's shoulder, and Truman Wickey, Rosetta's husband, took him aside. "It's not your fault," he confided. "Don't say anything, but we're going to announce later today that she's in the family way. The least little thing sets her off, so don't take it personally."

Isaac nodded gratefully. "I didn't mean to—I just thought since everybody's in such a *gut* mood—"

"I overheard you trying to apologize, and that's a fine idea," Truman interrupted gently. "Try again, in a quieter moment. That barn fire—losing a part of her family's history—cut her deep, Isaac."

Isaac glanced away, sorely disappointed that his attempt had failed—and that Vera had witnessed it. Had she guessed that Rosetta was pregnant? Did she consider him horribly insensitive for broaching such a personal subject in front of so many people?

Why does doing the right thing have to be so complicated? Now I have to apologize again.

Truman gave him a pat on the back and walked toward the kitchen to comfort his wife.

What should he do next? A few older fellows were coming for pie and cookies, unaware of the outburst he'd caused, and Isaac didn't want to look like a fool by hanging around, trying to make conversation with Vera. He was *so* hungry, but the dining tables were crowded with folks he didn't know. He didn't want to walk up and down the aisle with his plate looking for a seat—

"Um, would you like some pie, Isaac?"

Although Vera appeared too bashful to meet his gaze, her question sounded friendly. The sight of her graceful hands grasping the triangular server and shifting the filled plates toward the front of the table held him entranced. Was it any wonder she could create such exquisite bowls, pitchers, and vases? Vera's long, sensitive fingers fascinated him.

"A piece of pie would be wonderful," he replied. "How about apple?"

"How about two?" Vera deftly slid a second slice onto the plate she held, handing it to him with a shy smile. "I have no idea what came over Rosetta, but—"

"Let's let it be," Isaac said softly. "*Denki* for doubling my dessert, Vera. That's very sweet of you."

When her brown eyes met his and she nudged her glasses into place, his stomach filled with butterflies. He nearly dropped the loaded plate when his fingers brushed hers, so he stepped away before he could make a fool of himself.

What was happening to him? Isaac was always the

pursuer, always in control, yet Vera made his joints feel like jelly.

"By the way," he said as he took a dessert fork from the edge of the table. "You should bring more of your pottery into the store. Your pieces have been selling like gangbusters because—well, I've been telling customers a local girl makes them—"

Vera's face shone with delight—almost enough to make up for Isaac's blunder with Rosetta. "Oh, *denki* for telling me! I've been afraid to come in, thinking all of my pottery might still be there, untouched."

Her smile, and her sparkling brown eyes with those long, dark lashes, gave Isaac enough to dream about for weeks. He left the dining room with his pie, walking on air.

At a sink in the kitchen, Rosetta splashed cool water on her face and gratefully accepted the towel Beulah handed her. "I don't know what came over me—"

"You were having a moment," the older Kuhn sister put in gently. "Every one of us reaches a point now and then when the lid flies off."

"Having Isaac Chupp gloss over his apology for burning your barn down would make anybody blow her top," Christine muttered. "He could've chosen a more appropriate moment for the mission Dale is requiring of him—"

"But let's not forget he's a guy, and therefor clueless," Truman reminded them. "And he had no idea that Rosetta's mood can change in a heartbeat these days."

"He's got to be nineteen or twenty by now," Christine said tersely. "Old enough to know better—"

"Puh. I've known men who remained clueless their

entire lives," Beulah said with a wave of the spatula she was drying.

"Which was one of the reasons we decided to remain *maidels*, ain't so?" her sister Ruby chimed in. "It's all right, Rosetta. You look much better now that you've sipped some water and had a ham sandwich. Hunger does nasty things to us."

Rosetta sighed. She was pleased that her friends and family had come to her defense, yet extremely embarrassed about bursting into tears in a roomful of wedding guests. She knew Dale was expecting Isaac to request her forgiveness, yet when he'd mentioned her family's barn, the memory of her parents sitting on the front porch of the farmhouse had triggered an immediate reaction.

She'd been grateful to God that her *mamm* and *dat* hadn't lived to witness Isaac's destructive streak. Every now and then, however, a spark of grief flared, and Rosetta still burned with their loss, the same way flames had consumed the weathered barn that had been a landmark on their property for generations.

Truman smiled tenderly. "Might be time to, um, *say* something, *jah*?" he whispered near Rosetta's ear. "It would explain a few things. Folks wouldn't be worried about your mental state."

Rosetta laughed out loud. "You're probably right. And what better opportunity to announce it *once* instead of every time we see someone different?"

She gazed at Christine, Beulah, and Ruby, hoping to sound rational. "I'll tell you gals first—as practice," she teased. "I'm going to—well, *Truman* and I will be adding to our family soon—"

"I *thought* so!" Beulah crowed as she and Ruby slipped their arms around Rosetta.

"Oh, Rosetta, I'm so happy for you!" Christine blurted out as she, too, moved in for a hug. "But I've noticed little moods lately that made me suspect you were carrying. When are you due?"

"Early December, according to Minerva and the doctor at the Forest Grove birthing center." Rosetta wiped her eyes, letting another wave of emotion peak and then ebb. "We'd appreciate your prayers, of course. I'm older than most women starting families—"

"And you're healthy, and you'll be *fine*," Christine assured her. "Why not step out into the dining room and announce it while everybody's in one place?"

"The way Irene's been smiling—like the cat that ate the canary—I bet she already knows, *jah*?" Ruby asked as she removed another pan of ham from the oven.

"She figured it out before I did," Rosetta replied. "I was chalking up my queasy stomach and mood swings to the tornado's destruction—seeing the back wall of the lodge crushed by those two big trees. Thinking about all the rebuilding we had to do."

She reached for Truman's hand. "No time like the present."

"And no present like the time," he quipped.

With his warm hand grasping hers, Rosetta felt strong enough to face anything. And truth be told, announcing their news to a roomful of friends and family members was small potatoes, compared to preparing for a child and raising one.

As she approached the *eck* table, she wondered if her words might come across as inappropriate for the occasion—as Isaac's apology might've been—or if she'd be stealing Irene and Dale's thunder. The moment her mother-in-law winked at her, however, Rosetta realized that Truman's *mamm* had probably expected them to announce the baby while their church friends and family were all present.

Lord, I thank You again for giving me such an awesome mother-in-law.

As she and Truman stepped onto the dais behind the bride and groom, Dale glanced back at them with a big smile. "Irene's told me your news!" he said beneath the chatter that filled the room. "I'll get everyone's attention for you."

As Dale gleefully clanged his knife against his water glass, Rosetta's throat suddenly went dry and she wavered. "Truman, maybe you should be the one to— because what if I ruin the moment by crying again?"

Bless him, her husband slipped his arm around her shoulders as the crowd quieted. More than a hundred guests were watching them, half of them turning in their seats so they could see what was going on.

"First, we want to thank you all for joining our celebration today," Truman began in a clear voice that carried to the back of the crowded room. "And we want to express our appreciation to Beulah and Ruby Kuhn and all their helpers for putting on this fine meal."

Folks nodded, clapping loudly.

"We're also delighted that my *mamm* and Dale have finally tied the knot—"

Gentle laughter swelled as the guests applauded again.

"—and they want you to know that by early December, they'll be grandparents!" Truman finished jubilantly.

When everyone caught on, they began to cheer loudly.

Many folks rose from their chairs, beaming at Rosetta as they continued to clap. Back by the dessert table, Bishop Monroe raised his hands above his head to applaud exuberantly as he started forward. In the kitchen doorway, the Kuhns, Christine, and many of the Promise Lodge ladies were cheering and wiping away tears—as was Mattie, who hurried down the aisle with Amos close behind her. Rosetta's nieces, Phoebe and Laura, were wide-eyed as they, too, made their way to the corner of the dining room with their husbands, Allen Troyer and Jonathan Helmuth. Even her nephews, Roman and Noah Schwartz, and their wives, Mary Kate and Deborah, were stepping forward with toddler David and little Sarah on their hips.

As her family crowded in behind the *eck* table to congratulate her and Truman, Rosetta lost herself in their outpouring of love and joy. Why was she so concerned about age and pregnancy? The dear folks gathered around her would support her in every hour of her doubt, and they would cheer her on with each successful milestone of her baby's gestation, birth, and life.

There was simply no way to fail unless she lost faith. And the beloved people who were embracing her, blessing her with their presence, wouldn't allow that to happen.

Rosetta felt tears trickling down her cheeks, yet she no longer had to explain them, did she? When she could get a word in edgewise, she smiled brightly.

"I guess it's time to plan for a whole new level of happiness, *jah*?"

Chapter 6

When most of the guests had finished eating, Vera left the lodge with a picnic basket that surely contained enough food for a week, heavy as it was. She was learning firsthand about the Kuhns' legendary generosity: the two sisters were sending heartfelt greetings to Minerva along with ham, potato salad, and other dinner items, as well as an uncut pie and a platter of cookies.

Vera walked up the road quickly so Minerva's dinner would stay warm. She paused, however, at the bend where Uncle Harley's sheep were visible in his pasture. The afternoon sun was intense, so many of the sheep stood bunched together in the shade. Queenie, a black-and-white border collie that belonged to Noah Schwartz, surveyed the peaceful scene with her pink tongue hanging out.

It was like looking at a painting, perfectly balanced and arranged. Vera wondered if she had the skill to recreate the scene on a pottery tray and smiled at the thought. As she entered her aunt and uncle's house, however, she refocused on her role as Minerva's helper.

"I'm back from the wedding," she called out as she set the heavy basket on the kitchen table. "What can I bring you, Aunt Minerva? The Kuhns sent enough food to last us for days!"

"Glad to hear it," came her aunt's cheerful reply. "It means you get a break from cooking!"

Vera turned, surprised to see her aunt in the doorway. "Are you all right? Should I have come home earlier to—"

"Stir-crazy," Minerva put in with an impatient wave of her hand. "You'd think I'd be used to spending time by myself while your uncle works in the barrel factory, but I've had all the lounging I can handle today. I wasn't created to be a creature of leisure!"

Vera laughed, relieved that her aunt was in high spirits. In Minerva's situation, who wouldn't be stir-crazy?

"I'm sorry you missed today's celebration. What with Dale and Irene's church friends coming from Cloverdale, the meeting room was full and the dining room tables even had chairs at each end to accommodate the crowd."

"I'm glad it was well attended. Irene and Dale are wonderful people."

As Minerva eased into a chair at the table, Vera took a pitcher of iced tea from the refrigerator. "Everyone here seems so nice," she said, "although it was an odd sensation to be in a crowd where Eddie was the only person I really knew."

Her aunt watched eagerly as Vera put ice and tea in two glasses. "You and your brother have only been here a couple of weeks—and I keep you pretty isolated," she pointed out. "Let me know when you need to be with other people, all right? You could be getting better acquainted with your future students, after all. Or meeting the neighbors closer to your own age."

Vera sipped her tea, grateful for the way the cold liquid cooled her all the way down. "I was happy to help Rosetta at the dessert table today. And she and Truman announced that they're having a baby! I suppose you already knew."

"I'm glad she feels confident enough to tell folks about it now." Minerva took a long drink, her expression wistful. "After losing so many little souls myself, I understand her hesitation to announce her condition. But Rosetta's healthy. She should be fine."

"*You* look perfectly healthy," Vera pointed out. Her aunt had never dwelled on her miscarriages, but sometimes her secret sadness showed in her eyes when she watched other women tend their babies.

"That's the mystery of it. Looks can be deceiving," Minerva pointed out softly. "You don't know you'll have trouble carrying a wee one to full term until you lose one. Or two. Or more."

Nodding, Vera steered the conversation to a different subject. "Speaking of mysteries, what do you know about Isaac Chupp?"

"Only what I've heard from the folks who've moved here from Coldstream."

Minerva sipped her tea, lost in thought. "I hear Dale's hired Isaac to work in the store despite the irresponsible things he's done, and despite the way his *dat*—the bishop of the Coldstream district—allowed Isaac's behavior to go unpunished."

Minerva looked at Vera over the top of her glass. "But those things happened in a different town, before Marlin moved our family from Iowa to Promise Lodge. So it's not my place to judge Isaac, is it?"

It seemed like a tolerant way to look at Isaac's situation. As Vera reflected on what she'd heard the day Isaac interviewed at the bulk store, however, she wasn't sure she felt the same level of acceptance.

"He tried to apologize today for burning down Rosetta's barn—until she burst into tears," she added in a low voice. "And he told me to restock my pottery display—because he's been talking to customers about my work, helping to sell it."

"So Isaac's not an entirely bad apple." Aunt Minerva's lips twitched. "Not to diminish your pottery, because it *is* uniquely beautiful, but I suspect he's very interested in *you*, Vera. Most of the young women here are married, after all—are you interested in him?"

"Should I be? Or should I stay away from him—at least socially?" Vera asked. "Isaac's *gut*-looking, but he seems awfully confident. A little too smooth."

"Never hurts to trust your instincts, dear."

Vera sighed, swirling the ice in her half-empty glass. "I hate to ask Deborah about the night he left her in a ditch after she'd called the police because—well, maybe she doesn't want to be reminded of that nastiness."

"At least you'd be going to the source rather than relying on the grapevine," Aunt Minerva pointed out. "Pray on it, Vera, and God will give you His verdict on Isaac. Meanwhile what's in that picnic basket? Something smells awfully *gut*."

Vera chided herself for making her aunt wait for her food. As she lifted one large foil-wrapped container after another from the picnic hamper, Minerva carefully rose from her chair to fetch a plate from the cabinet.

"I can get that!" Vera protested.

"*Jah*, you could, dear. But if I don't keep moving, my muscles will get so weak I won't be able to push the baby out." As her aunt returned to the table with two plates, she smiled gently. "It's all well and *gut* for the doctor to recommend bed rest. It's another thing altogether to sentence me to total confinement when my belly's barely showing."

Vera stole a glance at her aunt's dark lavender cape dress. The bulge beneath her apron could still be taken for a few extra pounds rather than a baby.

"Will you join me, Vera?" Minerva asked as she removed the foil coverings. "Harley will load up on wedding food again tonight after the huge meal he just ate. Sometimes it seems he's the one eating for two."

She wasn't hungry, after eating some of the Kuhns' wonderful food while she'd set out the final slices of pie. Her aunt had spent a lonely day while her friends and family had attended the wedding festivities, however, so Vera took two sets of silverware from the drawer.

"What a lovely summertime meal," Minerva said as she stabbed a slice of ham and spooned potato salad beside it. "You can't go wrong with make-ahead dishes like this three-bean salad and—oh! My favorite mandarin orange and pineapple salad—"

As she chewed a bite of her dinner, her eyes widened. "Of *course* the Kuhns wouldn't set out ordinary potato salad. They put in dill pickle slices—and probably added pickle juice to the dressing! Very tasty!"

Vera smiled as she, too, savored a mouthful of the potato salad. "Would you like some ice cream to go with those dill pickles?" she teased.

Minerva waved her off. "I haven't reached that stage of craving yet. But I do anticipate making a big dent in the pie you brought home," her aunt said firmly. "Pretty as that crust looks, I bet Phoebe made it in her pie shop—and I wouldn't be surprised if Irene made some of the wedding pies, even if she *is* the bride."

Vera nodded as she fetched a knife. "Do you suppose she'll keep baking four days a week now that she's married? Some husbands wouldn't allow that."

"Dale doesn't impress me as the type to tell Irene what to do. Especially because he turns a nice profit from the Promise Lodge Pies display in his store." Minerva watched intently as Vera divided the pie into eight slices. "Look at those thin slices of apple—and so much cinnamon! The baby's telling me to eat my dessert now, so of course I must obey. It's all about the baby, you know."

Vera laughed out loud. Once again, she was pleased that Aunt Minerva was in fine fettle today.

And her invitation to come to Promise Lodge to help during her confinement might be a bigger blessing than I anticipated. Eddie found the love of his lifetime here, and maybe I will, too.

But it won't be Isaac.

Chapter 7

As Ezra entered the lodge Friday morning, he inhaled the heavenly scents of fresh bread, sizzling bacon, hot coffee, and something with cinnamon and sugar. He reminded himself not to wolf his food down as though he hadn't eaten for a week. He wasn't sure how Ruby and Beulah Kuhn could spend an entire day feeding a huge wedding crowd and then rise early enough to cook such a wonderful breakfast, but he was delighted. When he'd come to Promise Lodge, he hadn't realized what a bonus the meals would be on top of Christine's generous pay.

"*Gut* morning, ladies," he called out as he entered the empty dining room. The table nearest the kitchen door was set for six, but no one else had shown up yet. "Something smells indescribably delicious!"

"Oh, that would be me," Ruby teased as she carried a platter of cinnamon rolls to the table. "And how were the cows this morning, Ezra? I hope they appreciate it that you rise before the sun to milk them."

Ezra chuckled. "The cows are fine. Roman and I will be going to an auction sometime soon to buy more, now that Christine's expanding her operation. A small dairy north of here is dispersing its herd."

"I suspect the milk business runs on a mighty slim profit, from what I've heard about the government changing its policy on subsidies," Beulah said, placing a big platter of bacon beside the cinnamon rolls. "Takes a very committed family to keep a dairy going. No vacations from milking twice a day, rain or shine."

Ezra nodded. "This family doesn't have a son willing to take it over, and the *dat* is dealing with Parkinson's disease. Sad story—and getting to be more common these days."

At the sound of the front door, he turned to watch Isaac and the Brubaker kid walk in. Chupp was dressed for the day in clean trousers, suspenders, and a light blue shirt but Eddie had probably grabbed his rumpled clothing from the floor—and his wild bed head and half-open eyes made him look about twelve.

"Hey there, Isaac," Ezra said with a nod. "Ed, my man, what are you up to today? Just crawl out of the sack, did you?"

Brubaker blinked sleepily as he landed in a chair at the table. "What if I did?" he mumbled. "Don't have any painting to do here until the new cabins go up, so I'll go into Forest Grove later today. Put up some flyers so other folks will start hiring me."

Ezra nodded, choosing a chair across from the table from him. "That's an impressive green wagon parked behind your tiny home. How long have you been in business?"

Eddie yawned, swatting at Beulah's hand when she rumpled the brown hair that was standing straight up. "Couple of years. Had that wagon built with a bunk, so

I can stay onsite at jobs instead of heading home every night."

"Mighty impressive, if you ask me," Ruby put in. She placed a plate of fried eggs and a basket of sliced bread on the table, smiling at him. "Your sister tells me you're only seventeen, Eddie."

"Vera would know." He stared at the food as though he might be dreaming rather than awake. At least he had the presence of mind to bow his head in a silent prayer of thanks, and everyone followed his lead.

"You boys dig in while it's hot," Beulah said, slipping into her place closest to the kitchen. Rolling her eyes toward the ceiling, she added, "We don't know when Sleeping Beauty might make her way to the table, and you fellows have things to do."

"Hey, I heard that!"

The clatter of heels descending the wooden stairway announced Maria's arrival at the far dining room door. Ezra braced himself, noticing—too late—that the only vacant chairs were to his right. As she approached the table, a wave of perfume preceded her. When he stole a glance at her shoes, Ezra wondered how she kept them on her feet. They seemed to be a combination of a flip-flop and a sandal with a wooden heel that flapped loosely with every step she took. They made enough racket to rouse the dead.

"Ezra! *Gut* morning," Maria purred as she brushed against him taking her seat. She inhaled appreciatively as she flashed him a smile. "You showered for me. I like a man who—"

"I cleaned up so I wouldn't smell like the barn floor," Ezra corrected immediately. "I wanted *everyone* to enjoy this nice breakfast the Kuhns have cooked."

t to get out of bed!" Tears streamed
eks. "Do you have any idea how hard
he day to the next now that Lizzie's
ried in a wounded tone. "I get up in
night to start baking, and I run the
myself—and after the cleanup's done
mpty house, and I don't have enough
dinner.

h top of all that, I've lost my *car*!"
nd my bakery is a burned-out *mess*! I
up and die! Can you understand that at

om rang with silence. After Maria's
saac and Ed appeared shell-shocked—
he scene—except they had no graceful

een on listening to any more of Maria's
ailing, either, but he was curious about
d the Kuhns would do next. Apparently,
allowed Maria to reclaim her former
erday, to settle her down so Irene and
oy their wedding day. Ezra suspected,
the matter of Maria's rent had gone
and Ruby and Beulah had probably been
d to that topic when Rosetta arrived.

sorry you've lost your bakery and your
you've been lonely since Lizzie got
etta said gently. "Truman's working on a
g project these days, so to save him some
ng the facts about your circumstances—"
talk to Truman," Maria put in forlornly.
on't be so mean or yell at me about—"
se abruptly from her chair. "Young lady,

As he accepted the platter of bacon from Isaac on his left, he caught Chupp's smirk.

"I showered, too—but you can claim all the glory," the blond storekeeper said under his breath.

Across the table, Ruby helped herself to a slice of warm bread. She picked up a small plate that held an ivory-colored roll of cheese. "Well, Maria, now that you've settled in, you've probably noticed that the lodge has changed since you first stayed here, back when Mattie, Christine, and Rosetta lived upstairs," she said. "They've moved on—and you will, too."

Ezra nearly dropped the platter of fried eggs. He couldn't miss the hint in Ruby's words, and he liked the way she was thinking.

"This, by the way, is fresh goat cheese," Ruby continued, taking some from the small plate.

"You kids should try it," Beulah suggested as she cut a slice for herself. "We make it from Rosetta's goat milk—"

"And what a blessing, that she built her four goat girls a new pen at the Wickey place before the tornado came through last month," Ruby added with a shake of her head. "It was sad enough that Mose Fisher had to put down several of Christine's cows—"

"And sadder yet that Irene and Sylvia and we two sisters lost our homes in that storm." To drive her point home, Beulah gazed at the blonde who sat down the table. "It's fortunate that you arrived after our apartments have been completely rebuilt, Maria. Maybe you've noticed that you have new hardwood floors and freshly painted walls, and that the upstairs hallway and the rooms downstairs have been painted, too. And we've gotten new kitchen appliances."

"Not to mention younger guests sharing our meals!" Maria smiled brightly at Ezra, Isaac, and Ed as she filled her plate with bacon and eggs. "I probably shouldn't ask Rosetta if my apartment can be repainted the way it used to be. But *you're* a painter, Eddie, so maybe—"

"As much as Rosetta has invested in restoring the lodge," Ed interrupted firmly, "she won't pay me to repaint your walls, Maria. Not that I'd have time, with the other jobs I'm taking on."

Ezra nodded his silent support, flashing a quick thumbs-up. The kid across the table *would* have more work soon—and it was a sure bet Maria wanted him to donate his labor.

"But you should've *seen* my apartment!" Maria widened her blue eyes dramatically at Ezra, gesturing with a slice of bacon. "The lower walls in the front room were a deep raspberry and they gradually got lighter as they rose to the ceiling. And my bedroom— including the ceiling—was sky blue with puffy white clouds—"

"Amos and the other men outdid themselves to suit your whims when you lived here last time, Maria," a familiar voice said from the far end of the dining room. "But Eddie's got it right. We've finished the lodge, and we'll soon be rebuilding six of the cabins."

"Rosetta, *gut* morning!" Beulah called out. "We've got fresh cinnamon rolls, bacon, and eggs, if you'd like to join us."

"And goat cheese!" Ruby added. "It's delicious on this fresh bread."

"*Denki*, ladies, but I ate earlier," Rosetta said as she sat down across from Maria.

Ezra det
owner's voi
became muc

"With all
chance to vis
"But I overh
your car and
start?"

Maria spen
bread she'd ta
closed for the
mumbled. "Th
underside of m
exploded, the fl

"Your car w
your house?" Ro

Maria let out
up to the battery
going through the
it in."

Ezra finished an
quicksilver change
victim didn't surpr
either.

"And when did t
"Um, Monday,"
traught to eat anythi

Rosetta's eyebro
Ruby's. "And when
this? The building
meanwhile, your bus
you doing those two
wedding to—"

"I was too upse
down Maria's che
it is to get from o
married?" she qu
the middle of the
shop all day—by
I go home to an
energy left to fix

"And now, o
Maria wailed. "A
just want to curl
all, Rosetta?"

The dining r
escalating rant,
ready to leave t
way out.

Ezra wasn't k
weeping and w
what Rosetta an
the sisters had
apartment yest
Dale could enj
however, that
undiscussed—
working arour

"Maria, I'm
car—and tha
married," Ros
big landscapin
time, I'm gett

"I want to
"At least *he* v
Rosetta ro

it's time for you to grow up. You're at least twenty-five but you're whining like a five-year-old."

Maria's mouth dropped open, but no sound came out.

"I'll tell Truman that you'll present your plan of action—what you intend to do about your business— this evening after he gets home," Rosetta continued tersely. "But meanwhile, you're in an apartment in *my* building, so you'll talk to *me* about that. Shall we go upstairs and finish this conversation?"

"I think we'll join you, so we're all on the same page," Beulah said as she, too, stood up.

"That way you young men can finish your breakfast and get on with your day," Ruby put in, smiling at them. "Don't worry about the dishes. We'll get them later."

Maria looked like a deer blinded by headlights—or a trapped animal. She began to cry harder, muffling her sobs as she pushed back from the table. When she hurried through the kitchen and up the back stairway with a rapid *thump-thump-thump,* Ezra glanced at the floor.

Her sandals were under the table.

He and the other guys nodded at Rosetta and the Kuhns as they, too, went to Maria's apartment by way of the kitchen. When the women were out of earshot, Ed exhaled loudly.

"That girl's a piece of work. A disaster waiting to happen," he muttered.

"Oh, that train's already left the station," Isaac put in as he reached for the platter of bacon. "And lucky for Ezra, Maria thinks he's the solution to all her problems."

Ed's mouth curved as he spread some goat cheese on a slice of bread. "Is that why I saw you hightailing it out to the barn after the wedding yesterday, Ezra? She was hot on your trail—"

"And if you tell her that dairy cows don't get milked until much later in the afternoon, you'll be in deep trouble, Brubaker."

Ed's and Isaac's eyes widened. "That's what you told her you were doing?" the kid across the table whispered.

"And she believed it?" Chupp muttered in disbelief.

Ezra reached down and gingerly lifted a sandal by its strap. "Can you imagine what these shoes would look like after a trip through the barn? Next time Maria's chasing me down, maybe I should let her dash in and experience dairy cattle for herself."

"I want to watch that!" Isaac blurted out.

"*That* would convince her to go back to baking!" Ed put in.

As the three of them burst out laughing, Ezra sensed his companions would side with him rather than encouraging Maria to pursue him. He had no illusions, however, about the way she operated.

Anyone in pants was fair game.

And any single guy who appeared financially stable was apt to become Maria's love of a lifetime.

By midafternoon, Isaac felt that he and Marlene Lehman had found a comfortable routine for running the store without Dale. She had spent the morning restocking the shelves; then after her lunch break, she worked in the back room, unboxing a big shipment of baking supplies. This left Isaac to do some straightening out front, and then he ran the cash register as a steady stream of Friday shoppers came in. He was starting to recognize some of these regular customers, who already called him by name. It created a comfort zone he found strangely fulfilling.

Storekeeping was repetitive work—something he hadn't considered attractive until he'd needed a job on short notice. But it kept him too busy to think about being in a state of exile. And he didn't have time to ponder how he was going to reconcile with Rosetta—again—as well as Christine, and Deborah.

Isaac forgot about those three women, however, when Vera entered the store pulling a high-sided wagon. When she saw him at the cash register, she gazed around as though hoping to speak with Marlene. But after Isaac's last customer was checked out, she approached him.

"I—I hope this is a *gut* time to restock my pottery display—"

"*Jah*, you'll want to have more pieces out for tomorrow, because lots of English customers come in on Saturdays." He hoped he didn't sound *too* eager as he came around the front counter. "I can help you unpack—"

"Oh, I didn't intend to take you away from your work—"

"It's no trouble," Isaac quickly assured her. He smiled, hoping he didn't seem goofy or adolescent. "I enjoy seeing what you've created, Vera. Nobody else I know makes such colorful pottery. What've you got today?"

She pulled her wagon over to the open cabinet where the remaining pieces of her previous consignment were displayed. "Take a look while I decide how I want to arrange everything. I have four place settings of dinner plates, salad plates, and bowls as well as a couple of pitchers and some flowerpots."

When Vera pulled a folded sheet of paper from her apron pocket, Isaac lost all track of the shoppers in the store. Her bittersweet-orange dress complemented her chestnut hair and ivory complexion—and the color brought out the deep, appealing brown of her eyes as she shifted her glasses into place.

Isaac quickly focused on the inventory sheet she'd handed him. "I'll put this on Dale's desk, okay? He hasn't talked to me about keeping track of your pottery yet, so—oh! Do we owe you money from what's already sold?"

Vera's shy smile made him twinkle all over. "*Jah*, but that can wait until Dale gets back. It's not as though I need to pay the electric bill to keep my pottery wheel running."

"Electric bill?" Isaac blurted out. "Don't tell me Preacher Marlin and Harley run their barrel-making equipment with electricity! That would never fly in Coldstream—"

Vera's giggle told Isaac she'd pulled one over on him. "Do you really think they'd try that, living next door to Bishop Monroe?" she teased as she unwrapped her new pieces. "They allow me to plug my kiln into the solar panel on the shed roof, however. I form my pieces on a kick wheel, which runs on my own pedal power."

Isaac folded her inventory sheet and tucked it beneath his suspender. He could imagine Vera seated at her pottery wheel, intent on the moving clay as she formed it with her skilled fingers. He suddenly had the urge to find the shed where she worked so he could watch her. Sometime soon.

"With all the plates stacked and the other pieces on the shelf below them, everything is visible—" Vera quickly stood a salad plate on end, leaning it against the back of the shelf. "There. Now the pattern shows."

Isaac blinked. While he'd been lost in his visions of Vera and her clay-smeared hands, she had arranged her display very effectively—with no help from him. And she'd kept a straight face when she'd joked about paying the electric bill, which proved she had a sense of humor . . . and that maybe she wasn't as tongue-tied as he'd assumed.

Maybe Deborah hasn't given Vera the nitty-gritty about the night I left her in the ditch—or if she did, Vera doesn't seem completely repulsed. If I play my cards right, I might stand a chance—

"Young lady, did *you* make these fascinating dishes? I've never seen such a striking pattern!"

Isaac held his breath as an English woman in a ruffled yellow sundress picked up the salad plate on the top of the stack. He'd seen her in the store last week, and every detail of her flawless, tanned complexion and highlighted hair—not to mention the many rings that sparkled on her fingers—suggested that money was no object when she saw merchandise she liked.

"*Denki* for your kind words." Vera clasped her hands, gazing at the customer with a gentle smile. "I've always liked royal blue for a background color, and the red and yellow vertical stripes and tulips are a way to enjoy springtime all year long!"

"What a lovely thought! Will you have more of these? I'd like eight place settings—"

"I have four more place settings waiting to be fired, *jah*!" Vera put in happily. "They'll be ready on Monday."

The woman clapped her hands together, delighted. "And if you could make me two fair-sized serving bowls and a platter, that would be perfect, dear." She took a notepad and pen from her shoulder bag to write down her name and number. "How about if you set these dishes back for me and call me when the entire collection is ready? Oh, but you've made my day—made my entire week! It was wonderful to meet you—?"

"Vera. Vera Brubaker."

"Harriet Stoughton. You have such a talent—such an eye for color," she went on, shaking Vera's hand exuberantly. "When my friends in the art guild see these dishes, I suspect you'll be getting more orders. Let me give you a deposit—"

"You can do that when you check out," Vera said, nodding toward the cash register. "Isaac will make a note of your deposit and keep it separate for when the store owner, Dale Kraybill, returns from his honeymoon. He lets me sell my work on consignment, so we need to run the sale through his system."

As Mrs. Stoughton pushed her cart down the aisle, Vera stacked her packing material in her wagon. The ecstatic smile on her pretty face made Isaac fall in love with her all over again—yet he was puzzled.

"Vera," he whispered, "you should've accepted that lady's deposit, because—"

Isaac shrugged, trying to find the right words. "Well, it's *your* money, because you're the potter! You could be selling your pieces outright rather than giving part of your profits to Dale."

Vera straightened to her full height, frowning thoughtfully. "But if Dale hadn't allowed me display space in his store—space where he could be selling something else—I wouldn't have sold any of my pieces.

No one would even know I was a potter," she reasoned aloud. "It's only fair to pay Dale his percentage, *jah*?"

When Vera pushed up her glasses, nailing him with her sincere, nonjudgmental gaze, Isaac was struck by the fundamental difference in their natures: while *he* had seen a way for her to pocket all her profits, the thought of cutting Dale out of his percentage would never have occurred to her.

Vera was honest. He was not.

If Vera thinks about what we've just discussed, she'll figure out that difference. And I won't stand a chance with her.

Chapter 8

As Maria stared out the window of her apartment Friday afternoon, she grew more fidgety by the minute. What would she say when Truman quizzed her about her plans?

Puh. When have I ever made a plan and carried it through? I fly from one day to the next like a chicken without a head.

And if I don't figure out some answers, I'll be headed for the stew pot, just like that poor bird.

She sighed. She *had* made a plan, of sorts—to come to Promise Lodge again. To start over, again. But everything had changed since her last brief stay.

The apartment she'd loved now smelled of fresh varnish and ivory paint, and it was furnished with pieces other folks in the community no longer needed. The huge maple trees that had shaded the back side of the lodge had fallen during the storm, which meant the afternoon sun was beating relentlessly on her as she stood before the open window.

Rosetta had changed, as well. Maria had overheard Truman yesterday, announcing that she was in the family way, so that explained some of her moodiness—

But she might still be inclined to think I'm making a play for Truman—as she thought when I lived here before. It's not true, but her perspective might be even more skewed now that she's pregnant.

Maria sighed, pacing barefoot across the back of her main room. She had not been prepared for the tough talking-to the lodge's owner had given her this morning. Rosetta had no sympathy for Maria's situation, and she'd told her to stop whining and start doing something. The Kuhns had nodded, agreeing that Maria needed to pay full rent if she stayed. The business-women at Promise Lodge had started something called a Coffee Can Fund, but it was for women who were truly destitute, they'd said.

Why didn't *destitute* describe *her* situation? Hadn't she lost everything that mattered to her? When she paused in front of the window again, the afternoon sun felt even more merciless. The July humidity made her pink gingham dress cling damply to her body—and Maria *hated* to sweat.

As a Mennonite, she'd always wondered why the Old Order considered electricity so sinful. Did they sincerely believe God would deny their salvation if they had air-conditioned homes and modern appliances?

Fanning herself impatiently with a folded newspaper, Maria walked out into the hallway. Surely one of the empty apartments would be a cooler place to spend the afternoon. Because Irene Wickey, Marlene Fisher, and Sylvia Keim had vacated their rooms when they'd married recently, the upstairs level of the lodge echoed with her footsteps. Only the Kuhn sisters lived here now, and the rattle of pans and an occasional outburst of laughter told her they were in the kitchen preparing supper.

The vacant apartments stood open to allow for air

circulation, so Maria went to the front corner where Marlene had once lived. When she opened a window that overlooked the road, she saw Christine's new barn and the pasture where her dairy herd was grazing. Near the white plank pasture fence stood the little bakery building Maria had moved here from Cloverdale a couple of years ago—except it had been rebuilt after the tornado. Irene and her partner, Phoebe Troyer, ran Promise Lodge Pies there now, and a short distance away sat the small white building where Beulah and Ruby made their cheese.

When Maria looked more closely at both buildings, her eyes widened. They had air conditioners in their windows—because the Kuhns and Irene were Mennonites.

Maria's thoughts whirled faster, more hopefully. She had her answer! If she could—

The phone downstairs rang, and as one of the Kuhns answered it, Maria shook her head. Again, she couldn't understand why the Amish kept their phones in little sheds by the road. They thought it was a major indulgence that lodge residents got to share a phone in the kitchen. What was the big deal about having a phone in each apartment?

"Maria! Phone call for you," Ruby hollered up the back stairs. "It's Rosetta."

Maria swallowed hard. No doubt Truman was on his way to speak with her, and she had no idea what she'd say to him. As she descended the back stairs, it also galled her that her conversation wouldn't be private. Even if the Kuhns were cooking, they could hear every word she said.

When she reached the kitchen, she flashed the sisters a deceptively cheerful grin. She would do just about anything not to talk with Rosetta again today, but she picked up the old black receiver.

"*Jah*, hello?" she asked, as though unaware of who'd called. "This is Maria."

"Maria, it's Rosetta and we've had a change of plans." Her landlady sounded out of breath and concerned. "Truman had to take one of his landscaping employees to the emergency room, so he'll talk with you another time."

As the tension drained from Maria's body, she nearly whooped for joy—but she knew better with the Kuhns watching.

"You *do* know what you want to do, *jah*?" Rosetta continued, sounding more like the upbeat woman Maria had admired—mostly—during her previous stay. "And you can understand why it wouldn't be fair to allow you a rent-free apartment when everyone else in the lodge—and around the community—is pulling her weight and has a purpose."

Ah, there was the rub. Maria had no idea what her life's purpose was—but she wouldn't admit that when Rosetta seemed inclined to keep talking. At least she didn't sound angry or judgmental now.

"What would make you happy, Maria?" her caller continued in an upbeat tone. "You have the perfect chance to aim for that goal now, but you have some decisions to make—some loose ends to tie up. I'll remind Truman to call you when he's ready to discuss the bakery building in Cloverdale, all right? See you around, Maria." *Click.*

As she hung up, Maria felt like a schoolgirl who'd been excused from serving detention time for misbehavior—something she'd known about firsthand as a young scholar. When she noticed that the Kuhns were waiting for her to report what Rosetta had said—another troublesome invasion of her privacy—she strolled over to gaze out the window above the big stainless-steel sink.

"Truman had to take a guy to the emergency room, so he's not coming this evening."

"Oh, dear, I hope it wasn't something serious," Ruby said as she slipped a big roasting pan into the oven. "We met some of his crew when they were pouring foundations and clearing away underbrush. Nice fellows, every one of them."

Maria was only half listening, wondering how to ask the question that might determine her future—her *purpose*. Once again, she gazed over at the little building where the Kuhns made their cheese . . . in air-conditioned comfort. She took a deep breath.

"What would you ladies think about me helping in your cheese factory?" she asked in the sweetest voice she could muster. "I've worked in the kitchen all my life, you know, so I could be helpful at *something*, if you'd show me how—"

"It's not that you couldn't learn, Maria," Ruby interrupted earnestly.

"It's a matter of logistics," Beulah continued, sounding diplomatically kind. "When we had the cheese factory rebuilt after the tornado, we installed a couple more refrigerated units and mixing tanks, because we sell a lot of cheese at Dale's new store—"

"And because there was barely room for the two of us to turn around *before* the storm," her sister went on, "now one of us must step aside when we move from one area to the other. I'm sorry, Maria, but we can't take you on, dearie."

"We couldn't pay you what you've been earning at

your bakery, either." Beulah shrugged apologetically. "A young woman your age needs to be supporting herself and putting money away."

Maria pressed her lips together to keep from crying. The sisters were so adept at finishing each other's sentences—and so eager not to work with her—that they hadn't even consulted one another before refusing her a job. She'd been dismissed before she could even plead her case.

"Okay, fine," she muttered. Determined not to have another meltdown, Maria hurried through the mudroom to step outside.

She was again forced to face the changes the tornado had caused. The backyard was no longer the cool, shaded sanctuary it had been when the old maple trees were standing. As she shaded her eyes from the intense summer sunlight, Maria blinked back tears. She had no idea what to do next or where to go.

When she turned, the bakery building that had once been hers was yet another reminder of how she'd failed at running her business here. Without a nearby outlet for her breads and sweet rolls, she'd given away dozens of her goodies—or sold them at a discount to the young men who'd been living here, and who'd been happy to flirt with her.

Maria sighed. Those guys—Jonathan and Cyrus Helmuth and Allen Troyer—were all married now. The Helmuths were landscapers at the bustling nursery their twin uncles owned, and Allen built tiny homes. Along with their wives, the former Laura Hershberger, Gloria Lehman, and Phoebe Hershberger, they'd moved into new houses and were established as the next generation of Promise Lodge. Their lives had meaning because the six of them—all younger than she was—had found a purpose.

Why couldn't she seem to do that?

Maria wiped away her tears, still gazing at the small white building. Baking was all she knew. Was there a chance that Irene wouldn't want to make pies now that she'd married Dale? Or would Phoebe be carrying a child soon and give up working for Promise Lodge Pies? Maria had heard that the two partners sold every pie they baked—and could sell more if they worked more than four days a week. Perhaps Maria could find a new place for herself . . .

She sighed. She *hated* making pies. She could mix bread dough and frost cinnamon rolls and bake cookies in her sleep, but pie crust gave her nightmares.

What would make you happy, Maria?

As she heard Rosetta's voice in her ear, she saw Ezra coming out of the dairy barn—

And there's my answer. Ezra would make me happy!

Maria fought the urge to run over and greet him, because her cheeks were splotchy from crying. If she was to make any progress with handsome Mr. Overholt, she had to show him a happier face and disposition, didn't she?

As the aroma of roasting meat drifted out the kitchen window, she realized that she'd be having dinner with Ezra in a matter of hours—and because Truman wasn't coming, she had the entire evening free!

Bolstered by the hope of sitting next to Ezra and perhaps suggesting ways to spend the summer evening, Maria hurried inside. She bounded up the back stairway before the Kuhns could quiz her about her change of heart.

She didn't have time to answer to a couple of gray-haired ladies. She had a husband to catch!

Chapter 9

Near midnight, Isaac lay in a very comfortable double bed in an apartment cooled by a wall-mounted air conditioner, yet he was too wired—too fired up—to sleep. In the nineteen years he'd lived at home in Coldstream, he'd endured the winter drafts of his north-facing bedroom as well as the stifling humidity of summertime nights, yet he'd adjusted. The extremes of Missouri weather were all he knew.

Yet the relative luxury of Dale's new apartment wasn't the bonus he'd thought it would be. It was rather spooky to live above the store when it was closed, and to hear unfamiliar nighttime noises—real or imagined.

And it was another thing altogether to be totally alone. The Amish lived in family groups, in communities, that emphasized doing things together—which guaranteed that most people were rarely without another soul to talk to. Even earlier in his *rumspringa* when he'd taken off in his old rusted-out car to escape his judgmental family, he'd usually had a friend or two along for the ride.

For the first time in his life, Isaac didn't hear his parents' low conversations downstairs, or the occasional flush of a toilet, or the calling of the owls in the woods behind the house. Even the air conditioner was so quiet, he couldn't usually tell when it was running.

The silence unnerved him. His restless mind flitted from one subject to another, until one image became fixed: the three crisp one-hundred-dollar bills he'd placed in Dale's desk drawer. Never mind that they were in an envelope marked *"Mrs. Stoughton's deposit for Vera."* Ever since the lady with all the rings had handed him that money, he'd been getting ideas about what he could do with it. He had no business even *thinking* about those big bills, yet his fingers itched for the dry, flat feel of them.

Why would he even consider taking Vera's deposit?

Because Vera doesn't know that Mrs. Stoughton paid her way more than what she's charging for the dishes.

Because Dale doesn't know about the money yet. And neither does Marlene.

Because it's there.

Isaac chided himself, recalling his epiphany about Vera being honest while he was not. If he took the money, he would have to disappear—and wasn't that what most folks expected of him? He wasn't worried about Vera going unpaid, because once the theft was discovered, either Mrs. Stoughton or Dale would see that she got her money.

It gave him pause, however, that he had no easy way to hightail it down the road. He had a driver's license, but he'd sold his old car a while back. If he took the cash and hitchhiked the state highway at this hour, no one would pick him up—because the honest souls who lived in these parts were sound asleep, as he should be.

Isaac was also aware that anyone Amish he met would probably know whose son he was unless he gave a fake name. He resembled his father, and Obadiah Chupp had created quite a reputation for himself in this region, so it would be difficult for Isaac to escape unnoticed.

And although living English often sounded tempting, it would require more than three hundred dollars to establish himself elsewhere. He would have to travel quite a distance and stay away, too. He would no longer be able to go home—and he'd be cutting all ties to Promise Lodge if he disappeared like a thief in the night with Vera's money.

But I have more than a thousand dollars of auction money stashed in my duffel. And I took my Social Security card from Mamm's file box, so I could work for the English if an opportunity came along. Why am I in a sweat about starting over someplace else?

And why is Vera's deposit such a temptation?

Isaac sat up, vibrating with pent-up energy. Just to be sure, he checked beneath the false bottom of his duffel, and yes, the money he'd skimmed from auction profits over several months was still there, along with his driver's license and Social Security card. He told himself that if he checked to be sure he'd locked the store's doors, he could come back upstairs without handling Vera's money.

Right. Fat chance.

He swallowed hard as his feet found the cool hardwood floor. He could go to the frozen food section for a pizza, so he could pop it into the toaster oven for his breakfast tomorrow.

Uh-huh. The freezers are right next to the warehouse door where the office is, so where would the next stop be?

Somehow Isaac found himself at the apartment's door, his hand on the doorknob and his pulse pounding like a herd of stampeding horses. He assured himself that he could slip the money from its envelope—to be sure it was all there, and that he'd counted it correctly—and then put it back.

Liar, liar, pants on fire.

Isaac paused at the top of the stairway leading to the store. Rather than turning on a light, which someone might notice, he allowed his eyes to adjust to the dimness. With the numerous power lights glimmering on the refrigerator and freezer units and moonlight reflecting in the mirrors along the ceiling, the store glowed eerily beneath him.

But not eerily enough to keep him from descending the steps at a slow, careful pace. The last thing he wanted was for Marlene to discover him at the base of the stairs, dead from a broken neck, because she would *know* he'd been up to no good.

Once on the store floor, Isaac strode straight to the warehouse doors. Within seconds he'd slipped into Dale's desk chair, turned on the green-visored lamp, and pulled out the center drawer. As the envelope fluttered away, the three perfectly flat bills whispered when he separated them. Ben Franklin gazed at him in triplicate.

Happy now? Proud of yourself? Does it make you feel powerful and important to hold someone else's money, young man?

Isaac blinked. Although it was Franklin who'd challenged him, the voice in his head had sounded like Dale's. When he looked away from the bills, he saw that the white envelope had landed beneath a stack of papers so that only two words of his notation showed: *for Vera.*

For the hundredth time since this morning, Isaac

recalled the unsullied innocence on Vera's flawless face, the way her soft brown eyes had widened behind her lenses when he'd suggested that she could take Mrs. Stoughton's deposit.

If she saw him now—if she could read his mind— what would Vera think?

Isaac fell back against the wooden chair with a groan. It took several seconds to get his fast, shallow breathing under control. His white cotton briefs—he despised pajamas—clung to him because he was sweating.

What would Vera think? She would be disgusted. She'd realize that I've earned every scrap of my bad reputation. And she would never speak to me again.

Isaac rose from the chair. As he slowly put the bills back in the envelope, he realized that the physical pain he felt pointed to an addiction—the need to steal just because he could. The need to lie about it. The need to believe that he was smarter and smoother than the plodding, rule-bound Amish around him.

But a new emotional mission was taking hold. More than anything else in the world, he wanted sweet, virtuous Vera to love him—and to believe that Isaac Chupp was as honorable as she.

He replaced the envelope and closed the desk drawer. On his way to the stairs, he took a double-cheese sausage pizza from the freezer. As Isaac trudged up to the apartment, he felt old and heavy and used up from his near misadventure with those enticing C-notes.

Resisting temptation had exhausted him. He was ravenous from the effort of redeeming himself, so he heated the pizza and devoured every bite of it.

Isaac spent the rest of the night watching Dale's TV. Even with all the people on the screen, he was still alone, and lonelier than he'd ever felt in his life.

* * *

Sunday morning as Ezra milked the cows, he was thankful for a job that kept him in the barn, where Maria wouldn't seek him out. He'd agreed to take the early shift on this visiting Sunday so Roman could sleep late and enjoy the morning with his wife, Mary Kate, and their young son, David—which meant Roman would do the late-afternoon milking. Working alone gave Ezra time to think, and because there was no church service, he was concerned about how to deflect Maria's attentions for an entire day.

He refused to lie low in his tiny home. A rain shower had blown through, taking the high humidity with it, so it would be a perfect day—if only he didn't have to avoid the clingy blonde who wanted to lay claim to him. After two evenings of prying himself from her flirtatious advances, Ezra needed something to do—or somewhere else to be. Because, like Isaac, he had no family at Promise Lodge, he was almost tempted to see what Chupp was up to—

But not *that* tempted.

He'd be welcome at Christine and Bishop Monroe's home—or anyone else's—because he had a lot of friends here from Coldstream. But horning in on them didn't appeal to him. The Kuhns would be attending the Mennonite service in Cloverdale with Rosetta and Truman, and then they were going out for dinner. When Beulah had said they'd leave Ezra, Isaac, Ed, and Maria enough food for the day in the lodge kitchen, Maria had smiled brightly and offered to serve the meals.

Ezra, Isaac, and Ed had exchanged a look that said they preferred to fend for themselves.

Sighing, Ezra finished the milking and cleaned up the

equipment. If he went to his tiny home, it would only be a matter of time before Maria came calling, probably with a pan of food to get her foot in the door—which was the *last* thing he wanted. Why couldn't she take a hint that—

"Hey, Overholt! You in there?"

Ezra glanced over his shoulder. "Who wants to know?" he shot back, even though the voice and the body silhouetted in the dawn-lit barn doorway belonged to Ed.

"Somebody who's about to do you a huge favor—if you'll do one for me."

"How huge?" Ezra teased.

"I can take you where Maria won't find you all day."

Ezra's eyes widened. How had Brubaker known what he'd just been wishing for?

"What do I have to do in return?" As he crossed the barn floor, Ezra saw that his neighbor was neatly dressed in clean slacks and a fresh blue shirt, looking a lot better put together than usual.

When he got closer, Ezra also noticed that Ed was shifting from foot to foot, as though he wasn't sure Ezra would go along with his favor.

"Well, I sorta got you invited to spend the day with the Kurtz clan—"

"As in Preacher Marlin and his wife—and Fannie?" Ezra asked, accenting the name of Ed's girlfriend.

"Actually, we're all going to Harley and Minerva's place—beside the barrel factory," Ed said. "Aunt Minerva's my *dat*'s sister, and—maybe you already know this—she's on bed rest so she won't lose another baby. Everybody's going there so she won't be by herself."

"*Jah*, bed rest sounds pretty tiresome," Ezra quipped. By the light of the dawn's first sunbeams, he could tell

Ed hadn't yet revealed the whole favor, but he enjoyed watching the kid fidget.

"My sister and I first came to Promise Lodge last month because Vera's helping Minerva around the house—and she's to be the new schoolteacher this fall," Brubaker went on. "I came along, too, because, well—there was a girl I was trying to get away from, who swore God intended me to be her husband."

Ezra shrugged, although he wondered how Brubaker had gotten involved with someone like that at such a young age.

"She thought she was in the family way because some married fellow—well, anyway, Preacher Marlin got me out of that tight spot," Ed recounted. "So I know how you feel with Maria throwing herself at you."

Suddenly Ed Brubaker wasn't just a kid—he was another guy who attracted girls he didn't want. And he'd escaped the noose of a marriage built upon deception, by the sound of it. But that story could wait for another time.

"Wait a minute," Ezra said. "How come I didn't know you had a sister here?"

Ed shrugged. "Vera was at the Kraybill wedding, and she goes to church, of course, but then she heads back to Harley and Minerva's place to look after our aunt. She does the cooking now, so I hope you won't mind choking down whatever she's thrown together for us today—"

Ezra narrowed his eyes. "What are you not telling me, Brubaker? What's the catch?"

Ed cleared his throat, glancing away. "I was hoping that after dinner you'd come along with Fannie and me for a ride or—well, just about anything! Her *dat*—"

"Preacher Marlin."

"*Jah*, Preacher Marlin has declared that Fannie and I are too young to get married, and he suspects we're getting a little too—"

"Up close and personal?"

"*Jah*." Ed sighed, shaking his head. "So, if you and Vera would come along with us, as our chaperones—"

"You've set me up with your sister? Without asking me first?"

Ed coughed nervously. "Well, I haven't told Vera about this date either," he admitted. "But she's nineteen and she needs to get out with people our age. You're trying not to be with Maria, so I just figured—"

Ezra had lived at Promise Lodge less than a week; he racked his brain, trying to recall a young woman he might've seen at Dale and Irene's wedding. That was a useless exercise, however, because many folks from Cloverdale had attended, so he still had no way of knowing what Vera looked like. He exhaled loudly. If he declined Ed's invitation, the Kurtz family might think he was rude—or they might assume he preferred to spend his time with Maria or Isaac.

He looked Ed in the eye. "What's your sister like, Brubaker? How do I know she's not as desperate and irritating as Maria?"

His friend stood taller, scowling. "Vera's the eldest of five of us kids and she held our family together after our *mamm* died in a farming accident a few years ago," he replied defensively. "She also makes awesome pottery—which is selling like crazy at Dale's store—and she agreed to change her whole life to help Aunt Minerva during her bed rest, and to take over as the schoolteacher here this fall. Can you see Maria doing any of those things?"

Ezra blinked. "Okay, I get your point. But how's your family getting along without her?"

Ed relaxed, smiling again. "Our *dat* remarried a while back—and his new wife, Amanda, taught Vera about making pottery," he explained. "Between you and me, Ezra, when we came here, she said she was hoping to find a nice guy—and Isaac is acting interested in her. Nothing against Chupp, because I just met him when he came here a couple weeks ago, but he seems sort of—"

"If Chupp was sniffing around my sister, I'd be concerned," Ezra put in firmly. "Trust me, I've known him all my life. He says he's turning over a new leaf, but he's got some habits that are mighty hard to change."

"So, it's settled then? You'll join Fannie and me—and Vera—after dinner?" Ed said eagerly. "I thought we could drive to Minerva's house in my wagon, so Maria won't see you walking up the hill, if she's watching from the upstairs windows. She, um, does that a lot."

Ezra groaned. He could easily picture Maria going from one lodge window to the next—probably with binoculars—focused on his tiny home. And he had to admit that Ed had devised a great strategy for transporting him to the Kurtz place.

Chupp only chases after gut-*looking girls, so what've I got to lose? Isaac will be at loose ends—and he'd have the gall to show up at Harley's house out of the blue— so maybe I can rescue Vera from his presence today.*

"All right. Give me half an hour to shower and—"

"You're the best, Ezra!" Ed exclaimed, filling the barn with his excitement. "And don't worry about watching Fannie and me every single moment we're out and about, okay? We wouldn't want to distract you from getting to know Vera!"

Chapter 10

At the sound of her brother's voice coming through the mudroom door, Vera looked away from the breakfast dishes she was washing. Beside her, Fannie giggled and tossed down her flour sack towel.

"Eddie, you finally made it!" she exclaimed as she hurried across the kitchen. "And you brought Ezra! Oh, it's going to be a wonderful-*gut* afternoon."

At the kitchen table, Preacher Marlin looked up from his conversation with his two sons, Harley and Lowell. "Sounds as if you and Eddie have plans, daughter," he said in a purposeful, fatherly tone.

"*Jah*, we do!" Fannie grinned as she stopped beside Eddie, so excited she couldn't stand still. "Dat, this is Ezra Overholt. He just moved here from Coldstream—"

"I've met Ezra, *jah*. Welcome, boys, and come on in."

"—and he and Vera are going with Eddie and me for a nice long ride after dinner!" Fannie continued breathlessly. "You said that would be all right, as long as we had somebody else along. And with Ezra and Vera being older—"

The platter Vera had been washing slipped from her hand and landed in the dishwater with a sickening crash.

Never mind that she would have to remove broken china from a sink full of sudsy water: the young man standing beside Eddie was gazing steadily at her, as though assessing a cow in an auction barn.

As Vera turned away, her cheeks felt scorched and her glasses fogged over. Ezra appeared confident and handsome in fresh clothing that hugged his muscular frame.

He's everything I'm not. And I'm going to kill Eddie for not telling me—

"Vera, are you all right, dear?" Marlin's wife, Frances, asked as she stepped over to the sink. "Let's take the platter from the top of the dishes and then—"

"How about if I help you with that, Vera?" Ezra suggested. "Eddie has surprised you with this double date, just as he blindsided me."

Vera wanted to disappear between the floorboards. Frances now stood on one side of her and Ezra on the other, so she had no chance to flee before he could see how upset she was. When he lowered his hand into the steaming water, feeling for the knob of the drain plug, Ezra's powerful, warm body curved against hers. He smelled clean—enticing in a male way—and Vera prayed that the loud gurgling of the water drowned out the frantic pounding of her pulse.

"Ah," Frances said with a gentle smile. "It seems the platter and the top plate on the pile were the only ones broken. No harm done, Vera. Minerva and I have more dishes than we need."

Vera stood motionless as Frances took the two broken items from the soapsuds. Ezra then lifted the rest of the stacked plates effortlessly onto the countertop as the last of the water swirled around the drain.

"Why don't you kids get better acquainted, and I'll take care of this?" Frances suggested.

When Ezra stepped back, Vera turned to make her escape—but the tall fellow beside her gently grasped her shoulders. When she looked up at him to protest, her glasses were still so fogged from steam and anxiety that she couldn't even discern his facial features. "You—I—"

Ever so gently, he removed her glasses. As he wiped them with the towel Fannie had tossed aside, Vera's mouth dropped open. "You can't—this isn't fair—"

"It's not," Ezra agreed kindly, catching her off guard again as he tenderly positioned her glasses on her nose and replaced the earpieces. "Maybe we can get even with your brother this afternoon, *jah*? Meanwhile, you probably want to, um, change your clothes."

Frowning, Vera followed Ezra's glance and saw the huge wet spot that was making her dress cling to her bust and waist. The platter had splattered her after Fannie's revelation about their double date, and now Vera was even *more* mortified. She sprinted across the kitchen and up the stairs to the safety of her room.

When she saw her reflection in the dresser mirror, Vera knew she couldn't go back downstairs. The big wet spot wasn't the worst of it: the steam from the dishwater had loosened her hair so it drooped beneath her *kapp*. She looked like a frightened little girl. She was so aghast at all that had gone wrong in the past minute, she wanted to curl up in a ball on the bed until this day was over.

But it wasn't even ten in the morning.

The sound of footsteps on the stairs made her stiffen. Fannie peered around the door.

"I—I didn't mean to upset you, Vera," she blurted out. "But Dat's been so dead set on Eddie and me not being alone together—and I got so excited about—well, I thought the four of us could have some fun this afternoon."

Vera swallowed hard. She couldn't remember the last time she'd been out with kids near her age, having fun.

"Eddie's been telling me about Ezra—how much he *likes* him. You see, they eat supper together at the lodge," Fannie continued earnestly. "And you can't ignore the fact that he's super cute, Vera."

Oh, but I'd like to. A shy, messy mouse like me has no business believing a fine-looking man like Ezra could be interested in me. And the nerve of him, taking off my glasses!

"And it isn't as though you're going out alone with a stranger on a blind date." Fannie went to the closet and brought out Vera's newest dress, a lightweight knit the color of terra-cotta. "Wear this. It suits your complexion and brings out your pretty eyes. And when you come downstairs, Minerva wants to see you."

Before Vera could respond, Fannie flashed her a smile and hurried down the hallway—to spend more time with Eddie.

How was it that Fannie, who'd recently turned seventeen, had fallen deeply in love with Eddie yet had taken Vera under her wing like a mother hen? Shaking her head, Vera removed her wet dress. She still had the overwhelming urge to stay in her room, but if Aunt Minerva had requested a visit, she couldn't do that.

After she'd changed her clothes and tidied her hair, Vera stood before the mirror to put on a fresh *kapp*. She was *not* primping to impress Ezra. He was too bold by half, and he would soon tire of her reticence, her tongue-tied and bashful lack of conversation.

But the young woman in the mirror at least *appeared* to be more in control of her emotions. Maybe if she focused on avenging the underhanded trick Eddie and Fannie had pulled on her, the day would somehow pass, and she could return to her normal routine on Monday.

When she stepped into Aunt Minerva's room, however, Vera received an unanticipated warning.

"Fannie and Frances have told me about your reaction to being tricked into a double date," the slender woman sitting up on the bed remarked calmly. "Keep in mind that once you're in the classroom with Lowell and his best buddy, Lavern Peterscheim, those two will do everything in their power to derail your teaching plan— or to embarrass you in front of the entire class."

Vera blinked. This wasn't at all what she'd expected.

"You need to roll with the punches, Vera," Aunt Minerva continued. "And you should have a few responses ready, because if those boys learn they can upset you, they'll do it every chance they get."

Vera's eyebrows rose, and so did her pulse rate. On this humid July Sunday, teaching school seemed a long time away—something she had plenty of time to prepare for. And what did this have to do with Eddie and Fannie setting her up for a date with a total stranger?

Her red-haired aunt was apparently just getting warmed up to her subject, however. She patted the mattress beside her, waiting for Vera to sit down. Minerva gazed into her eyes, so there was no backing down— and no escape.

"I've heard a bit about this young man, Ezra Overholt," she began in a low voice. "When Christine comes over to visit, she often remarks about what a *gut* worker he is—how he genuinely cares for her cows, and how his lifelong experience with his family's dairy has been such a benefit as she's expanded her herd. What's your impression of him, Vera?"

Vera's eyes widened. "Well—at least he doesn't *smell* like a cow!" she blurted out. "I—I just met Ezra. How would I know about—"

"Your intuition is sharp, young lady, so don't tell me you haven't formed an opinion," Aunt Minerva countered. When she smiled, her freckled face lost its tension. "You also have a kind and generous heart and a *gut* head on your shoulders. You have no reason to feel ashamed or unworthy of Ezra—or any man."

Vera looked down at her lap, unsure of how to respond to her aunt's praise.

"When the right fellow looks into your soulful eyes, he won't be able to look away."

Vera shrugged, thinking her aunt's gentle lecture sounded like one of the fairy tales Mamm used to read, about impoverished girls who captivated princes and were whisked away to live happily ever after in a castle.

"And after today's date, maybe you'll realize Ezra's not the man God intends for you," Minerva continued gently. She took Vera's hand between hers. "They say you have to kiss a few toads to find the handsome prince—"

Startled, Vera met her aunt's eyes. Was this more fairy-tale talk? What could it possibly have to do with *her* situation?

"—but if Ezra's not the one, then at least you're on your way to meeting the next potential prince, *jah*? No harm done by spending this afternoon with him, ain't so?" Minerva pointed out. "And I'm glad you'll be out with young people instead of hanging around the house all day."

"But I *like* your house—"

"And you love to make your pottery. You're the best helper I could have possibly asked for," her aunt insisted, "but after the baby comes—Lord willing—and after you're settled into the classroom a few months from now, what'll you have to show for *yourself*? And besides, who else might you go out with here at Promise Lodge?"

When Isaac Chupp's image came to mind, Vera had a hunch that Aunt Minerva had also heard Christine Burkholder's opinion of Dale Kraybill's blond store assistant. She seemed to be finishing her little pep talk.

"Approach Ezra with an open mind, sweetie. And most of all, get out and have a *gut* time. If there's one thing your brother Eddie can show you, it's how to have fun."

Ezra knew the afternoon wasn't off to a good start when Ed and Fannie climbed up to the driver's seat of the big green horse-drawn wagon Brubaker drove to his painting jobs.

"You and Vera can sit in the back," he said, gesturing toward the enclosed wagon. "Sorry, but there's no more room on the bench with Fannie and me."

"Edward Lewis Brubaker, you know I'm not riding back there!" Vera blurted as she glared at her brother. "There's nowhere to sit but—but a *bunk*! And it's a hundred degrees inside that wagon. And it smells like varnish and paint."

After trying to coax pretty, shy Vera into a conversation during the never-ending noon meal, Ezra stepped back. Ed's sister had a voice after all—and a touch of temper, now that her little brother had pushed her beyond her comfort zone.

He suddenly saw Vera in a different light.

She'd made some valid points, too. And she'd saved him the awkwardness of bouncing around on the bunk with her—which was totally inappropriate, even if he found her attractive—inside a wagon that did indeed resemble a furnace.

Ezra crossed his arms, frowning. "Hey, buddy, it was one thing to put me back there this morning so Maria wouldn't see me. But if you think your sister and I will spend the afternoon in that wagon while you and Fannie are enjoying the fresh air, think again."

Ed glanced at Fannie and then shrugged. "Well, I guess that means you can drive, Ezra, so it'll be Fannie and me riding in the—"

"Not while *I'm* along on this trumped-up escapade, you're not! What were you thinking, Edward?"

It was the first time Ezra had ever seen Ed at a loss for words, and it did his heart good to know that Vera could put her brother in his place. He had a horse and a rig, which the Burkholders kept at their place for him, but he didn't feel inclined to offer that as a solution— because this wasn't his problem. Ed's gelding stomped its foot and whickered, which sounded like a disgusted sigh.

Fannie's brow puckered. "What do you suggest, Vera?" she asked. "If you and Ezra don't come with us—and Dat finds out—Eddie and I will be in serious trouble."

Vera shrugged, as though she didn't feel it was her problem, either. "I guess you either find a different vehicle to drive, or we'll stay at Promise Lodge."

After the young couple on the driver's seat studied one another's perplexed expressions for a moment, Eddie brightened. "I know, we can go to my place! I've got a dock on Rainbow Lake, and we can paddle around in the canoe or go fishing or—"

"Awfully hot to catch much," Ezra pointed out. "The fish are probably staying near the bottom, where it's cooler. And I'm not in the mood to fry myself out on the lake either."

Eddie threw up his hands. "Oh, come on, Overholt! I didn't think you were so ancient that you'd forgotten how to make some entertainment on a hot summer's day. Is this what I can look forward to when I'm the ripe old age of twenty-one?"

"Hey! You wrangled me into this situation without asking first, Brubaker—and now you've invited everyone over for a dose of sunstroke," Ezra said tersely. "You sound like a boy who has trouble making a workable plan."

Scowling, Ed turned to Fannie. "Come on, honey-girl, let's park the wagon behind my house. We'll be in plain sight—and maybe our *chaperones* can decide whether they want to join us. Meanwhile," he added, "if Maria's gawking out the lodge window and sees Overholt wandering around alone, I guess he'll get what's coming to him."

The big green wagon had lurched away from its spot

and started down the hill before Ezra realized what Eddie had just said.

During their dispute, Vera had slipped away.

He looked toward the Kurtz place, the barrel factory, and then over to Bishop Monroe's pasture, where the Clydesdales grazed. Where could Vera have gone so quickly? Ezra couldn't blame her for running out of patience—or for wanting to get out of the intense afternoon heat.

But Brubaker had made a point: if he wandered around looking for Vera, Maria would probably spot him.

Chapter 11

Maria washed her dishes at the sink, feeling supremely sorry for herself. In the Kuhn sisters' absence, she'd offered *so* nicely to serve breakfast and Sunday dinner for the three guys who ate their meals at the lodge, but not one of them had shown up. Eddie had probably joined the Kurtz family on this visiting Sunday, because he was obviously head over heels for Fannie.

But what were Ezra and Isaac doing? Had they holed up alone, one in his tiny home and the other in his apartment, rather than spend time with *her*?

"I can't be *that* hard to get along with!" she whimpered as she rinsed her solitary plate and utensils. "I came to Promise Lodge to be with other people, but I'm no better off than I was in Cloverdale. I am *not* spending the rest of this day all by myself!"

Having gazed out the upstairs windows for most of the morning with binoculars she'd found, Maria had formulated a last-resort plan. The sound of her footsteps echoing in the upstairs hallway had driven her crazy—and the air conditioner in the bakery window was further incentive to leave the lodge.

I'll bake Ezra a pie! If I work in the little bakery building, I won't mess up the Kuhns' kitchen—and I'll be cooler, too.

As Maria stepped out onto the lodge's porch, she looked toward the bulk store. No sign of Isaac. Although the Helmuth twins and their twin wives would be spending the day in their double-sized home next to the nursery, she couldn't imagine they would invite Isaac to share their Sunday—and she couldn't envision him spending the day with their two toddlers, either.

What does he do *over there above the store—especially with Dale not coming back until this week?*

Maria shrugged. The murmurings she'd heard about Isaac's checkered past didn't fascinate her nearly as much as thoughts about what Ezra might be doing today. Was he over there by the lake, in his red tiny home? How did he occupy his time in a place that didn't appear big enough to turn around in?

The only movement she saw in that direction was the rippling of the lake's surface. A rowboat was tethered to the dock next to Eddie's blue house, but she'd never seen anyone use it. A shed behind the tiny homes housed several different outdoor games and fishing poles, yet no one was out playing croquet or badminton. The two houses appeared unoccupied . . . which was all the incentive Maria needed to do some snooping before she made Ezra's pie.

Not wanting to be spotted, she crossed the lodge's front lawn and walked between two tall rows of Mattie Troyer's sweet corn. When she reached the private road, however, nothing offered her any cover.

"Nobody can fault me for taking a walk," Maria

reasoned aloud. She glanced up the curving road and saw no one out on their porches or in lawn chairs, which suggested folks were still eating a leisurely noontime meal or cleaning up their dishes.

The closer she got to the lake, the more clearly she realized that if Eddie or Ezra *were* at home, they might have spotted her and suspected what she was up to. Maria was lonely and bored enough not to care, however. She strolled toward the blue house, which resembled a railroad car with a small compartment perched on its top.

She took a moment to get her nerve up and peered through the house's front window.

"Oh, my word," Maria murmured as she gazed into the compact living space. "I'll give you this much, Eddie. You keep a tidy home—but then, you have no choice. There's no room to be messy."

Still seeing no one else around, she walked nearer the shore of Rainbow Lake. The water lapped gently against the wooden dock. Maria was tempted to sit on its edge and dip her feet into the lake, except she'd be easy to spot—and there was no shade; the trees stood behind the two little houses.

She quickly made her way over to the red home, which was built with a slightly different design. Hoping Ezra might be inside, she knocked loudly on the door. After a few moments, she looked through the window. A stray towel lay on the tiny bathroom floor, along with a pile of work clothes outside the door.

"And where did you go in such a hurry?" Maria mused aloud. "Who did you shower for, Ezra? And why wasn't it me?"

The creak of wheels startled her. When she saw the big green wagon with **BRUBAKER PAINTING & STAINING** in large yellow letters, Maria quickly ducked behind Ezra's house. Eddie and Fannie Kurtz sat on the wagon seat, so engrossed in each other that they would never spot her if she timed her escape carefully.

Why did Eddie drive up the hill this morning instead of walking? And why would he be bringing his girlfriend back with him, unless—

Maria wanted to be well away from either tiny home before the young lovebirds spotted her. She could guess what they had in mind—even if Fannie *was* a preacher's daughter—so she listened carefully. When the big rig had rumbled behind Eddie's blue tiny home, Maria made a beeline for the dairy barn. She walked in the building's shadow until she could cut in front of the corral and enter the bakery.

"Close one," she whispered. All that sneaking around had left her breathless.

The little building was stuffy from being closed since Friday, when Phoebe had baked pies to sell at the bulk store. The flip of a switch made the air conditioner hum to life, and soon Maria felt refreshed.

Being inside the bakery brought back a lot of memories. She didn't dwell on the day she'd had this building moved from Cloverdale—when the truck driver had taken out the arched metal Promise Lodge sign and several trees at the entry. She didn't think about all the baked goods she'd been unable to sell, either, or the way the Kuhn sisters had said she didn't have much of a head for business. And she certainly didn't want to take the blame for Rosetta's breaking her engagement to Truman—because Rosetta had assumed, incorrectly, that Maria was trying to win him for herself.

"Today is different," Maria promised herself as she went behind the counter to find the flour, lard, and fillings she wanted. "Today is the first day of the rest of my life with Ezra!"

Isaac shook his head as he gazed out his apartment's back window. After peering into both tiny homes, Maria had entered the bakery, no doubt with another plan for enticing Ezra into her clutches. Before that, Brubaker and his girlfriend had parked the green wagon in the shade behind his house. It bugged Isaac that *he* had nothing to do and nowhere to go on this visiting Sunday.

It bothered him more that Overholt wasn't at home.

He figured Vera had spent the day with her family at the Kurtz place. But now that her younger brother and Fannie had escaped the older generation, what was Vera doing? Was she really such a recluse that she preferred her aunt and uncle's company to that of the younger folks at Promise Lodge—namely *him*?

Or is she secretly seeing Ezra? And is he smooth enough to be kissing her and holding her without letting on about his love life during our meals at the lodge?

In his fantasies, Isaac had kissed Vera dozens of times, so the possibility that Ezra might actually be receiving her affection annoyed him. A lot. As he went downstairs and through the warehouse, Isaac was so disturbed by his mental images of Overholt making out with Vera that he could almost forget about the three hundred dollars in Dale's desk drawer. Almost.

As he strode past Dale's new home and the lodge, his main motive was to find Vera and spend the rest of the afternoon with her. He'd given her plenty of time to assess his past wrongdoing—to talk to Deborah, Rosetta, and Christine. It was time to make his move. Talking to her in the store about her pottery didn't count.

Especially if Overholt had lured Vera beyond the *talking* stage.

Chapter 12

As Vera removed the fired dishes from her kiln, she told herself this activity didn't count as work on the Sabbath. After all, Uncle Harley had tended his sheep and Bishop Monroe had fed and watered his Clydesdales early this morning—just as Ezra had milked Christine's dairy cows. She'd become so exasperated by her brother's behavior, on top of breaking Aunt Minerva's plates, that it seemed wise to duck into the shed where she made her pottery.

Everyone needs a time-out now and then. By the time Eddie, Fannie, and Ezra have left, I'll be settled enough to return to the house.

She was lifting the second royal blue serving bowl from the kiln, however, when a tall, broad shadow blocked the sunlight coming through the doorway.

Vera froze. She carefully set the beautiful piece on her shelf before she turned to greet her visitor. Considering how quickly her pulse had shot into high gear, along with her anxiety level, it was a miracle that Mrs. Stoughton's bowl wasn't lying in pieces on the concrete floor.

"Ezra," she murmured. "You found my hideaway."

"I wanted to apologize for anything I might've done to—oh, wow," he whispered as he spotted the plates, bowls, and other pieces in various stages of completion. "Ed told me you were a potter, but I had no idea that— well, these are fabulous, Vera!"

"*Denki*," she said, clasping her hands so she didn't appear as agitated as she felt. "A nice customer at the store ordered these serving bowls to go with a set of dishes I'd added to my display on Friday. I was so fed up with Eddie—playing matchmaker and then expecting us to ride in the back of his wagon—"

"They're on their own now," Ezra put in with an easy shrug. "I don't understand why Preacher Marlin insists that Ed and Fannie can't be alone together—or get married. Lots of kids their age do that."

"*Jah*, Marlin's being very protective," Vera agreed. "I suppose it's because Eddie and I have only lived at Promise Lodge since early June—although, because Minerva is our *dat*'s sister, the Kurtz family has known us since she and Harley married several years ago. Minerva says Fannie fell in love with my brother the first time they met. And Eddie has done some fast catching up these past few weeks."

Ezra nodded, moving closer as he looked at her pottery pieces. It unnerved her, having a tall, muscular man invade the workspace she shared with Harley's lawn equipment—even if he was considerate enough to study the plates and bowls without touching them.

"This is a beautiful shade of blue," he said. "I'm not a guy who goes for flowery dishes, but I really like these red and yellow tulips. They're bold and they don't back down."

I could say the same for you, Ezra Overholt.

Vera would never voice her thought aloud, but because Ezra sounded sincerely interested in her work, she was warming up to him. He wasn't backing her into a corner, either, nor was he behaving as though he would use his size and superior strength to compromise her.

"Vera, I'm sorry Ed's plan for our afternoon didn't work out. But I'm glad I've met you," Ezra said as he straightened to his full height. "You'd probably like to look over your pottery without me horning in, but I hope I can see you again. Sometime soon?"

Her eyes widened and her mouth went dry. "I—I'd like that," she stammered. Nudging her glasses back into place, Vera added, "I'm sorry I overreacted when you took off my specs and wiped them dry, Ezra. I suspect I've blown a lot of things out of proportion today."

When Ezra shrugged, he looked boyishly appealing. "Your brother has a way of lighting little fires and leaving them for other folks to put out. See you around, Vera."

As he stepped out of the shed, Vera released the breath she didn't realize she'd been holding.

Your brother has a way of lighting little fires . . .

Vera sensed a flame had indeed been kindled, but Eddie had nothing to do with it.

Ezra strolled toward the pasture where Harley Kurtz's sheep grazed with a border collie lying in the shade watching them. When the dog spotted him, it sat up, focusing intently on his movements even though Ezra didn't intend to visit the herd. He hoped to avoid Maria by winding through the trees to loop around the bulk store and approach his tiny home from the road. It was a long, hot walk to elude her scrutiny—and her binoculars—but what else did he have to do this afternoon?

At least Vera agreed to spend time with me again. Considering our rough start, we've made some progress.

A lone figure on the road made Ezra pause and instinctively duck behind a tree. Isaac's long strides and tense expression were sure signs that he was on a mission—and would not be deterred.

Ezra doubted that Isaac was joining the conversations at the Kurtz home today to spend time with Vera. Did the angular blond know where she worked on her pottery? Ezra hadn't gotten the impression that Vera was expecting a guest, so he doubled back toward the shed, remaining hidden.

When Chupp topped the hill and passed the Burkholder place, he glanced toward the Kurtz home and the barrel factory but stepped off the road. The way he looked around, zigzagging from the stable to the chicken house, told Ezra this was Isaac's first time on the property. And when Chupp beelined toward the machinery shed, the triumphant expression on his face warned Ezra to move in closer.

He noticed that Bishop Monroe and Christine were sitting on their back porch with Preacher Amos and Mattie, but this was no time to go for a visit.

When a slender silhouette cut the light coming through the shed's doorway, Vera stiffened. She kept facing the wall and her pottery pieces, telling herself to remain calm. This visitor's rapid breathing—the way he stared without greeting her—told her that Isaac had come calling. And he had a specific agenda in mind.

Her mouth went dry. Goose bumps prickled on her arms and back. It was one thing to deal with the smooth-talking blond in a store filled with shoppers, when Marlene or Dale were nearby. Getting cornered in a shed on the far edge of Harley's property was another situation altogether.

Get outside. If I act as though I was leaving anyway—returning to the house—

"Vera."

His proprietary tone made her swallow hard. She stepped away from the shelves covered with pottery pieces, hoping she appeared more confident than she felt.

"Hey there, Isaac," she said with a tight smile. "I was just going to the house for some lemonade. Care to join me?"

"Nope. I came to see *you*, girl."

As her pulse raced, Vera searched for the right words—and a way to get around Isaac. "Let's go sit in the shade," she suggested, gesturing toward the lawn. "It's way too warm in here to—"

"Is that because you and Overholt were heating things up, getting hot and bothered—"

"No!" she cried out. Had Isaac been spying on them, waiting for Ezra to leave?

"—and I've had these mental flashes of you kissing him and giving in to—"

"That's not true!" Vera protested, hating the telltale tears that sprang to her eyes. She tried to rush past him, but his arm shot out to block her escape.

"—everything he wants when it's *me* who's helped sell your pottery, Vera!" Isaac continued in an escalating, manic voice. "I fell in love with you the first time I saw—"

When he clutched her close, Vera screamed—until Isaac smothered her outcry with a hard, crushing kiss. As his fingers gripped her head, her glasses snapped. She flailed at him with her free hand, trying desperately to turn her head away from—

"Let her go, Chupp! Turn her loose!"

Suddenly two strong hands were prying Isaac away from her. She gasped for breath, relieved that Ezra had arrived before Isaac could take any further advantage of her. When Ezra roughly shoved him out of the shed, Vera heard someone else approaching.

"What's going on in there?"

"Vera, honey, are you all right?"

Her face was aflame. She'd never felt so mortified. The coppery tang of blood meant her lip was bleeding, and here came Bishop Monroe, Christine, and Mattie to witness her embarrassment.

"I—I'm okay," she rasped, gingerly removing her glasses. The side piece had broken off, but she was too upset to look for it before Ezra gently led her outside.

Preacher Amos was standing sternly beside Isaac, who lay sprawled in the grass. "What do you have to say for yourself, young man?" he demanded. "Vera wouldn't have screamed if she'd been having a *gut* time with agreeable company."

"We'll have a meeting of the minds, right now, at my place," Bishop Monroe put in, pointing toward his porch. "Ezra, please join us to add your perspective. Christine, if you and Mattie would see to Vera—"

"Of course, we will," the bishop's wife said as she slipped an arm around Vera's shoulders.

"And we'll speak to Dale about this when he returns home tomorrow, too," Mattie put in, glaring at Isaac. "Could be you'll lose your job, Mr. Chupp."

Chapter 13

As Isaac sat on the Burkholders' back porch, perched nervously on the edge of an Adirondack chair, he knew Preacher Amos and Bishop Monroe would send him away without further ado.

How do I explain what just happened with Vera? I never intended to—

"Shall we bow our heads for a word of prayer?" the bishop said softly. "Dear Lord, Father of us all, forgive our foolish, impulsive ways and help us understand Your will for each of us. Give us the grace to admit when we've made mistakes, the gumption to ask forgiveness for them, and the strength to move forward on a more honorable path. Amen."

Isaac kept his eyes squeezed shut beyond the prayer's closing. Monroe Burkholder was so different from his *dat*—so compassionate and patient. He even spoke to God with a reverence that inspired Isaac to believe the Lord cared for him, personally. Did he dare hope this bishop might listen to him, rather than condemning him and ordering him to leave?

"Isaac, how did you come to be inside Harley's shed?"

Isaac focused on the bishop as he framed his answer.

"I didn't intend to—I don't *know*, sir," he stammered. "I was tired of being alone above the store—and it *is* a visiting Sunday—so I walked over to spend some time with Vera.

"Although," he added, glaring sourly at Overholt, "I had a feeling Ezra might already be there. And since I'd told Vera that *I* wanted to be the guy who—"

"And had you been there, Ezra?" Preacher Amos interrupted. "When Vera screamed, you got to the shed mighty fast."

From the porch swing, where he sat beside Amos, Ezra flashed Isaac an irritated glance. "I'd been there, *jah*," he replied. "But then, I'd been at the Kurtz place most of the morning and for the noon meal, because Ed Brubaker invited me."

Isaac's stomach roiled with acid and envy. "So, you and Vera slipped out to the shed—as though she was going to show you her pottery—but you, of course, had to kiss her and—"

"I did no such thing!" Ezra protested. "I just met her this morning, and it didn't go well. Her brother roped us into a blind date to chaperone him and Fannie, and neither of us appreciated it."

"Isaac, it sounds like you've let your imagination run away with you," Bishop Monroe remarked with a frown. "Your story doesn't match up with Ezra's at all."

"And you have too much time on your hands in that upstairs apartment," Preacher Amos chimed in. "It's unnatural to be alone so much. We need to find you a different place to live."

"That depends on whether Dale will keep you on, after what you've done," the bishop pointed out. "You can't go around forcing yourself on—"

"I only wanted to kiss her," Isaac muttered, slumping in the chair.

"You made her lip bleed! And you broke her glasses," Ezra blurted out. "What kind of a kiss was that?"

Truth be told, Isaac had gotten so carried away on a wave of need—to win Vera for himself rather than letting Ezra have her—he didn't remember what had happened after he'd spotted her inside the shed. And that scared him a little.

"I loved her the moment I saw her," he confessed, shaking his head. "And the first time Vera looked at me and nudged those glasses up her nose, I—I was hooked. Is it any wonder I wanted to kiss her? I've been so patient—I've given her a couple of weeks to get acquainted with me—"

"Maybe so," Ezra butted in, "but you have a nasty way of expressing your so-called love—especially when Vera didn't invite you into the shed. After what you did to her, why would she ever want to look at you again?"

Even as Isaac shot daggers at Overholt, he had a sick feeling that his rival was right. And it didn't set well.

"Sometimes we men need to realize that the way *we* see a relationship—the way we feel—might not match up with what the woman of our dreams is thinking."

Isaac blinked. Who could have anticipated Amos Troyer making such a statement about *feelings*? It seemed downright un-Amish for a grown man—especially a preacher—to wax romantic rather than to expect his woman to go along with his wants and needs. His *dat* had been preaching the gospel of submission since before Isaac was born.

Bishop Monroe shifted in his chair. "The next move

is yours, Isaac. An apology is in order. And the sooner you express it, the better, as far as helping Vera—and the rest of us—see you in a more positive light.

"But I won't tell you what to do." Burkholder leaned his elbows on his knees, holding Isaac's gaze. "If your apology is to be sincere, you need to initiate it. Not Amos or me."

Another apology. Because he'd lost his head over Vera—succumbed to his overwhelming need to kiss her—Isaac now had to beg for *four* pardons. How was it that he'd rubbed so many women the wrong way? And how could he face Vera now that he'd injured her?

Isaac hung his head. Why were Burkholder and Troyer speaking to him in such reasonable voices? Why weren't they ranting at him, promising that God would condemn him to eternal damnation if he didn't do what they told him? For the first time in his life, Isaac glimpsed a faith that made it worth the trouble of doing the right thing rather than doing as he pleased.

"All right. I'll go over there and talk to her," he mumbled.

"God bless you, and *gut* luck," the bishop said with a nod. "If your apology doesn't go the way you want it to, be patient and try again, Isaac. Life is a road, and every step along the way is a lesson."

"And if you choose *not* to ask Vera for forgiveness," warned Preacher Amos, "we'll be hearing your confession at church next Sunday, so the congregation can vote on your penance."

After the way he'd made Rosetta cry, Isaac knew all about apologies that hadn't gone well. The last thing he wanted was to go down on his knees in front of everyone in the Promise Lodge district, to be questioned about this very personal incident—especially because Vera would be there watching the inquisition. Witnessing his humiliation.

Isaac stood up. He looked toward the Kurtz place, wondering what to say—how to explain himself to Vera, especially if other folks were listening. He started off the porch but paused.

"*Denki* for your help," Isaac said, looking first at the bishop and then at Preacher Amos. "I have a lot to think about. And don't *you* even think about following me over there to hear what I say to Vera," he added with a scowl for Ezra.

Overholt's expression didn't waver. "Wouldn't dream of it. You got yourself into this mess. You're on your own."

Isaac walked across the clipped grass toward the Kurtz home. His body and soul felt so heavy, he could've been wearing a concrete overcoat. He dreaded the glares he'd get from Preacher Marlin and the rest of the Kurtz clan—not to mention Mattie and Christine—

But what do I care about them? I just want Vera to understand my feelings for her so she'll return them someday.

Bolstered by his hope for the future—and his male pride—Isaac stepped up to the back porch of the Kurtz house. He knocked tentatively on the screen door.

Harley answered, but he didn't seem inclined to let Isaac in. And if the tall, heavyset man of the house denied him entrance, what would he do?

"What's on your mind?" Vera's uncle demanded. "I'll tell you this much, Chupp. If you ever enter my machine shed again—"

"I—I've come to apologize to Vera!" he blurted out.

Harley scowled, but he pushed the door open. "I should hope so, considering the way you split her lip. After you beg her forgiveness, you won't be visiting Vera again, either. Follow me."

Isaac felt like a prisoner being led to his execution. Because Harley's bulky form blocked his view, he didn't see who was in the kitchen—until Preacher Marlin and Lowell stopped talking to watch him from the table. Their somber, judgmental stares made Isaac glad he was entering the front room—

Until Harley stepped aside. Christine and Mattie were sitting on the couch, comforting Vera as she held an ice pack to her lower lip. Minerva sat nearby in a rocking chair, pale and shaken. Isaac was expecting their disapproving glares, and they didn't skimp on scorn, either.

When Vera's brown eyes widened and she reached for Mattie's hand, however, Isaac's heart lurched. She resembled a frightened fawn facing her predator, fearing for her life. Without her glasses she looked even more vulnerable.

I did that to her. She's scared to death of me, and she'll never trust me again.

Rather than accept a future without Vera, however, Isaac told himself to man up and say how sorry he was. Before, when the Bender barns had caught fire and he'd wrestled with Deborah in a ditch, he'd been drunk. And he'd walked away from the aftermath.

I wasn't in love with them. Their feelings didn't matter so much because I didn't suffer along with them.

"Cat got your tongue, Isaac?" Christine demanded in a low voice. "We're not in the mood for your presence unless you've come for a *gut* reason."

Isaac let out the breath that had stuck in his throat. He didn't like to show emotion in front of others, but maybe if these women saw how miserable he was— maybe if he groveled enough—they'd tell Bishop Monroe and Preacher Amos how penitent and sincere his apology had sounded.

"Vera, I'm so sorry—I never intended to hurt you," he began, pleading with his eyes and an emotion-choked voice. "I was lonely for you, and I lost my head, and—well, can you please forgive me?"

The room went silent, except for the ticking of the mantel clock. Vera was trembling, looking at her lap and trying not to cry.

Isaac got an inner glimpse of hell. He felt the flames of remorse licking at his lonely soul. As the silence stretched on—except for the infernal ticking of the clock—he began to worry.

What if she didn't accept his apology? He'd always believed that when a guilty party pleaded for forgiveness, the victim was supposed to grant it, because that's how the Bible said the situation should play out.

But what if Vera said *no*? What if she—like Rosetta— told him to beg again when she was in a better frame of mind? With four other sets of eyes focused on him, Isaac wasn't sure how much longer he could remain in the room if Vera refused to look at him.

She finally glanced up, blinking rapidly as she removed the ice pack. "I accept your apology," she rasped. "Now please go away."

Not allowing himself to deflate in front of Vera, Isaac left the front room. He wasn't surprised that

Preacher Marlin didn't let him escape without getting a word in.

"You've taken the first step, Isaac," he said sternly, "but your apology means nothing if it doesn't lead to some serious soul searching about why you feel compelled to hurt others—especially women—with such utter disregard for their well-being, and with no apparent remorse or intention of compensating for their losses. You're old enough to leave that habit behind you. If you can."

Isaac stalked out the way he'd come in, seething. The nerve of Kurtz, to forget that his whole motivation for coming to Promise Lodge had been to start fresh. And what did the preacher mean about his *habit* being so ingrained that he couldn't stop hurting people?

"I can do anything I decide to do," Isaac muttered as he strode away from the Kurtz place. "I don't have to listen to—"

But he did have to listen. Harley had told him he wouldn't be seeing Vera anymore. And Vera herself had told him to go away. Maybe she'd only accepted his apology so he would leave.

And what if Marlin was right? What if I become so fixated on my own wants that I don't care—or even realize—what I'm doing until the damage is done? I never intended to split Vera's lip. I just got a mental picture of Overholt kissing her and went berserk.

Trouble was, Isaac didn't even recall what Vera's lips had felt or tasted like. All those times he'd fantasized about kissing her until she was crazy in love with him had led to his banishment from her life. His romantic imaginings had gone very wrong, and he didn't recall the exact moment he'd lost control. He didn't want to think about what might've happened if Overholt hadn't pried him away from the young woman of his dreams.

By the time he was striding down the hill toward the lodge, Isaac was in such a state of emotional disarray, he didn't know what he felt or what he thought—or what he was going to do about the hot mess he'd become.

Until the store opens tomorrow, I'll just hole up in my apartment . . . which was where this whole problem started.

Chapter 14

When Maria stepped out of the bakery with a picture-perfect cherry pie, she was so elated—in such a hurry to find Ezra—that she barely felt the aluminum pan singeing her fingers. There was no time to waste if she wanted to present her creation in its freshest, most fragrant form.

But where had Ezra gone? While she'd done her baking, she'd peered out the windows every minute or two to see if he was walking home. She had to find him, because she couldn't leave a pie on his doorstep with a note. It would be just like Eddie to watch her put it there and then snatch it away as a joke.

When she spotted Isaac striding down the hill, she hurried toward him. "Isaac, hi!" she called out. "Have you seen Ezra today?"

The slender blond blinked, as though he'd been lost in thought. "*Jah*, I have," he said as he kept walking.

Maria frowned. Isaac had his moods, but she'd never seen him scowling so intently. "So, where is he?" she asked earnestly. "I made this pie—"

Isaac's curdled expression silenced her. He stopped

in the road, looking her over as though deciding whether he wanted to respond—and appearing upset enough to knock the pie out of her hands.

"If you really want to know," he began ominously, "Overholt has spent the entire morning up at the Kurtz place—with Vera Brubaker. He doesn't want anything to do with you, Maria. Just as Vera has nothing more to say to me. There you have it!" he added with a sneer. "Happy now?"

Maria felt as though a snake had struck without warning, stunning her with its venom. After her initial shock wore off, she burst into tears. How had Ezra gotten up the hill without her seeing—

He was in the back of Eddie's wagon.

Her eyes widened. Eddie, who'd had no logical reason to drive his big wagon the short distance to the Kurtz place, had been hiding Ezra in the back. Both boys had conspired to spend the day away from *her*. And Isaac had gone up there, too, apparently because this Vera—Eddie's sister, whom Maria hadn't met—was so beautiful and enticing that guys just couldn't resist her.

With a sob, Maria threw the pie to the ground and hurried toward the back door of the lodge. During her startling exchange with Isaac, she hadn't noticed Truman's white pickup parking beside the front porch, bringing the Kuhn sisters home from their Sunday morning in Cloverdale.

"*Gut* afternoon, Maria!" Ruby exclaimed cheerfully.

"How was the meat loaf we left you?" Beulah chimed in.

Maria waved and walked faster. The last thing she

wanted was two old busybodies horning in on her pity party.

"Maria, I stopped to look at the bakery building," Truman called out from the driver's side window. "Would this be a *gut* time to discuss your plans for—"

"*No!*"

Maria jogged the final few steps to the mudroom door and let it slam behind her. Would these people *never* figure out that she wanted to be left alone?

Well, except for Ezra. But he apparently doesn't want anything to do with me.

When she reached her apartment upstairs, she slammed that door, too. Not that it made her feel any better.

Isaac swooped down on the discarded pie, grateful that it had landed right-side up. He'd seen the Wickeys' pickup pulling in while he'd set Maria straight about Overholt. He was hoping the truck's occupants would be so distracted by her drama that they wouldn't notice him hurrying along to duck between the tall rows of sweet corn growing near the road.

No such luck.

As he reached Mattie's nearest garden plot, he heard the low rumble of the truck slowly coming up behind him.

"Isaac, I've had an uplifting morning in church, so I'm ready to reconsider your apology," Rosetta said out her window. "Would you like a ride to the house? We'll talk about it over coffee and—"

"*No!*"

It was pointless to continue down the corn rows now

that he'd been caught, but Isaac went anyway. Holding
the pie out in front of him, he hurried toward the far end
of the plot, heedless of the long, green leaves slapping
his face.

*I'll pay for this. Rosetta won't let me forget that she
offered me another chance. But how can I talk to her
about all the sins she'll dredge up from my past when
I've been banned from ever seeing Vera again?*

At the end of the garden plot, Isaac broke into a run
and didn't stop until he'd reached the bulk store. He was
breathless as he raced up the stairs—but he still had
enough air to release a torrent of swear words when he
reached the apartment. He cussed Ezra at the top of his
lungs and then added a phrase or two for Harley and
Preacher Marlin before he ran out of steam and flopped
down on the sofa.

Panting, he gazed at the pie on his lap. Its beautiful
golden crust glistened with sugar. Beneath the five perfect leaf-shaped holes Maria had cut, red cherries and
thickened juice completed the picture of deliciousness.

Isaac let out a short laugh. Who knew that ditzy, airheaded Maria Zehr had the patience or skill to produce
a pie that could've won a medal at the county fair? Sure,
she ran a bakery, but he'd assumed her finished prod-
ucts came up as short as her administrative skills—at
least the way Beulah and Ruby had described them.

As he fetched a fork, he chuckled again. Overholt
was missing out on Maria's love offering, and Isaac
intended to enjoy every sweet, fragrant bite of the pie
she'd baked for the handsome, hardworking pillar of
Coldstream's youth community. It had always irked him
that folks couldn't say Ezra's name without remarking

how well he'd turned out—and how his parents surely must be proud of him.

No one had ever said such things about Bishop Obadiah's youngest son.

Isaac sat down at the table to better enjoy the only meal he'd had today. Without bothering to cut the pie in slices, he placed his fork in one of the leaf-shaped holes and pushed down—*hard*. Scowling, he tapped the top crust with the fork. The loud *thunk-thunk-thunk* told him it was as solid as a rock. When he'd cracked the top and lifted a piece of the broken crust, he saw that it was about half an inch thick.

"Well, Overholt, you can thank me later. I just saved you from breaking a tooth," he muttered.

Isaac devoured the warm cherry filling. It was very sweet, and its deep red color suggested that it had come from a can.

No surprise there. He couldn't picture Maria standing at the stove, patiently stirring cherries and sugar—although she could've found those ingredients in Phoebe and Irene's bakery, because they made their delectable fillings from scratch.

"Another fantasy bites the dust," he joked as he tossed the inedible pie crust in the wastebasket.

But it wasn't so funny that his beloved fantasies about Vera had also been trashed today.

As he paced from one window to the next, he saw nothing through his haze of anger and bitterness. By this time tomorrow, Dale would be back in the store—and he would've heard about his new employee's misbehavior. Word traveled fast around Promise Lodge.

And because Vera was to deliver her finished dishes

for Mrs. Stoughton tomorrow, Kraybill would see exactly how brutal Isaac's kiss had been.

Isaac's sigh ended in a whimper. If the storekeeper dismissed him, he had to be ready to hit the road with nothing but his duffel. Again.

Chapter 15

Dressed and dragging herself into a pointless Monday, Maria closed her apartment door with a sigh. She'd arrived five days ago and was still in a state of limbo: she didn't want to go back to Cloverdale and face her burned-out bakery, but she hadn't found the happy new life she'd dreamed of at Promise Lodge, either.

Aromas of perking coffee, sweet cinnamon, and sizzling sausage drifted up the back stairs from the kitchen—along with a strident female voice.

"I can't believe it, Beulah! I went in this morning to bake pies for the bulk store, and the kitchen was a *mess*! Flour all over the floor and strips of raw dough left on the worktable—and the oven was on! Thank *gut*ness there wasn't a fire!"

At the top of the back stairway, Maria winced. In her excitement about taking the cherry pie to Ezra—and then having Isaac ruin her day—she'd totally forgotten about returning to the bakery. And now Phoebe Troyer was demanding answers.

"I know *you* ladies didn't leave the bakery in such a

state," the young woman continued. "Do you suppose Maria was baking—and on a Sunday?"

One of the Kuhn sisters cleared her throat loudly. Ruby's voice rang in the enclosed staircase. "You might as well come on down, Maria."

"*Jah*, we know you're up there," Beulah put in. "And we saw you carrying that pie yesterday afternoon."

For the umpteenth time Maria muttered about having no privacy here—the Kuhns heard every closing door and creak of the floor, and there were no other tenants to blame things on. As she descended the stairs, her mind raced. Phoebe had every reason to be upset—especially because she'd found the oven burning—but Maria needed to turn her apology into a plea for employment. If she messed up again, the Kuhns and Rosetta would send her away because she hadn't found a *purpose*.

As she reached the bottom step, Maria put on a depressed expression—which wasn't difficult, considering the way Isaac had shot down her dreams about Ezra. With a sorrow-filled sigh, she looked at the attractive blonde who awaited her with crossed arms and a scowl.

"Phoebe, I—I'm *really* sorry I left your bakery in a mess yesterday," Maria began, hoping she sounded pathetic enough. "As I was taking a pie from the oven, I received some devastating news—"

A short, sarcastic laugh in the dining room told her Isaac had come over for breakfast, and she kicked herself for not thinking of that possibility. Maria went on with her apology, however. If Ezra wanted nothing to do with her, it was even more important for her to find meaningful work, wasn't it?

"—and I completely forgot that I'd left your oven

on," she continued forlornly. "Please figure up how much I owe you for the ingredients and the propane I used, and the trouble I've caused you.

"Or—or better yet," Maria said, her eyes widening with a brilliant idea, "I could make it up to you by *working*—baking things for you to sell! Pastries and breads and cookies like I've made in *my* bakery! And then you and Irene could take me on as a partner—"

"Stop right there," Phoebe put in, holding up her hand. "We call our business Promise Lodge Pies because we bake *pies*. And besides, Irene also decides about anybody else working with us—and she called this morning to say she and Dale are extending their trip for another week."

Maria's shoulders fell. For a few seconds, she'd envisioned herself happily baking her favorite pastries and sweet rolls at Promise Lodge and selling every last one of them at Dale's bulk store—capitalizing on Phoebe and Irene's success. She was a genius for thinking of it, because she'd no longer have a building to maintain, and—

"I've already cleaned up your mess, of course, so I could bake my pies," Phoebe said. "I'm sorry about your bad news, Maria, but please don't use our bakery again. Especially without asking us first."

Nodding to the Kuhn sisters, Phoebe walked briskly through the mudroom and out the back door. Ruby and Beulah were putting sausages, pancakes, and eggs on platters. Their expressions suggested that they had plenty to say to Maria, but they were saving it for later.

"If you'll bring that syrup, please, we're ready to eat," Beulah said as she started toward the dining room.

"*Jah*, sounds like Ezra and Eddie are coming in," Ruby put in with a nod. "Timing is everything!"

Sighing, Maria picked up the warm pitcher filled with pancake syrup. *Her* timing wasn't so good, because now she had to sit through a meal with Ezra, Eddie, and Isaac—all of whom she had issues with.

Should've stayed in bed. Should've just rolled over and waited until later to eat by myself.

As Isaac helped himself to three feather-light pancakes, he glanced at his tablemates and kept his mouth shut. Eddie was brooding, not making eye contact. Ezra nodded a curt greeting but still seemed put out about Isaac's behavior with Vera. Maria—not surprisingly—was ready to burst into tears, probably because Ezra didn't seem inclined to talk to her. The Kuhn sisters were in their usual upbeat moods, but they were no doubt considering the information Phoebe Troyer had revealed about the state of her bakery this morning.

Isaac, too, was reviewing what he'd overheard during Phoebe's visit. One line in particular made him thrum like an electrical wire.

. . . *she called this morning to say she and Dale are extending their trip for another week.*

All last evening Isaac had stewed over how Dale would react to his incident with Vera, but now he had a reprieve! Dale had surely spoken with Marlene about how things were going at the store and had decided he could stay away several more days—which meant Marlene had given a good report! By the time the newlyweds returned, Vera's lip would be healed and the immediate tension about Isaac's inappropriate behavior would've eased. He had apologized to Vera, after all—in front of witnesses—and she had accepted it.

Forgive and forget *is the key phrase here. Emphasis on the* forget *part.*

Ruby passed the sausages to Eddie, her brows furrowed with concern. "You look like a fellow who's lost his last friend, dearie," she said softly. "Is everything all right?"

When Eddie stabbed a couple of sausage links, three others rolled onto the table. "You're close," he replied morosely. "Fannie's been grounded, and I'm not allowed to see her again. We, um, sort of defied her *dat*'s orders yesterday so I had to call my parents—like I'm a schoolboy in trouble with the teacher. They're coming to Promise Lodge next weekend to straighten things out."

"Ah. Well, Preacher Marlin's a man of his word," Beulah observed gently. "If you went against his rules, there were bound to be consequences, *jah*?"

Eddie glanced darkly at Ezra. "Fannie and I invited my sister and Ezra to be our chaperones—*following* Preacher Marlin's rules. But they ducked out on us."

"And that's all we're going to say about that," Ezra put in bluntly.

Isaac focused on his breakfast, making quick work of the savory sausages, three eggs, and pancakes as light and feathery as his new mood. When he'd scraped the last of the syrup from his plate, he stood up.

"*Denki* for a really fine meal," he said, smiling at the Kuhns. "Can't let Marlene think I'm slacking while she gets the store ready for another day."

Isaac strode through the dining room and out the lodge's front door before anyone could delay him. He dashed across the lawn, his heart pounding as he entered the warehouse.

Sure enough, the red message light on Dale's office phone was blinking. Holding his breath, Isaac pushed the button.

"*Gut* morning, Isaac! Irene and I are having such a fine time in Kansas City that we're staying an extra week. Marlene has assured me that you two have everything under control, so keep up the *gut* work and we'll see you next Sunday."

Isaac was over-the-moon elated. Dale had praised him—was so confident about the way things were going in his absence that he was vacationing for another week! Isaac felt as if he'd been given a new lease on life—a chance to compensate for the way he'd come on too strong with Vera. He played the message again, basking in the sunshine of Kraybill's compliments.

From now on he would toe the line. He would work diligently—do even more of a sales job when customers noticed Vera's pottery. He would prove that Isaac Chupp had overcome his shady past and could be trusted with the large amount of money that came into the cash register every day. And he would tackle those apologies he owed Deborah, Christine, and Rosetta—with extra confidence and sincerity because God would give him the right words to convince those women that he meant what he was saying.

He turned around and stopped short. How long had Marlene been standing outside the office, observing him through the glass window?

As she opened the door for him, Isaac was once again aware that—like her twin brother, Mose Fisher—Marlene stood head and shoulders taller than he was.

She wasn't the least bit fat, but she was *substantial*. Not a woman he wanted to challenge, either physically or verbally.

"I nearly bit my tongue in two, not telling Dale about what you did to Vera yesterday," she said as she raised one dark eyebrow. "I didn't keep quiet for *you*, Isaac. I wanted Dale and Irene to enjoy another well-deserved week together—and I figured that after they return, Bishop Monroe or Preacher Marlin will tell him what you did. Then it's between you and Dale, whether you still have a job."

With difficulty, Isaac willed his big breakfast to remain in his stomach. "Um, *denki*," he said hoarsely. "I—I owe you, Marlene."

"*Jah*, you do. Let's get to work."

Chapter 16

Vera entered the store at ten o'clock Monday morning with her loaded wagon, relieved to see Marlene coming to greet her—and even happier that Mrs. Stoughton had arrived early. Isaac was talking to a customer at the cash register, and Vera thanked God that she didn't have to use any of the lines she'd rehearsed in case she had to deal with him.

"Oh, Vera, look at all these beautiful dishes!" Mrs. Stoughton gushed as she gazed into the wagon. She carefully lifted one of the serving bowls. "I love it that you made this piece with a brim—like one of my summer hats!—and that it's irregular in shape. It's unique! I can't thank you enough, dear."

Vera hoped Mrs. Stoughton couldn't tell how much her scabbed lip hurt when she smiled. "I'm glad you like them," she said. "I enjoyed making them for you."

The woman's necklaces jangled softly when she carefully returned the bowl to its padded spot in the wagon. When she noticed Vera's lip, she frowned. "Oh, dear, what happened to you, sweetie? And how'd you break your glasses?"

Vera exhaled slowly, focusing on another line she'd

practiced. "I, um, wasn't paying attention," she replied softly. "Got hit by—"

"Oh, Vera, are these the dishes your aunt was raving about?" Rosetta sailed through the store's front door to admire the plates and bowls. "I'm glad I got to see them before they went to their new home! We need to talk about something bright and cheerful for Truman and me—but sorry! I didn't mean to interrupt your transaction."

"Don't apologize for recognizing a bright, wonderful talent," Mrs. Stoughton put in. "I'm so delighted to have this set. And here—"

The vibrant blonde's bracelets whispered as she reached into the pocket of her rainbow-striped sundress. "This is more than we agreed upon, Vera, but I want you to keep it all for yourself. My initial deposit more than paid the store owner's consignment fee, after all."

As she accepted the white envelope, Vera's pulse shot up. It wouldn't be polite to protest her customer's positive intentions, so she slipped the envelope into her apron pocket. "You're very kind, Mrs. Stoughton. If you'd like me to help you load these into your car—"

"I'll bring out the four place settings we set back for you," Marlene put in eagerly. "We'll arrange them in your trunk so they'll arrive safely, and you can enjoy your new dishes for years to come!"

"I'll help, too," Rosetta said as she picked up the wagon handle and started for the door. "Many hands make light work!"

Vera walked ahead to open the door, grateful to God and her good friends that they'd helped her past her fears about talking to Isaac. It was truly a joy to create colorful pottery that made her soul sing and dance—and now Rosetta wanted dishes, too!

When she worked at her wheel, Vera felt closest to God, so earning money for her pieces was an extra blessing. Despite the unpleasant incident with Isaac, she believed with all her heart that He had led her to Promise Lodge earlier this summer.

God had surely made her a promise. Now she had to live into it.

"Isaac."

He turned from the shelf he'd been stocking and sucked in his breath. Vera was standing a few feet away—so close that the dark, hard scab on her lip made him wince. Her glasses sat askew on her nose, held together with a band of gray duct tape where one arm joined the frame.

I did this to her. How can she even stand the sight of me?

Vera handed him a white envelope. "Put this with the rest of Mrs. Stoughton's money. Please."

"But she intended—I heard her say this money was for *you*, Vera!" he protested, waving it away. "And she's right. The three hundred dollars she's already paid includes more than Dale's share of—"

Her brown eyes widened, as though she'd had no idea how much her enthusiastic customer had already put down. "But it was the agreement Dale and I made, Isaac. It's the right thing to do."

He blinked. "How much did she give you today?"

"I have no idea. I'm trusting Dale—and you—to pay

me my share when the transaction's been entered into
the books."

Isaac's throat squeezed shut. His heart hammered
painfully in his chest. After the way he'd so thoughtlessly
injured her, Vera had made a point of giving *him* the
envelope rather than Marlene. He was so stunned that
he had no idea what to say.

*Is this what happens when someone truly forgives
you? Are they really able to set aside their hurt feelings
and physical pain to trust you again?*

Isaac looked away, blinking back tears. The real
stinger was that he'd lost all chance of ever being with
Vera—Harley and Marlin Kurtz would see to that.

It was all his fault, of course. And the way Vera
stood before him now, shy and vulnerable yet looking
him in the eye without a single sign of malice, was the
ultimate proof of just how much he'd lost.

He accepted the envelope, being careful not to brush
her fingers with his. "Vera, I'm so sorry about what I
did," he whispered. "You're a saint to even speak to—
you have every reason to hate me."

"No, Isaac," she murmured. "My hatred would eat
me away from the inside out, while it probably wouldn't
even faze you. I've chosen to let it go, and to let God be
in charge."

Vera left him standing in the aisle, more than awed
at what she'd revealed. He'd listened to his *dat*'s sermons all his life, but Isaac had never encountered the
extreme faith Vera had just displayed. She'd set him free
from his guilt—but she'd also relieved her own mental
anguish by calling God in to handle it for her.

It was a minor miracle that made him stare at his
unstocked shelf for several minutes, contemplating the

difference between Vera's beliefs and his lifelong version of religion as it was preached in Coldstream.

Man, but I've screwed up. Why did I have to fall for a girl who's so far out of my league that I never stood a chance?

On Friday afternoon, Ezra signaled for his gelding to turn and take the buggy beneath the arched metal Promise Lodge sign, heading for home. With Vera sitting beside him, he felt like a million bucks—partly because her bright smile reflected her own fine mood and her growing confidence in his presence. It had been the right thing, to offer her a ride into Forest Grove to pick up her new glasses.

"I really appreciate your taking me into town, Ezra," she said as the two tiny homes came into view beside Rainbow Lake. "It felt so awkward to have my glasses taped together—"

"And your new frames are really cool, Vera," he put in with a grin. "They're so—well, so *you*."

Her cheeks flushed prettily. The injury on her lip had almost healed, and Vera appeared physically recovered from her run-in with Isaac. She hadn't mentioned him all day, so Ezra sensed that she'd somehow put the unfortunate incident behind her.

"Do you think they're over-the-top?" she asked warily. "With my parents coming later today, I still want to look like a respectable Amish girl who's joined the church—"

"Instead of like an *artiste*?" he teased lightly.

"Well, *jah*. Maybe I should've chosen the dark brown frames—"

"The turquoise is bright and happy," Ezra hastened to reassure her. "No one can fault you for loving pottery and bright colors—because God created colors, after all.

"And besides," he added, slowing the horse when he spotted Ed coming out of his tiny home, "my brother Raymond kept his red glasses after he joined the church and married Lizzie. So far, no thunderbolts of judgment have come through the ceiling to strike him dead."

When Vera laughed, Ezra got a fluttery feeling in his stomach. He was glad he could relieve some of her concern about what might happen to Ed and Fannie once their parents discussed their recent defiance of Preacher Marlin's rules.

"Hey there, Ed! What's happening?" Ezra called out. It was easy to see that his friend lacked the usual spring in his step as he approached the road.

"Saw the parents' rig heading up to the Kurtz place about ten minutes ago," the kid replied, pushing his hair back from his face. "Figured I'd better make an appearance rather than waiting for them to come fetch me."

"Hop in. We just happen to be heading in that direction."

Ed stopped, staring at his sister. "Hoo-boy, what'd you go and do, Vera? With glasses like those, maybe *you'll* be the topic of conversation and the folks'll leave Fannie and me alone."

"Don't count on it," Vera shot back. "And unless someone else brings up the subject of Isaac Chupp, I don't intend to rehash what he did. Got it?"

Ed clambered into the back of the buggy. "I'll stand by you if you'll do the same for me, Sis," he replied. "We've gotta stick together—and you *know* Fannie and I haven't done anything wrong or immoral. We can't help it that we're a couple of kids in love."

Ezra smiled as the horse started up the hill. Ed might be young, but he knew what he wanted to do with his life, and he'd met the young woman he wanted to spend it with. "Would you rather I dropped you both off? So your folks don't see the bad apple you've been hanging around with?"

"Absolutely not!" Vera insisted. "They might as well meet you, Ezra, so they'll know exactly who we're talking about when your name comes up in conversation. No one will be spared by the time the weekend's over."

"*Jah*," Ed put in behind them, "you know how it is when parents—or aunts and uncles—start playing matchmaker."

Ezra blinked. Although the siblings' comments had rung with good humor, the underlying truth of them startled him. Did folks around Promise Lodge already consider him and Vera a couple?

"Well, that can work both ways," he said. "Maybe if I meet your parents, I'll understand why you Brubakers have turned out the way you did."

"And what do you mean by that?" Vera demanded, playfully swatting his arm. "I thought you *liked* me, Ezra!"

Once again, he was taken by surprise. He'd never anticipated shy, reticent Vera saying such a thing in front of her brother—and in such a casual, lighthearted tone, as though his feelings were obvious to everyone around them.

Must be her new glasses putting her in such a gut mood. Go with it.

As they topped the hill, the Burkholder and Kurtz homes came into view. Ezra gazed at Vera full-on, mere inches from her face. "Oh, I do like you, Vera," he whispered. "A *lot*."

Chapter 17

After Ezra had met Eddie and Vera's *dat* and step-*mamm*, Amanda, he'd chatted over lemonade for about half an hour before excusing himself to do the afternoon milking. Vera wished she had such a solid excuse for leaving. It wasn't that she thought the conversation would turn ugly. But she'd never enjoyed confrontation or having to defend her actions—or Eddie's.

Deep down, she saw no reason that Eddie and Fannie shouldn't marry soon. But that wasn't her bone to pick. Poor Eddie was seated in a lawn chair exchanging glances with Fannie when he thought the adults weren't watching, and Preacher Marlin's daughter appeared just as uncomfortable while sitting on the porch swing between her step*mamm*, Frances Kurtz, and Minerva.

When her father leaned his elbows on his knees, focusing intently on Vera, she prayed for the cool confidence Ezra always radiated.

"What possessed you to get new glasses, Vera?" he asked. His dimples made his smile boyishly engaging. Wyman Brubaker was a big, handsome fellow and she'd always adored him—but how much had he already learned from Uncle Harley or Aunt Minerva? Did he know that Isaac had broken her other pair?

"The old ones snapped," she replied with a shrug. "I'd had them a long time—"

"I think they're awesome!" Fannie put in.

"Vera's selling a lot of her pottery here—wild, colorful pieces," Eddie added with a supportive nod. "There's no law that says you have to wear boring specs, just because you're Amish."

Her father and Marlin exchanged a glance. "There *is* the unwritten rule about not calling attention to yourself. We Amish believe in conforming with others of the community," the preacher pointed out. "Although we've seen the red glasses Ezra's younger brother wears, I'm surprised his very conservative bishop, Obadiah Chupp, hasn't told Raymond to get more suitable frames now that he's married and running a store."

Vera tried not to wince at the mention of Isaac's surname. Had Preacher Marlin brought it up as a lead-in to further interrogation?

"How did you pay for them, dear?" Amanda asked gently. "If we owe Uncle Harley for—"

"I bought them with money I've earned from my pottery," Vera replied. And it was true—although she'd borrowed some of the cash from Mrs. Stoughton's envelope and asked Marlene to put an I.O.U. in its place.

"You should've seen the colorful dishes she sold this past week," Aunt Minerva said proudly. "Eight place settings, along with two custom-designed bowls and a platter. Several local gals are saying they'd like dishes now, so between her pottery and teaching school in the fall, Vera's going to be a very busy young woman."

Vera kept her smile carefully in place, hoping to

escape further questions. "Eddie will be busy, too," she
said, smiling at him. "He's got a couple of big commercial jobs in Forest Grove, and then he'll be painting
the walls and staining the floors of the cabins Rosetta's
rebuilding."

"*Jah*, the managers at the hardware store and the old
mom-and-pop motel on the state highway have hired
me," Eddie elaborated.

"Which means you'll be working—out of town a
lot—so you'll not be tempted to slip away with Fannie
when I've explicitly told you not to," Preacher Marlin
said without missing a beat.

Vera sighed. She hadn't intended to put Eddie in the
spotlight—but then, it was only a matter of time before
one set of parents or the other mentioned the topic that
had brought Dat and Amanda to Promise Lodge.

Dat cleared his throat, addressing his son. "Exactly
what did you do, Edward?"

Eddie let out an exasperated sigh. "Last Sunday,
when I asked Vera and Ezra to spend the afternoon with
Fannie and me—as Marlin had requested," he continued earnestly, "our chaperones decided not to stay with
us. And I, um, took Fannie to Rainbow Lake anyway."

"You were alone together, inside your tiny home?"
Dat asked in a disapproving tone.

"No!" Fannie whimpered. "We stayed outside in the
shade the whole time. We've done nothing wrong!"

"But you were alone together," Marlin said sternly.
"You disobeyed the rule I set for you."

Vera ached for her younger brother and Fannie. They
were so sincere—trying so hard—and they were obviously crazy for one another.

"Maybe I'm missing something," she began with a

cautious glance at Preacher Marlin, "but when kids Eddie and Fannie's age attend Singings in larger districts, those guys often drive girls home—alone. It's an acceptable way for them to spend time with one another."

"Fannie and I intend to get married—and we'd do that in a heartbeat if you'd let us, Preacher Marlin," Eddie blurted out. "I earn a *gut* income, and I've already saved up enough for a down payment on a house—and we'd be living right here at Promise Lodge, where you could see that I was taking *gut* care of her!"

"She's too young," the preacher insisted. "Fannie just turned seventeen—"

"But I'll be eighteen in a few months!" Eddie protested. He seemed ready to go into a rant—until Dat leaned closer, gently grasping his arm.

Eddie exhaled loudly and went silent.

"As a parent with a fifteen-year-old daughter, I understand your concern, Marlin," their father said in a low, steady voice. "She's riding home with boys from youth gatherings, and we've had some tough talks with her about how she's to behave when she's alone with one."

Vera nodded, smiling at the thought of Amanda's Lizzie, who'd stayed home with Pete and the three younger Brubakers. The trip would allow Dat and Amanda some time alone together—and it gave them a chance to talk to Eddie without his adoring younger siblings disrupting this conversation.

"But I have to say that when I married Viola—the mother of my five children," Dat continued in a nostalgic tone, "I was eighteen and she was sixteen. We lived with her parents for the first five months—which was incentive for me to take a better job so we could rent a house!"

As everyone chuckled, Vera prayed that her father's calm recounting would persuade Preacher Marlin to reconsider. Marlin was a reasonable man, and his laughter eased the taut expression on his face.

"I'm not saying Eddie and Fannie should defy the rules you've set," Dat put in with a purposeful look at each of them, "but our families have known each other for years, Marlin, so our kids are more aware than most of whom they'll be spending the rest of their lives with if they marry."

"And by marrying younger, maybe they'll have a better chance at starting a family."

Aunt Minerva's wistful observation, spoken softly, brought the conversation to a momentary halt. Vera didn't know how old Minerva and Harley had been when they'd tied the knot, but it was apparently an issue that had haunted the couple their entire married lives.

Preacher Marlin gazed apologetically at his red-headed daughter-in-law, who was now confined to the house—and her bed—most of the time.

"We've made some points that are worth praying about," he said softly. "I'm sure we'll revisit this conversation over the next few days while you're here, Wyman and Amanda. Meanwhile, the sun has shifted and I'm all for finding some shade—"

"And more lemonade," Harley put in, holding up his empty glass.

Frances stood up, chuckling. "I think that's our cue to start rustling up some supper, ladies," she said. "Shall we get Minerva in out of the heat and continue our visit in the kitchen?"

Vera felt enormously relieved. Her *dat* and Amanda hadn't pressed her any further about her encounter with Isaac—if they knew about it—and their avid support of Eddie and Fannie might turn the tide of Preacher Marlin's opinion in their favor.

"Shall I help you get comfortable in your room, Aunt Minerva?" Vera asked, slipping her arm around the shorter woman's shoulders. "And how about if I bring you a snack? You look a little pale."

Her aunt preceded her into the house, where they felt immediately cooler after getting out of the sun. "*Gut* ideas, both of them," Minerva agreed, taking Vera's hand.

Back in the bedroom, Minerva eased herself to the edge of the bed and Vera helped her swing her legs up onto the mattress. She leaned back into the pillows propped against the headboard. A breeze was rippling the simple blue curtains, and a large tree shaded the side of the house.

"Tell me how it is between you and Isaac now," Minerva said in a low, confidential voice. "Your lip is nearly healed, but sometimes the inner scars from unfortunate incidents never really go away. Maybe it's your new glasses, but you look confident—and you've seemed that way ever since you delivered the rest of those dishes to Mrs. Stoughton."

Vera smiled. Her aunt might be in bed most of the time, but Minerva Kurtz missed nothing.

"Isaac and I had a chat at the store that day," she said. "He was amazed that I didn't hate him. When I told him that hatred is harder on the person who feels it than the one who's supposed to receive it, he was speechless."

"Ah. The old biblical strategy of being so kind to

your enemy that he feels you're heaping burning coals on him." Minerva smiled, settling deeper into her pillows. "You're a wise young woman, Vera. And maybe," she added with a secretive smile, "your newfound feelings for Ezra are helping, as well."

Vera felt her cheeks turning hot pink. "Maybe."

"Why don't you invite him to join us for supper tomorrow night? Harley plans to grill hamburgers and brats, and there will be plenty to feed one more of us."

Vera's eyes widened. Did Aunt Minerva already consider Ezra one of the family?

"We'll see," she hedged. "Maybe it's best to keep the focus on Eddie and Fannie, rather than having my parents fuss over *me*. Let me get you a glass of iced tea and that snack we talked about."

Chapter 18

On Saturday night, Maria did her best to help the Kuhns cook a light supper without arousing their curiosity about how she'd been spending her time or what she planned to do with the rest of her life.

"If you'll melt these chocolate chips with this sweetened condensed milk, Maria, tonight's dessert will be ready," Beulah suggested.

"*Jah*, it's fudge, which isn't just for Christmas anymore! And you don't turn on the oven or heat up the kitchen to make it," Ruby quipped as she stirred mayonnaise into her potato salad.

Maria went to the stove, where a double boiler was already heating over a pan of water. She resisted nibbling some of the chocolate chips, because the Kuhns would catch her.

I could make this fudge in two minutes flat if there was a microwave in this place!

She kept the remark to herself, however, and figured on foraging for leftover fudge after the Kuhns had gone to bed. What better way to soothe her soul during another long, lonely night?

"It'll just be four of us this evening," Ruby said,

placing her bowl of potato salad in the fridge. "Eddie's eating with his family up at the Kurtz place, and Ezra has gone home to celebrate his *mamm*'s birthday."

"That means more food for *us*!" Isaac called from the dining room. He peered in at them from the kitchen doorway, smiling brightly.

"You're early tonight," Beulah noted. "Did you close up because folks have bought everything in the store?"

"Marlene gave me time off for *gut* behavior. I've stayed late all week to close out the cash register, so she's taking her turn this evening." Isaac glanced behind him at the table that had been set for supper. "With Ezra and Eddie gone, I'll have to behave myself, *jah*? You women won't let me get away with anything."

"And don't you forget it!" Ruby teased.

"Might be a *gut* evening to pay more attention to Maria," Beulah suggested slyly. "She's been mighty quiet these past few days."

Maria nearly dropped the pan of hot fudge she was pouring. When she'd scraped the last of the steaming chocolate into a glass pan, she glanced up.

Isaac was watching her closely.

Time to change the subject.

"So, Isaac—if Ezra was driving back to Coldstream, I'm surprised you didn't go with him to visit *your* family," she said cheerfully. "You're the youngest, and I bet your *mamm* really misses you. Does she call you often?"

Isaac quickly covered his stricken grimace with a smile, but Maria had seen his pain. She nipped her lip. She didn't like Isaac as much as Ezra or Eddie, but she hadn't intended to hurt his feelings, either.

"I, um, was so eager to declare my independence, we agreed that nobody would call me for a while," Isaac hedged. "You know how it is when folks think you have an *attitude*. Right, Maria?"

Her mouth dropped open. She was ready to tell him where to put his attitude—except he was right, wasn't he?

"I do," she admitted, glancing at the Kuhn sisters. "Sometimes it's best to lie low and do as you're told—for as long as you can stand it, anyway."

"That pan of fudge needs to chill, missy," Ruby teased, pointing to the refrigerator. "Let's sit down to supper. Everything's ready, ain't so, Beulah?"

"Everything's ready to boil right over," her sister put in with a shake of her head. "Is it me, or are we all going crazy with this heat?"

Maria recognized a mood softener when she heard one. Her apartment had been stifling today from the lack of breeze, and she'd thought about slipping over to the bakery to enjoy some air-conditioned comfort—except the little building was probably still warm from Phoebe's Saturday morning pie baking.

And the hum of the window unit would alert any passersby to my presence. I've got nowhere to go and nothing to do but sweat tonight, it seems.

"What about your family, Maria?" Isaac asked after they'd sat down and said grace. "I haven't heard you talk about the folks you've left behind in Cloverdale."

"That's because there aren't any." Maria sensed that the young man across the table was sincerely interested, for once, rather than trying to push her buttons. She explained her situation as she passed the platter of chicken and the bowls of potato salad and slaw.

"You know, of course, that my little sister, Lizzie, married Ezra's youngest brother and they live in Coldstream," she began. "We had an older sister, but she died of multiple sclerosis a while back. Our parents have been gone for years, so it's just me now, rattling around in that big old house in Cloverdale. Which is why I decided to start over at Promise Lodge after my bakery burned down."

Isaac had stopped eating to listen to her story, nodding in comprehension.

"What about you, Isaac? You have sibs, *jah*?" Maria asked. She bit into a chicken leg so he wouldn't think she was watching him too closely.

"Ten of them—most a lot older than I am," he replied. "And because the auction business is already supporting my brothers' families and my parents, I had to find another way to make a buck. So here I am."

Maria suspected there was more to his story. She also sensed that his so-called *independence* hadn't been totally voluntary. It was highly unusual for a bishop's kid to suddenly go off on his own, because the Amish believed in community rather than solitude.

The Kuhns were following the conversation, eating rather than injecting their spot-on observations. In the silence that filled the dining room, Maria searched for another topic to quiz Isaac about before he could delve deeper into *her* situation. She was about to ask how he was getting along at the store, but everyone looked up when the lodge's front door opened.

Truman Wickey strode between the rows of long wooden tables, smiling as he approached. "Sorry to interrupt your meal, but I had a few spare minutes."

"We'll fetch you a plate," Beulah offered. "I bet you had a big landscaping job—"

"And we can pour you some iced tea," Ruby put in as she rose from her seat.

Truman slid into the chair beside Isaac, across from Maria. "You ladies are very generous! Tea sounds fabulous, but Rosetta will have my supper ready."

Maria maintained a smile despite her racing pulse. She'd hoped to postpone any talk about her bakery for as long as possible.

"Maria, a crew is cleaning up the mess from the fire and will soon be reconstructing the damaged parts of the building," he began, gazing at her patiently. "I can't replace your car, of course, but it's on me to restore the structure."

Maria nodded. At least he was speaking kindly—not blaming her for the fire or expecting her to pay for the damages.

"I need your decision," Truman continued. "If you no longer want to run your bakery in my building, I'll advertise for another tenant—and I won't replace kitchen equipment the next person might not want. Do you see where I'm coming from?"

Blinking rapidly, Maria inhaled to settle her nerves. Truman had just given her some positive news in a very kind way, so she had no reason to cry.

"*Jah*—sorry," she added, blotting her tears with her napkin. "It's nice of you to—I appreciate your understanding."

Maria almost asked when he needed her decision, yet that would force her to make one, wouldn't it? Instead, she bit into her chicken leg again. Better to let her landlord set a date and go with his flow.

Truman accepted the glass of tea Ruby brought, nodding his thanks. He gulped it thirstily before smiling at Isaac. "How's it going at the store? Rosetta tells me you and Marlene have your act together."

Isaac's eyes widened in surprise. "Storekeeping is a lot more involved than I'd anticipated," he admitted, "but Dale has all the inventory and recordkeeping on his computer. We can tell by each day's cash register transactions how much we've sold and what we'll need to reorder. But we'll still be glad when Dale's back."

Truman nodded. "*Jah*, he's very organized and progressive. I suspect you'd feel a lot more stressed if you had to tally sales receipts by hand every evening."

With a final swallow, he finished his tea. "Better head on home, folks. *Gut* to see everyone—and I'll keep you posted on the progress in Cloverdale, Maria. Let me know what you're going to do, all right? And if you'd like a ride to church tomorrow, we'll be coming for Ruby and Beulah at nine."

Still chewing her chicken, Maria nodded. As Truman's footsteps echoed in the open dining room, she relaxed. She'd expected a lecture—and she wouldn't have been surprised if he'd presented her a bill for some of the renovation expenses. After all, if her car hadn't exploded, his building would still be intact.

"Nice fellow, Truman is," Beulah said with a nod. "He and Rosetta were the first folks Ruby and I met when we came to Promise Lodge. Their welcoming attitude—and their happiness—were sure signs that we should come here to live."

Maria braced herself, in case Beulah or her sister reminded her that her friendship with Truman had almost caused Rosetta to cancel their wedding.

Ruby, however, returned to the table with the pan of fudge. "Didn't want us to forget about our dessert," she teased as she cut the candy and placed pieces of it on a plate. "Sometimes out of sight is out of mind."

"Puh!" Maria exclaimed as she snatched a square of the fudge and popped it into her mouth. "Chocolate refuses to be forgotten. It calls your name until you answer it."

As her three companions burst out laughing, Maria realized that her outlook was suddenly on the upswing. She was among friends here. Her fears had come to nothing because Truman and the Kuhns had chosen not to dredge up her shortcomings or remind her of all the things she'd done wrong.

Is this what acceptance feels like? Do these people think I belong here now?

Maria blinked. Maybe her life wasn't so terrible after all.

She still didn't want to go back to Cloverdale, where she'd be alone, yet she had a business there. She really did need to give Truman an answer.

But for now, I'll just have another piece of this awesome fudge.

Chapter 19

On Sunday morning, Isaac stood at the apartment window grinning. Over at the lodge, where the windows were open to let in the meager breeze, the congregation was singing the opening hymn.

But he was not!

After a lifetime under Bishop Obadiah's relentless thumb, Isaac was skipping church. It was sheer indulgence to be doing what *he* wanted rather than to be sitting on a hard wooden bench for three hours wishing he were somewhere else. He felt so deliciously lazy and free that he went back to bed and dozed off with the cool hum of the air conditioner playing him a lullaby.

Next thing he knew, it was nearly noon. Isaac congratulated himself on truly enjoying his Sunday morning—until he saw the men carrying tables outside into the shade so the common meal could be enjoyed picnic-style.

His stomach rumbled. He'd returned from last night's supper with some cold chicken, but he wasn't in the mood for it. If the Kuhns saw the snacks and quick-fix items in his fridge, they would laugh and say he kept a bachelor's kitchen. An entire store full of possibilities awaited him downstairs, but he didn't want to cook.

And he certainly couldn't join the others for lunch— or even go outside for a stroll—because everyone knew of his absence from church. The bulk store's doors were locked, but it would be just like Bishop Monroe or one of the preachers to phone him to see if he was ill. And when they realized he was perfectly healthy, the lectures would start.

You have too much time on your hands in that upstairs apartment. It's unnatural to be alone so much. We need to find you a different place to live.

As Preacher Amos's words echoed in his head, Isaac sighed. He was glad Troyer hadn't yet relocated him, but he'd made himself a prisoner for the day. When he'd played hooky from church, he hadn't realized he'd be cutting himself off from eating with other people— unless he wanted to endure their chastisement by only showing up for lunch.

He didn't.

From behind his window curtain, Isaac ate pork and beans from the can, watching the folks below. He noticed that Maria wasn't there, either. Had she gone to church in Cloverdale?

He doubted it. As Truman had talked to her, Isaac had sensed her hesitation about returning to her bakery. But how would she support herself if she didn't? Maria Zehr was one of the most airheaded young women he'd ever met. Beautiful but clueless.

Isaac forgot all about her, however, when he spotted Vera and Deborah chatting together. Vera was wearing new turquoise glasses that matched her dress, while her companion bounced a baby girl on her hip. It made quite a picture when Deborah's little daughter reached for Vera, who swung the child into the air to make her laugh.

Had I behaved differently—twice—maybe Deborah or Vera would be playing with my *child.*

Isaac's spoon paused above the bean can. Until he'd met Vera, he'd never seriously considered marrying anyone. But now that these two attractive young women were out of the running, it made him keenly aware of the opportunities he'd thrown away.

Were the girls comparing notes, rehashing the way he'd mistreated them? Or had they moved on? By all appearances, they were happy—

And when Christine joined their conversation, Isaac had the sudden urge to rush downstairs and tell them all he was sorry. Maybe Vera's forgiving mindset would rub off on Deborah and Bishop Monroe's wife! Maybe he could score two more of his apologies before Dale returned to the store tomorrow!

But Isaac lost his nerve, and Christine walked away to speak with other friends.

A few minutes later, when an unfamiliar couple joined Vera and Deborah under the tree, Isaac immediately saw that the man was an older version of Eddie. With a pang of regret, he realized that the Brubakers had driven all the way from Bloomingdale—at least a couple of hours—to visit their kids for the weekend.

None of the Chupps would do that for him.

Vera laughed at a comment her *dat* made. As her parents pointed at Eddie and Fannie, who were walking hand in hand among some of the younger couples—and apparently being congratulated for something—it was easy to see that the Brubakers were a tight-knit bunch. A happy family.

Isaac had no more appetite for his cold beans. He'd left home nearly a month ago and had heard nothing—not a letter or a phone call—from his brothers or his *mamm*. His *dat*, of course, would be too stubborn and proud to reach out to him—

The apple didn't fall too far from the tree, ain't so?

With a sigh, Isaac threw away the rest of his sorry excuse for a meal. He could've picked up the phone in Kraybill's office—could've jotted his mother a note—these past few weeks, but he'd been determined to prove to his family that he didn't need them. More than once he'd called his father arrogant and bullheaded . . . but weren't those the exact traits keeping him from joining his friends on the lawn right now?

So what if they teased him for sleeping in? Deep down, Isaac knew that moments after his morning's behavior had been revealed, the women would urge him to fix a plate. Some of the men would probably admit to pulling the same stunt when they'd been younger.

But Isaac spent the rest of his day watching mindless television shows, trying not to think about the pleasant Sunday he'd missed out on.

Later that evening, however, after the Promise Lodge homes were dark, Isaac slipped into the lodge. Although the Kuhns often ate dinner in Cloverdale after church, they would've cooked something on Saturday for a simple Sunday night supper. The big stainless-steel fridge always contained leftover food, and anything the two *maidels* had concocted would taste so much better than unheated beans.

Pausing in the lobby, Isaac removed his shoes. He allowed his eyes to adjust to the dining room's darkness so he wouldn't bang into a table. As he padded down the center aisle, he hoped some of Ruby's potato salad was in the fridge—and if he was lucky, he'd find some of that fudge. Even their leftover chicken would taste better because he'd had the adventure of foraging for it. It would *really* be hitting the jackpot to find some pie.

Once he reached the kitchen door, the hum of the big refrigerator welcomed him. Very carefully he made his way between the shadowy cabinets and counters. He'd never actually been in this room.

Where was the pantry? Most likely the Kuhns stored a lot of great food—

"Slipping in like a thief in the night, Isaac? We missed you at supper."

A surprised yelp escaped him as he turned toward the familiar voice. Beulah was seated at the worktable on the back wall, deep in the shadows.

"Sitting in the dark, figuring to catch me at it?" he retorted. He didn't know whether to resent her "thief in the night" description or to laugh it off, because he detested getting caught doing things he wasn't supposed to do.

Her gentle chuckle smoothed his ruffled feathers.

"At my age, I sometimes get up in the night," she explained. "Rather than tossing and turning—and waking my sister next door with the creaking of my bed—I come down here. There's something very peaceful about a kitchen after the day's work's been done and everything's put away," she mused aloud. "Sit down, dear. I won't bite."

Exhaling the last of his huffiness, Isaac found the chair across the table from her. What harm would it do to admit he'd held himself prisoner all day? This kindly

Mennonite *maidel* couldn't hold him accountable for skipping an Amish church service, after all.

"Okay, so I missed supper—as well as the common meal—today because I skipped church," Isaac confessed. "Then I realized I couldn't show up for lunch, or anything else, because Bishop Monroe or the preachers would call me out on it."

Shaking his head at his foolishness, he met Beulah's gaze in the darkness. "Being a bishop's son, I could *never* miss church or even pretend I was sick. My parents made sure my butt was on the pew bench even on Sundays when I had the flu. Or a hangover."

"*Jah*, I can imagine they did," she said as she eased up from her chair. "Let's see what we can find for you to eat."

As she walked toward the fridge and a door next to it—which turned out to be the pantry—Isaac saw that she was wearing a summer-weight robe over her nightgown. Even in the shadows, its fabric appeared as splashy and colorful as Beulah's daytime dresses. Her hair, gathered into a loose ponytail at her neck, hung all the way down her back.

Beulah returned with an armful of plastic containers. Then she fetched two paper plates and some utensils.

"Wouldn't want you to eat alone," she teased as she set everything down on the worktable. "Nothing *gut* would come of it."

Isaac laughed out loud and then covered his mouth. "Sorry. No sense in waking everybody else up."

"You've got that right. The two gals upstairs need all the beauty rest they can get," she quipped with a perfectly straight face. "We've got a dab of potato salad here, and fruit salad, and slices of ham—and the rest of the pizza we brought home from Cloverdale after church. And coconut custard pie."

"I've died and gone to heaven," Isaac murmured as he popped the lid off the nearest container. "Which surely must mean you're an angel, Beulah. *Denki* for being so nice—"

She waved him off. "Somebody's got to eat this stuff. Might as well be us."

Beulah spooned some food onto her plate. "I can't imagine you raided the fridge a lot while you were living at home, either. Not that I condone some of the things you've done, Isaac—and it's not my place to judge your *dat*—but I suspect you've been held to some mighty high standards.

"I've met your father a time or two," Beulah added softly. She gazed across the table at him. "I can't imagine he was keen on your coming to Promise Lodge, where so many of his former church members have moved to get away from him."

Isaac stopped wolfing a piece of pizza. Beulah didn't sound judgmental. She was taking his side, expressing what she assumed had been his lifelong plight. But she'd gotten one thing wrong,

"He, um . . . Dat doesn't know where I am," Isaac admitted softly. "He's a—a *difficult* man to live with, and—and he convinced my *mamm* that I shouldn't be allowed to live at home anymore. She called me a thief. Told me to leave. So I, um, didn't feel the need to tell them where I was going."

Isaac's mouth clapped shut. What had possessed him to reveal his story to Beulah? He'd danced around the truth when other folks had asked about his coming to work at Dale's store. And if Kraybill—or anyone else—

learned why he was really here, they'd jump his butt for lying or send him away.

Beulah exhaled softly. "I guess that doesn't surprise me. You're of an age where young men shoot first and ask questions later, so to speak. Or they decide to jump the fence."

She smiled, as though recalling a fond memory.

"Ruby and I did something similar, two years ago when we came here," she recounted. "We were living with our brother, Delbert, in a house bursting at the seams with people—because he felt it was his place to take care of his two unmarried sisters. When we couldn't stand it another minute, we packed our bags and hired a driver without telling him. Didn't call him until we'd rented our apartments here and settled in.

"And truth be told," she added conspiratorially, "running away from home was one of the smartest things we ever did. So, see? There's hope for you yet, Isaac."

He'd stopped eating, fascinated by the Kuhns' own declaration of independence. "What happened after you called him?"

Beulah chuckled. "Delbert being Delbert, he drove up here intending to haul our contrary selves back home," she replied. "We informed him that everyone was better off with us gone, especially because there was only one bathroom for a houseful of people. We also told him we were tired of riding herd on his rambunctious kids when their *mamm* didn't see fit to control them herself."

Isaac's eyes widened. He couldn't imagine an Amish woman saying such a thing—nor would an Old Order brother tolerate that attitude. "I had no idea," he murmured. "So now, instead of being live-in babysitters, you and Ruby run a successful cheese business."

"You said that exactly right, dear. But more importantly, we're living the life we choose, rather than having a man dictate what we do and where we go."

Beulah plated a generous wedge of coconut custard pie and slid it toward Isaac. "I know several Mennonite and Amish men who'd put me in my place for saying such a thing—"

"My *dat* would be first in line."

"—but Ruby and I decided life was too short to ignore the gifts God has given us. Instead of staying crammed into a shoebox of a life, we live in this magnificent old lodge amongst friends who love us."

Beulah reached across the table, gently grasping his wrist. "You're restless and bored and very lonely right now, Isaac. You're a fertile field where the seeds of change have been planted," she whispered urgently. "God's given you a sharp mind and He's led you to Promise Lodge for a reason."

Isaac was ready to protest her sermonette, yet he was too enthralled to make a sound. And Beulah didn't seem inclined to let go of him.

"It's up to *you* to become a productive, thriving garden, dear." Her voice was barely audible, and her eyes were riveted to his in the dimness. "Nobody else can do it for you. And nobody else can take the blame if you grow into a patch of weeds.

"And one last thing," Beulah put in as she released his wrist. "Call your *mamm*. Better yet, send her a letter to tell her where you are, so nobody can erase your message before she gets to the answering machine," she suggested. "I guarantee she'll welcome you home, Isaac. She'll be too relieved that you're safe and employed to hold her grudge against you—no matter what your *dat* says."

Long into the wee hours, after Isaac had returned to the apartment above the store, the *maidel*'s words ran through his mind like a continuous, repetitive loop.

You're restless and bored and very lonely right now, Isaac . . . you're a fertile field where the seeds of change have been planted . . . it's up to you to become a productive, thriving garden, dear . . . nobody else can take the blame if you grow into a patch of weeds.

All his life, adults had preached at him. Their judgmental expressions and angry words had repelled him—made him more eager to find bigger trouble, just to spite them. Yet in a few short minutes, gray-haired, grandmotherly Beulah Kuhn had reached inside and caught him up, heart and soul.

He suddenly felt *valuable*, as though his life mattered to someone.

Isaac was wiping away tears while he wrote his mother a quick note. As he put the letter in the mailbox by the road, dawn was splashing the sky with brilliant ribbons of pink, peach, and fuchsia that reminded him of the Kuhn sisters' vibrant dresses.

It seemed like a sign.

He told himself to pay attention, because maybe—just as Beulah had said—the God he'd tried so hard to ignore all his life really had led him to Promise Lodge for a reason.

Chapter 20

Vera smiled as she spooned more breakfast casserole onto Minerva's plate and set it in front of her. All around the table, happy faces lit up the kitchen—with Eddie's and Fannie's shining the brightest.

"Dat, we can't thank you enough for changing your mind about us getting married!" Fannie exclaimed as she clasped Eddie's hand. "It's such a relief, not to go around as though we've done something wrong, having to hide our feelings."

Preacher Marlin glanced briefly at Vera's *dat* before responding. "Always helps to talk to God when other people's opinions differ from your own," he said softly. "And after another chat with Wyman, I realized it was my own fear getting in the way."

Eddie's brow furrowed. "What were you afraid of? You surely know I have the best intentions—"

"I was afraid of losing my little girl," Fannie's *dat* admitted ruefully. "She's grown up so fast, and there are no more coming along behind her."

Vera's heart went out to the preacher as he shared his feelings so openly. Not many church leaders—or fathers—would admit to such a sentiment.

"Don't forget, though," she said, placing her hand on Minerva's shoulder. "You'll soon have a wee one in this household to coddle. Minerva and Rosetta both got *gut* reports during their doctor visits last week."

"And for that we're all thankful!" Frances put in. She smiled at Amanda and Wyman, across the table from her. "Can I send some of these pastries with you? To tide you over until you get home?"

Vera chuckled. Just as Amanda appeared ready to refuse the offer, Dat's eyes lit up. "What a fine idea, Frances! You folks have been generous hosts and we really appreciate it. I'm sure the kids back home will gobble up what we don't eat along the way."

Minerva put her fork on her plate. She seemed tired. Vera suspected that she'd slip back into her bedroom the moment their visitors left. "So, we're having the wedding here, in the lodge, on August thirtieth," she confirmed. "That should give us plenty of time to invite our far-flung relatives and prepare for the big day."

"And Vera, we want you and Ezra to be side-sitters!" Fannie blurted out.

"We're going to ask Pete to pair up with Lily Peterscheim," Eddie added with a mischievous grin. "It wouldn't be right to leave out my brother or Fannie's best friend."

Vera's mouth fell open. "Um, that—that's quite an honor, but what if—"

"No *buts*," Fannie insisted. "Anybody can see that you and Ezra are probably next in line to exchange vows, so our wedding can be a rehearsal for you."

Vera prayed that no one could hear how frantically her heart was pounding. It was one thing to ride alongside Ezra to get her new glasses in town. It was another thing altogether to spend the day as a *couple* in front of all their new neighbors and friends.

"Not to worry, dear," Amanda said kindly. "I know girls who've been *newehockers* in several weddings and didn't marry *any* of the young men they stood up with. You're there to make the bride's day happier. It's no more than that."

Vera smiled at her step*mamm*, grateful for the way she'd put Fannie's invitation into perspective—and thankful, as well, for the pottery wheel, kiln, and lessons Amanda had given her.

After everyone had finished eating, Frances insisted that the Brubakers should be on their way rather than washing dishes. As Dat loaded their luggage into the buggy and Amanda said her goodbyes, Vera realized that the two families had made a lot of progress over the weekend. Eddie and Fannie *were* young to be getting married, but they were more emotionally prepared than most couples—and the parents had agreed to put money toward a house for the newlyweds, as their wedding gift.

Vera was also extremely relieved that no one had mentioned her run-in with Isaac Chupp. The focus had remained on her brother and Fannie—as it should have.

Right before her father climbed into the buggy to drive home, however, he hugged Vera and held her for a few extra moments. "Your new glasses are very attractive, daughter," he whispered near her ear, "but when Marlin and Harley told me how the old ones got broken, your true beauty came shining through. I'm proud of you for showing that misguided young man your forgiveness, Vera.

"And," he added, holding her gaze, "I have no doubt

that the Kurtz men—and Ezra—won't let Isaac near you again. But be careful, sweetheart. If something bad happened to you, I—I couldn't be so quick to forgive. And my heart would be broken."

After quickly kissing her temple, Dat and Amanda climbed into the buggy. Vera waved until the rig was beyond the curve in the road, her heart full of love for the father who never ceased to amaze her. Eddie came to stand beside her, holding Fannie's hand.

"Well, *that* turned out better than it could have," he remarked.

"*Jah*, it did," Vera agreed for her own reasons.

They were walking toward the house to help clean up the kitchen when someone called her name from down the road. Dale Kraybill waved, smiling as he covered the distance between them with long strides.

"Can we chat for a moment, Vera?" he asked, offering her a thick white envelope. "I thought you should have your money for the dishes you sold while I was away. And there's another matter I'd like to discuss, as well."

As Isaac sat across the office desk from Dale mid-morning, his damp shirt was clinging to his back beneath his suspenders. The meeting, a review of what had happened in Kraybill's absence, was going very well. But Isaac was waiting for the other shoe to drop.

"Marlene has told me you've been a fast learner, and that she was willing to entrust all the data entry to you after only a few days," the storekeeper summarized. "After looking through the daily transactions this morning, I believe everything's in *gut* order. Thank you for your diligence and your attention to the details of running my store, Isaac."

Isaac nodded. His throat was cotton-dry, so when he responded, his raspy voice made him *sound* guilty even though he wasn't. "I—*jah*. You're welcome," he said softly. "I learned a lot while you were gone."

Kraybill nodded. "I believed you were perfectly capable of handling this business, and you've proven me correct."

Afraid to comment for fear he'd appear boastful, Isaac pasted a tight smile on his face.

"I also appreciated the way you set aside the money Mrs. Stoughton paid for Vera's dishes. Your note was very helpful, and I'm delighted that a customer has taken such a shine to Vera's work—for her sake as well as for the store's."

Here it comes. If he fires me, I have to accept it and roll with the punches.

"I did, however, receive a call from Marlin Kurtz last week." Dale paused, watching Isaac's face. "I almost came home to dismiss you, Isaac, but the positive reports about your work ethic and computer skills—plus the fact that Marlin, Amos, and Bishop Monroe had already counseled you about your behavior with Vera— convinced me to wait until I returned this morning."

Isaac cleared his throat. "So here we are," he mumbled.

"Here we are."

Kraybill leaned back in his chair, clasping his hands on the desk as he assessed Isaac for several seconds. "Care to tell me what happened? I've already heard, but I'd like to know your side of it."

Isaac's eyes widened. What could he say without

further incriminating himself? "I, um, fell for Vera—hard—the day I came to interview—"

"*Jah*, I recall that."

"—and when I decided to pay her a visit that Sunday afternoon—and I got it in my head that Ezra Overholt might already be laying claim to her—I, um, went a little crazy," he continued in a ragged voice. "I only meant to kiss her—honest—but I . . . I lost control. Had no intention of breaking her glasses or splitting her lip, and then suddenly Overholt was pulling me away from her—"

Isaac exhaled harshly, shaking his head.

"You know, of course, that I find your violence repulsive."

"*Jah*," Isaac whispered. "So do I. But it won't happen again—partly because Preacher Marlin and Harley have forbidden me to see her anymore."

"And how do you feel about that, Isaac?"

His eyes widened. Was that a trick question? Why did it matter what he felt?

"I, um, can understand why the Kurtzes are keeping me away from her. Even though Vera herself has accepted my apology and forgiven me," he added in his own defense.

"Would you have been so aggressive if Ezra hadn't been in the picture?"

Once again Isaac was taken aback. Why was Kraybill digging so deeply into his mental and emotional state rather than chastising him for the physical harm he'd done Vera? "I don't—why do you ask?" he demanded suddenly.

Dale leaned forward, his arms on his desk. As always, he wore an impeccably pressed dress shirt with the sleeves rolled to his elbows, and his salt-and-pepper hair was neatly trimmed in a style that looked more English than Plain. His gaze didn't waver.

"From what I've heard about you two young men from Coldstream," he began, "I suspect you resent the way folks have always admired Ezra while you have been notorious for making trouble. So why *wouldn't* you be jealous if Ezra was winning the young lady you wanted for yourself?"

. . . *why* wouldn't *you be jealous* . . .

"I—I never thought of it that way," Isaac admitted. As he recalled his mental images of Overholt kissing Vera, holding her close, he briefly relived the turmoil that had driven him to express his need for her—the one-sided, unreturned passion that had overridden all rational thought.

Jealousy—because Ezra had what Isaac wanted. And envy—because Ezra was who Isaac wanted to be. How many times had preachers spoken about those sins? Yet he'd never understood how they'd taken over his life.

"I suggest you ponder your feelings about Ezra. And I think you owe God a few prayers of thanksgiving that Vera was so understanding—to the point that she entrusted all of Mrs. Stoughton's cash to *you*." Dale's eyebrows rose. "In her place, I wouldn't have been so gracious."

"*Jah*, there's a lot of truth to that."

"In fact, Vera was so gracious," Kraybill continued, "that when I asked her this morning whether I should fire you or let you stay on, she thought I should give you another chance."

Isaac felt lower than a worm's belly. Vera had stood up for him after the physical and emotional distress he'd put her through. Once again, he was sorely aware of the wonderful young woman who'd slipped away because of his inappropriate behavior.

"So, I'll give you another chance, Isaac. But now that you've been the recipient of her forgiveness," the storekeeper continued with a warning in his voice, "I'm even more adamant about you reconciling with Deborah, Rosetta, and Christine—as we agreed upon when I hired you. Find it in your heart to say those two words *I'm sorry*."

Swallowing hard, Isaac nodded. After all the times he'd thought about the three apologies he needed to make, he'd discovered that those two words were the biggest hurdle—the one he couldn't seem to approach without turning tail.

"Let's get out there and get to work so Marlene isn't running the store all by herself," Kraybill said as he rose from his chair.

Chapter 21

August began with a much-needed day of slow rain that soaked into Mattie's garden plots and everyone's parched lawns. As the front passed through, it took the heat and humidity with it. Aunt Minerva was lounging comfortably in her bedroom, and it wasn't yet time to prepare supper, so Vera took a walk. Because she rarely left the Kurtz property, it felt good to stretch her legs and gaze at parts of the Promise Lodge property she didn't often see.

It didn't hurt that Christine had returned that afternoon from an auction at an Iowa dairy that was dispersing its herd.

"I was glad Ezra pointed out warning signs in some of the cows that suggested they weren't as healthy as they should be, or wouldn't produce as much milk," she'd told Aunt Minerva during her quick visit. "He saved me a lot of money in future vet bills—and on today's acquisitions, too, because I didn't bid on all the cows I thought were cute!"

Still smiling at Christine's observations, Vera strolled past Lester and Marlene Lehman's new home, and Frances and Marlin's place, as well as the smaller house where Preacher Amos and Mattie lived. By the time she could see the tall, white dairy barn, she heard the lowing of the black-and-white Holsteins waiting to be milked. Apparently, a dozen or more cows had just been released from the milking stations because Ezra was escorting them out of the barn.

Vera could only distinguish a red shirt in a sea of broad, white backs with black splotches on them, but she instantly recognized his strong shoulders and thick, dark hair. He was pressed between the cows' large bodies as they walked, yet he appeared totally confident as he stroked their backs and talked to them. The moment he glanced up and saw her, he stood still.

When he raised his hand, Vera's heart thumped erratically. She waved and walked faster, eager to see him—yet hoping she didn't appear *too* eager.

By the time Vera had passed the little bakery and the Kuhns' cheese factory, Ezra had come through a side corral gate and latched it behind him.

"Vera! I was just thinking about you, hoping we could take a walk after Roman and I finish the afternoon's milking," he said in a low voice.

"We can do that," she agreed. She stopped a few yards away from him, shyly returning his smile before gazing at the cattle in the corral. "Christine sounded pleased about your trip to the auction."

"We did well. Brought home twenty milk cows and five calves."

She racked her brain for something else to say that wouldn't sound utterly clueless, for she knew very little about dairy cows. Then she focused on the cattle between a couple of the corral's fence planks.

"What would it be like to design bright white plates

and bowls with random black splotches?" she wondered aloud. "Would customers think they looked odd, or—"

"From what I've seen of your pottery, Vera, people will go crazy for them." Ezra came over to stand beside her as she continued to gaze into the corral. "If nothing else, you could make a sample place setting and show it to Christine—she's sure to want them. She continued her husband's dairy business partly because she thinks polka-dot cows are adorable.

"Of course," he continued, "because the Kuhns make cheese, she has a market for some of her milk that costs her nothing for transportation. It's a sweet deal."

When Ezra clasped her hand, jolts of supercharged current ran up Vera's arm. Even in his mucking boots and work clothes that smelled like livestock, he was such a handsome young man—and so supportive of her work and ideas.

"I'll work up some sketches and make a dinner plate, a salad plate, and a bowl or two—maybe a different shape from the blue dishes with the tulips," she mused aloud. "I'm already getting mental pictures of kitchen accessories like spoon holders and salt-and-pepper shakers and trivets—"

"And I'm getting ideas about something totally unrelated to your business or mine," Ezra said with a playful smile. "But we'll save those for after I've showered and we're on our walk—"

"Ezra! Ezra, you're back from the auction! Oh, but it's *gut* to see you!"

When his face fell, Vera turned to see who'd shattered the intimate mood between them. Maria Zehr, decked out in a pink gingham dress with a matching kerchief tied over her blond hair, was rushing toward them in a state of high agitation. Her cheeks and lips were pink, too, and her eyelashes were augmented with mascara. *Lots* of mascara.

Ezra still held Vera's hand as he braced himself for the encounter. "Maria," he acknowledged with a nod, "have you met Ed's sister, Vera Brubaker? She and I were just—"

"Oh, hi," Maria said, but her gaze never left Ezra's face. "I wanted to be sure you're coming to the lodge for supper tonight, because *I'm* roasting the chicken and I've made my special recipe for scalloped potatoes, and after we eat, I thought we could take a ride into—"

"But Maria, I've already asked—"

"—Forest Grove to pick up a few supplies and go to that ice cream place before we—"

Vera slipped her hand from Ezra's. Although *pushy* only began to describe Maria, the vivacious blonde was also cute and curvy—not the wallflower type who sat home alone wishing for dates or working at her pottery wheel. The longer Vera stood near Maria, the mousier she felt. As her heart folded in on itself, she eased away from the one-sided conversation and started up the hill.

It was a sure bet that Maria wouldn't even notice she'd gone.

Would Ezra be sorry she'd left?

Ezra held up his hand but there was no stopping the blond chatterbox—and no way to get his protests in edgewise. He felt horribly inconsiderate as Vera stepped away from him. He should just break away from Maria's intrusive talk and catch up to the gentle, slender young woman whose head hung low as she strode up the road—

But Roman was in the barn doing all the milking. Ezra had only stepped outside with a group of the new cows to help them become acclimated to their new home. He'd taken a moment to talk with Vera—and then Maria had spotted him.

"Maria," he interjected loudly, "I need to get back to work. Now."

Her blue eyes widened. "Weren't you listening to a thing I said?" she bleated. "I was just explaining how lucky you are to have your new position with a nice boss like Christine, while I'm still trying to figure out what to do with myself. She's even provided you with a tiny home to live in, and I—I've lost everything! I just wanted you to be my friend—"

As her chatter took on its habitual whine, Ezra's patience snapped.

"Let's not forget that Christine lost her barn and part of her herd, while the Kuhns, Phoebe, Irene, and Mattie lost their businesses in the tornado," Ezra pointed out curtly. "But those women have rebuilt and moved on, while *you* seem to be—"

Her blue eyes filled with tears. "But they didn't face their losses *alone*," she said with a whimper. "Now that Lizzie's married to your brother, I have no one—and I don't do well by myself. I feel like such a misfit here."

Ezra knew he should just turn and go back to the barn, but he took her bait. Again. "Lizzie has talked about your home in Cloverdale—"

"I can't go back there!" Maria declared in a quavering voice. "I've just told you I don't want to live by myself!"

Ezra frowned. She wasn't even letting him finish his sentences. "But if it was your parents' house, it's probably paid for, right?" he pointed out tersely. "If you sold it, you'd have enough money to live on for a long time—or to open another bakery, or whatever sort of business you wanted."

Maria's mouth dropped open. Then she lit up like a full, yellow moon. "Ezra, you're a genius," she exclaimed, grabbing his hand. "I could build a bakery of my own with an upstairs apartment—and without Truman's help—and you could come to Cloverdale to live with me!"

Ezra blinked. Had he ever met a more clueless, self-centered young woman in all his life? "Really?" he blurted out. "I should just quit my *gut* job to live in a little apartment with *you*? Get real, Maria!"

He stalked toward the corral gate, but when she called his name in her heartbroken voice, Ezra turned toward her again. "I'm going to finish the milking—with Roman," he added purposefully. "Don't even think about coming into the muddy corral or the barn that's full of cow manure, Maria."

Her brow puckered. She was ready to launch into a big crying jag when Ruby hollered out the lodge's kitchen window.

"Better come rescue this chicken, Maria! The kitchen's full of smoke and I'll pitch the roaster out the back door rather than let you set *this* place on fire!"

With a squeal, Maria jogged toward the lodge.

Ezra exhaled his frustration, grateful that Ruby had given Maria a reason to leave. If her food was going up in smoke, it sounded like a good evening to eat supper elsewhere.

After he and Roman finished the milking and mucked out the barn, Ezra rushed home to shower. On his way up the road toward the Kurtz place, he stopped to pick some summer flowers blooming along the pasture fence. Would the bright orange tiger lilies and purple coneflowers convince Vera that he was interested in her rather than Maria? At least it would be a peace offering.

As he passed near the Burkholder pasture, Ezra paused to admire the team of Clydesdales Lavern Peterscheim and Lowell Kurtz were training. As Lavern drove the black show-style wagon, Lowell jogged alongside the three pairs of horses to instruct and encourage them. Bishop Monroe and his assistant, Mose Fisher, were standing several yards away to observe the boys and the Clydesdales—watching as the next generation of Promise Lodge learned a valuable skill that might some-day become their trade.

Ezra smiled. It was yet another example of how the people here worked together to ensure the productivity of their neighbors' sons and daughters. The sight of the majestic horses always inspired him, but as he approached Harley Kurtz's house, he saw another vision that made him glad he'd come to this community.

Vera was sitting in the porch swing with a sketch pad. She was so engrossed in drawing that she wasn't aware of his approach, so Ezra held the flowers behind his back. He walked more slowly, observing how her brow puckered slightly above her turquoise glasses as she concentrated. She was so lost in her creative trance, he almost hated to intrude—but he really wanted to make amends.

Ezra cleared his throat.

When Vera looked up, a smile slowly transformed her face. When she was working, she was a comely young woman, but as she focused on Ezra, she became stunning.

"Ezra! Come and tell me what you think of my new cow dishes!"

He felt as though she'd invited him to a big party—an exhibition of her work—and that he was to be the only guest. Vera had made him feel special, even though she'd walked away from Maria's rude intrusion only an hour ago.

"Do you know how fabulous you are?" he whispered. "I came to apologize and—and to give you these flowers—"

"But mainly, you came to see me. You left a much prettier girl behind—"

"Maria?" Shaking his head, Ezra stepped up onto the front porch. "She's become such a nuisance that I don't even see her anymore. I just see red."

"Let me put these in a vase! I'll be right back." Vera accepted his handful of flowers as though they were a precious gift and went into the house.

Ezra eased onto the swing, stealing glances at her sketch pad. It wasn't his place to snoop—and besides, he wanted Vera to tell him about her ideas while she sat beside him. As he gazed out over the lawn and the rosebushes blooming profusely along the porch railing, the fragrance of the deep pink blooms heightened his awareness of the beauty around him.

Of course, anything smelled better than a dairy barn. As Vera returned to the porch and placed the quart canning jar of flowers on the nearby table, he sighed with gratitude.

He was in his happy place. And he was wise enough to realize it.

"What do you think, Ezra? The plates I'm making all need to be the same size and shape, so they'll stack correctly in a cupboard," Vera said as she sat down beside him. She picked up her sketchbook and shared it with him. "But should I go with squares or ovals? I'd like this design to have a unique look, so round plates seem too ordinary."

Ezra leaned closer to her, pleased that she was asking his opinion. Truth be told, he'd never thought about plates being anything except round, yet Vera's creative mind was miles ahead of his assumptions. As he looked at her sketches, his answer came immediately.

"If you want your dishes to look more natural—more cowlike," he ventured cautiously, "wouldn't oval be better for setting off your irregular black spots? The square edges, even though you've rounded them a bit, seem harsh. But then, I handle the softest part of the cow when I attach her to the milking apparatus, so maybe my opinion—"

"You've got it!" Vera said with a grin. "I was thinking about the square plates fitting better into a cabinet— which is all straight lines and flat surfaces. But anyone who'd want these playful cow dishes probably wouldn't care about such practicality, ain't so?"

When she beamed at him, Ezra felt ecstatic. His breath left him in a rush and all he could think about was pulling Vera close for a kiss—except Isaac had made that mistake, hadn't he? Her split lip had healed, but that didn't give him license to take what he wanted.

"Whatever you say, sweetie," he murmured. "I, um, lost my train of thought when you looked at me that way."

Her brown eyes widened behind her turquoise glasses. "What way was that, Ezra?"

The innocence of her question was too sincere to be faked. Had Maria spoken the same words, they would've sounded deliberately coy, and she'd have been fluttering her lashes at him. All thoughts of Miss Zehr left him, however, when Vera rested her head on his shoulder.

"You probably think I'm pretty clueless, being nine-teen and—"

"I think you're wonderful, Vera," Ezra whispered, slowly slipping his arm around her shoulders. "I—I really want to kiss you, but after the way Isaac came at you, maybe you're not ready for another guy to—"

"You're not just another guy, Ezra."

When she closed her eyes and her lips drifted slightly apart, Ezra's heart thrummed. She was trusting him with so much.

He gently pressed his mouth to hers. Her soft sigh told him she wasn't going to push him away or scream for help, so he relaxed, prolonging the kiss for several long, blissful moments. When he eased away from her, Vera's hand cupped his cheek, guiding him back for another taste of her gentle eagerness to please him.

Several moments later, when they eased apart, Ezra saw that her sketch pad had slid onto the porch floor. With a nervous laugh, Vera leaned down to pick it up.

"Guess my cows thought we'd caught fire, and they couldn't stand the heat," she quipped. "I should go in and start cooking, but you can come with me—if you want to. Aunt Minerva would be tickled to chat with you, or you could help me, or—"

Vera squeezed his hand, blushing. "I'm trying to invite you to stay for supper, Ezra, but my brain seems to be running at the mouth. Sorry."

"Don't be sorry," he said as he stood up beside her. "You've just made my day."

Chapter 22

When Isaac arrived at the lodge for supper on Wednesday evening, he knew immediately that part of the meal had burned. Ruby and Beulah were carrying a relish tray and a gelatin salad to the table, and they looked up when they saw him.

"*Gut* evening, Isaac! We're glad you've come for supper," Beulah said rather loudly.

Ruby met him at the table, rolling her eyes. "Time will tell if *you'll* be glad," she hinted under her breath.

"Our extra places are set for Irene and Dale," Beulah continued, speaking like a woman who was hard of hearing. She held Isaac's gaze, nodding toward the kitchen. "Maria offered to cook tonight, so it's a shame Eddie will be eating with Fannie at Preacher Marlin's place—"

"And I just saw Ezra hiking up the hill," Isaac put in, matching the volume of Beulah's speech. "I suspect he'll be eating at Harley's house. With Vera."

When Maria appeared in the kitchen doorway to frown forlornly at him, Isaac realized the Kuhns had been preparing him for more of a roller-coaster ride than usual. It was clear that he'd just burst Maria's bubble, where Ezra was concerned, and he expected the tears to flow at any moment. As the lodge door opened and the newlywed Kraybills entered, however, Maria smoothed her pink gingham dress and smiled brightly.

"Irene, welcome back!" she said too cheerfully. "Oh, and you, too, Dale! I—I hope you folks won't mind that I was the cook this evening—"

As though afraid something else might burn to a crisp, the blonde disappeared into the kitchen. Isaac chatted with the Kraybills as they settled into chairs at the table, and then Maria came from the kitchen with a large tray of pastries. She focused on Irene.

"While you were away, Irene, I—I was wondering if you and Phoebe would let me join your Promise Lodge Pies business," she said hopefully. "I'd leave the pies to you two, but I was hoping you'd let me expand the menu by baking my best-selling pastries—my mainstay varieties in Cloverdale—"

"What time of day would you want to bake?" Irene interrupted. "Phoebe mentioned that you'd spoken to her about this idea. We've agreed that our little building doesn't have enough workspace—or ovens—for pies and pastries to be made at the same time."

Maria's face fell. Dale had the presence of mind to gently take the tray from her hands before she dumped its contents on his wife.

"I'm still wondering why you don't return to your own bakery," the storekeeper said kindly. "Folks at church have been asking when you'll reopen, Maria. Everyone really misses your breads and sweets."

Maria pressed her lips into a thin line and retreated to the kitchen again. Isaac saw that she wasn't happy with the way the conversation was going, so she'd abandoned it, as was her habit.

Ravenous, Isaac snatched an apple fritter from the tray. He took a big bite.

It melted in his mouth. The luscious confection contained enough cinnamon and apples to convince him to take another big bite to savor the soft chew of the pastry. When the Kuhns came to the table with a platter of scorched chicken pieces and a pan of scalloped potatoes with the top layer scraped off, Isaac sensed that Maria's pastries might be the most appetizing part of this meal.

As they all bowed to give thanks, Isaac silently prayed that Maria would be able to regain her cheerful demeanor, even if most of her food suggested she'd had a rough afternoon. After the prayer, folks politely took helpings of the chicken and potatoes, and Isaac did, too. He wasn't a fan of fruity gelatin salads, but he took a large helping before passing the bowl along.

When Maria emerged from the kitchen to sit down with them, she gazed hopefully at Irene again. "What if—what if I waited until you and Phoebe finished baking for the day before I made my pastries?" she asked softly. "That way, you wouldn't even have to clean up, because *I* would do it after I finished!"

The clean-up idea must have just occurred to her, because her blue eyes lit up like sparkling crystals. Before Irene could reply, however, the lodge door opened and Rosetta entered, followed by Truman.

When Maria blinked, it was as though she'd dimmed the high-beam headlights on her car.

"Welcome, Wickeys!" Ruby called out, waving to

them. "You're just in time for supper. Shall I fetch a couple more plates?"

Rosetta, whose belly was getting noticeably rounder, glanced at the chicken and the potatoes but graciously didn't reply. Truman, however, plucked a Danish from the tray.

"We stopped by to see if you'll be returning to your bakery," he said to Maria. "The construction crew's making *gut* progress—"

"And Ruby and I want to make a contribution from our Coffee Can Fund," Beulah told Maria with a kindly smile. "You could put it toward new appliances, or whatever your business needs, Maria. That's why we businesswomen at Promise Lodge started the fund."

Isaac braced himself. The blonde's expression had gone from bad to worse in the past few seconds, and she looked like a teakettle at full boil, ready to spout off.

"You just want to get rid of me—all of you!" Maria blurted out. "I've been working hard to improve— trying to be helpful and find a new purpose at Promise Lodge—but you don't want me around! If I had my car, I'd be gone in a heartbeat!"

Irene gazed intently at the young woman seated across from her. "It's this impulsive, immature behavior that has prevented your success ever since your parents passed, Maria," she said, shaking her head sadly. "You surely realize that Phoebe told me about the mess you left our bakery in—without asking her to use it in the first place—"

"And I'm simply asking for the decision you were to make a while back, Maria," Truman pointed out gently. "I'll be getting an insurance settlement that could pay for some of your equipment, too. But I need your commitment."

As Maria hung her head, stifling sobs, Isaac badly wanted to leave the scene of this emotional head-on crash. He felt bad for Maria, however, because he understood how it felt to be shut out—or to believe you'd been shut out. And he certainly knew firsthand about the loneliness she was enduring.

He also knew that Truman and Irene had made valid points. And the Kuhn sisters had made a very generous offer to help Maria. But she'd interpreted their remarks as condemnations and criticism—neither of which she handled well.

Dale sighed as though he, too, wished to be somewhere else. "One of the reasons Irene and I joined you tonight," he began cautiously, "was to tell you that Lizzie's motor scooter is still parked in my garage. She left it behind when she joined the Amish church and married Raymond, so I've pulled it out onto the driveway, thinking you might want to—"

Maria stood up so fast that her chair fell backward. "It's a *sign*," she declared, tossing her fork onto her plate. "Maybe I'll drive off and never come back!"

Isaac wasn't sure why, but when the blonde bolted toward the front door, he wasn't far behind her. "Maria, wait! You're in no condition to drive—"

She was already down the porch steps, however. She sprinted past the six cabins that were under construction toward the Kraybills' new house.

Isaac had the advantage of longer legs, but Maria was moving at full speed, driven by adrenaline. When she spotted the pink scooter, she ran faster than he'd ever imagined she could.

Who in the world would drive a pink motor scooter?

He laughed. Knowing what he did about Maria, her sister—and even Raymond Overholt—he should've figured any vehicle they owned would be quirky. When Maria put on a bright pink helmet, he called out, "Hey, maybe I ought to drive! You're upset, Maria—an accident waiting to happen!"

She turned her back on him, redoubling Isaac's determination to save her from herself. He didn't like her all that much, but the thought of her getting hit, lying injured and bleeding on the pavement, spurred him on. Before Maria could climb onto the seat, Isaac shoved her aside and swung his leg over the scooter.

"Hey!" she protested. "I didn't invite you along—"

"Too bad!" Isaac shot back. "I'm not letting you go anywhere—"

"But you're Amish," Maria argued, planting her fists on her hips. "You're not supposed to be driving."

"I have a license—and I'm still in *rumspringa*," he informed her.

Dale had left the scooter's key in the ignition, so Isaac turned it, grabbed a hand brake, and then pushed the Start button. He revved the engine a few times, stoked by the sound of the scooter's power—and by the possibility of getting away from Promise Lodge, if only for a while. He'd forgotten how much he loved to drive.

"If you're going anywhere, Maria, you'll be going with me," Isaac informed her over the engine's low roar. "Better hang on tight, because if you fall off, I won't go back for you."

She scowled, thrusting a second pink helmet at him. "You've got to wear this—"

Isaac laughed. After his weeks of quiet life in a

lonely apartment, he was suddenly primed for a wild ride and an adventure. "If you think I'm wearing a pink helmet, think again. You coming, girl?"

As her driver accelerated down Promise Lodge's private road, barely slowing down to make a left turn onto the county blacktop, Maria clutched him for dear life.

Isaac had a need for speed. He hadn't been driving two minutes before he was traveling faster than she'd believed the scooter could go.

What if he crashed? What if the local sheriff saw him driving without a helmet and came after them? Would Isaac pull over, or would he shoot off down the road even faster?

What if he doesn't really have a license and we're heading toward our death?

As the engine whined louder, however, she reveled in the feel of Isaac's taut, muscled body as he leaned forward, totally focused on the road. When he laughed wildly, Maria realized that she no longer felt like crying. She was too scared to cry.

No, I'm too excited.

When he pulled into a gas station, however, her doubts took over again.

"How do I get to Cloverdale?" he asked as he fitted the nozzle into the scooter's tank.

Maria scowled. "Why would we go there? If I wanted to be back in—"

"Why do I suspect you're overlooking some things?" Isaac shot back. He leaned down until his nose was mere inches from hers. "Humor me, Maria, because I'm still driving. Which way to Cloverdale?"

Her mouth dropped open. Who did this guy think he was, telling her to go places she didn't want to go—and all but stealing her scooter? She had *not* invited him along on her pity party—

But Isaac barged in anyway. And he was probably right. Considering my mental state, I'd probably be a bloody puddle in the road by now if I'd driven off by myself.

"Fine," Maria retorted. "If you have to be such a hot shot about it, just stay on this county road. And if a cop spots you speeding without a helmet, the ticket is on *you*, Isaac."

He shrugged. "I can handle it. Lord knows I've done worse things."

After Isaac climbed back onto the scooter, they shot off down the blacktop again. As farmland and woods flashed by them in a blur, Maria fearfully wrapped her arms tighter around him—while he had the nerve to whoop and holler over the whine of the engine. He was obviously having a fine, fun time at her expense—

But he took over. He's a fabulous driver. I've never heard Isaac laugh this way, and . . . he's kinda cute when he's bossing me around. He's a daredevil show-off, but he knows exactly what he's doing.

As they entered the Cloverdale city limits, Isaac slowed to the proper speed. They passed the Laundromat and the local gas station, where George Dillard waved as he watched them go by, a puzzled expression on his face.

"Which way to your bakery, Maria?" Isaac asked over his shoulder.

She sighed. There was no sense in lying, because in a town this small, Isaac could drive up and down the streets until he found the burned-out building. "Keep going. We're only a couple blocks away."

Her stomach clenched. She didn't want to see the charred remains of her business or the blackened skeleton of her car, but Isaac seemed set on putting her through that torture. Maria closed her eyes and leaned her head against his sturdy back, determined not to cry again. She was so tired of crying.

A few minutes later, the scooter slowed to a stop. Maria figured if she kept her arms locked around Isaac—refused to move—he would eventually give in and drive away.

But no.

"So, your store is on the corner of the county highway and Main Street," he pointed out. "I bet the guys coming out of that barber shop and the women in that beauty salon next to it are some of your best customers. And the folks who work at the bank down the way probably serve your pastries at their staff meetings."

How did Isaac know these things? Maria sat up with a sigh, allowing him to gently pry her arms from around his waist.

"Come on, girl, let's go in," he said softly. "The renovation crew Truman hired has cleared away the worst of the damage."

Reluctantly, she removed her helmet and handed it to Isaac. The bakery's walls were scorched in places, but the structure was intact. The debris had been cleaned off the street and the new front windows facing Main still had their stickers on them. After Isaac hung her helmet on the handlebar, he reached for her hand.

"It'll be easier if you just look it in the eye, Maria," he said with an encouraging smile. "I'm here to walk you through it, and we don't have to stay long."

Was this the same Isaac Chupp who'd been bossing her around? As she took his hand, Maria swallowed the smart remark she'd been ready to hurl at him. He was probably a smooth talker—knew exactly what to say to get what he wanted from every young woman he met— but at this moment, he was offering to be her friend. Her guardian angel.

"Maria! Hey, it's good to see you!"

She turned, finding a smile for Dan Schumann, the bank president.

"Our last staff meeting wasn't the same without your fried pies and apple fritters," he put in as he nodded at Isaac. "Lots of folks are hoping you'll be back in your kitchen soon."

When Dan had walked down the street, Maria followed Isaac toward the opening where the bakery's front door had been. "You couldn't possibly have paid him to say that, right?" she teased.

"I didn't have to," Isaac pointed out. As he stepped inside the building, he looked at the walls and the empty kitchen. "If you took the Kuhns' offer and bought new appliances, I'm guessing you could be baking again in another week or two, Maria. Truman would be sure the workmen have finished by then if you tell him you're coming back. And he said something about replacing some of your equipment, as well. It's a sweet deal."

Maria shrugged noncommittally. Isaac was right— but her heart wasn't in it. "Um, would you look out the back kitchen window and see if the carcass of my poor little car is still there? I don't have the heart to do it myself."

With a nod, he passed through the room where the sink, refrigerators and ovens had once stood. "Nope. All gone."

"Poor Ruby," she whispered. "I had no idea I was going to blow you to smithereens—"

"Let's stop at your house," Isaac said, holding her gaze. "You probably left in a hurry and didn't think to shut off the water or the gas—"

Maria hung her head. Once again, Isaac was right—and once again, she'd acted like a complete fool. Out of habit, she probably hadn't even locked the doors when she'd hurried to catch her ride to Promise Lodge more than a week ago. Someone could've taken up residence—or pulled up a truck and loaded her furniture into it.

"Yeah, we should," she admitted under her breath. "I—I've seen all I want to see here."

They were getting back onto the scooter when Sally Swanson, the business teacher at the high school, waved from the sidewalk. "Awfully sorry about your fire, Maria," she said. "Let me know how I can help you get your bakery going again!"

Isaac started the engine, then spoke over his shoulder. "The folks here sincerely wish you'd reopen, Maria," he observed gently. "Lizzie's gone to Coldstream, *jah*, but if you don't want to work alone, would it be so hard to hire an assistant?"

Maria shrugged. Truth be told, she hadn't considered that possibility.

As they pulled out onto Main Street, she pointed in the direction Isaac was to turn. Every fiber of her being warned her against going to the house—that poor, empty shell of a home that no longer rang with laughter or girl talk.

But Isaac was as hardheaded as she was. If he was determined to check the place over, there'd be no stopping him.

When he pulled into the driveway on Maple Street, Maria was embarrassed at how messy the uncut lawn looked. Isaac again offered his hand, so she couldn't refuse to go inside, no matter how many ghosts and memories might haunt the unoccupied rooms. With a sigh, she followed him up the walk and through the front door.

And no, she hadn't locked it.

Chapter 23

As Isaac looked around the Zehr place, his entire body relaxed. He'd lived in such a sparsely furnished house all his life that the soft femininity of Maria's home welcomed him with open arms. Graceful lace-edged curtains hung at the windows. Colorful afghans were folded over the two overstuffed chairs. The soft hint of scented candles—and maybe Maria's shampoo—lingered in the air. He had the sudden urge to stretch out on the couch and put his feet on the coffee table, but if he did, he knew he might never leave.

This place feels like home to me. I could be very happy here.

Startled by his thoughts, Isaac released Maria's hand. He'd come to Cloverdale on a whim, to save her from herself, yet he suddenly yearned to live here—in this friendly town, in this cozy old home.

But he knew better than to suggest such a thing. He'd seen the way Maria had latched on to Ezra, once she got the idea that Overholt was the man who'd take care of her.

He wasn't ready to become Miss Zehr's next victim. He hadn't come here because he *liked* her, after all.

"Well," she said with a shrug. "Here it is."

Isaac nodded, proceeding cautiously. "And you grew up here? With your parents and Lizzie and your other sister?"

"They're all gone now, except for me," Maria reminded him with a hitch in her voice. "Ezra suggested that I should sell this place and use the money to—"

"Why would you do that? I'd live here in a heartbeat!" Isaac blurted out. "I mean—I couldn't possibly afford to buy this house, but if I could—"

Maria's blue eyes widened at his show of emotion, but she was shaking her head. "Well, I might have to sell the place anyway, to repay Truman. Since the bakery fire was my fault, I should at least replace the equipment and appliances he provided when he first bought the building."

Before Isaac could protest, she held up her hand, holding his gaze.

"You see, Truman set me up in this building to get me away from Promise Lodge, because Rosetta believed I was luring him away from her." She looked away sadly. "My business was a total failure there anyway—not that I've done any better in Cloverdale. Everyone loves what I bake, but a lot more money seems to flow out than comes in. I'm such a loser, Isaac."

"That's not true!" Isaac sensed Maria was getting ready to cry again—something he'd rather avoid—and she had no reason to put herself down. "You have options! Ruby and Beulah and Truman—and the folks we've seen here in Cloverdale—all want to help you get going again. You could—"

"None of those options will make me better at running my business, Isaac," she pointed out ruefully. "And I'd still be all alone."

"What if I set you up with a computerized system like my brothers use for their auction business? Like the one Dale has in his store?" Isaac said, his voice rising with excitement. "It would keep track of your inventory and your expenses—"

Maria stared at him as though he'd grown a second head. "Do you think I'd know how to *run* a computerized system? I used an adding machine and wrote out paper receipts—"

"*I* could help you maintain it!" Isaac blurted out, as though the solution ought to be obvious. "I've been doing computer stuff since I was a kid—"

"Even though you're Amish?"

Isaac threw up his hands. "I learned from the English guys who help us with our auction business, all right? Before long, I was showing them shortcuts they had no idea about! And again," he added, "I've not joined the church—and I don't *own* the computers. My family never objected because I helped them run their business more efficiently."

His words burned a little. Like hellfire.

We won't go into the way I skimmed some of the profits without Dat or my brothers knowing for a long while. That's behind me now.

Maria's wide-eyed wonderment alerted Isaac that she'd latched on to his words.

"You would do that, Isaac? For me?"

The wistful desperation in her voice made Isaac go soft inside. Maria was sincerely astounded that he'd offered to help her set up a very basic system—

Or maybe she's playing me for a big fool. She's had plenty of practice at getting guys to do whatever she wants by flashing those baby blues on high beam.

When she stepped up and kissed him full on the lips, however, Isaac gained a new appreciation for Maria's techniques. Maybe she *was* playing him. But as he pulled the curvy blonde close to kiss her until they were both senseless, he didn't really care.

This woman knew how to please a man.

As Isaac cupped her head in his hands, kissing Maria with all his pent-up need, he knew she wouldn't cry out or run scared. He'd been attracted to Vera—and to Deborah before that—because their naïve innocence had set him afire. But he'd gotten scorched when they'd reported his advances.

Maria Zehr wouldn't kiss and tell. She'd initiated their intimate contact, and she could give as good as she got—or better. She was older than he, and Isaac was willing to be the one who learned rather than the one who led. For now, anyway.

When they stepped apart, exhaling hard, Isaac prayed he wouldn't be sorry for what he'd said and done in this quiet house.

Maria held his gaze, catching her breath. She had a dazed look about her. Their kisses had apparently boggled her mind, as well.

"You've given me a lot to think about," she admitted in a breathy voice. "We—we'd better go back to Promise Lodge so I can consider my options. And if you didn't mean what you said about setting up a computer system and maintaining it for me, you'd better tell me sooner rather than later. Like, now."

Isaac blinked. If this was Maria's voice of authority, he liked it. It was certainly an improvement over a pity party.

"Are you sure you want to watch me make a sample plate?" Vera asked Ezra after supper. They were strolling toward the little shed where her pottery equipment sat waiting. Her body was on high alert because she was with such a handsome young man, but she was also anxious.

She hadn't allowed anyone to watch her create new designs—except for her step*mamm*, Amanda, because she was an accomplished potter herself. Ezra, on the other hand, claimed he had no artistic talent whatsoever.

But he'd immediately sensed a connection between an oval plate and a cow's soft, flexible udder and irregular black spots. He instinctively knew that art often mimicked natural elements—and he seemed genuinely interested in watching her work.

Vera prayed she wouldn't freeze up in front of him. Or create an out-of-kilter plate that wouldn't stack correctly.

She was thankful for the evening breeze that freshened the shed as she propped the door open. Vera rummaged through a large box of pottery tools until she found an oval template and its corresponding wooden mold, as well as a large, flat block of foam and a rolling pin. When she removed a lump of clay from her supply, it felt cool and damp; heavy with promise as she held it between her hands.

"How do you know how much clay you'll need for a plate?" Ezra asked, leaning against the wall nearby.

She shrugged. "I go by feel, mostly. For the plates I have in mind, the most important thing is to roll the clay into a flat, roughly rectangular piece—like dough for cut-out cookies, but thicker. I'll use these flat rods on either side, so it'll be the same thickness all over."

Ezra was watching with interest as she stepped over to her worktable with the clay, the rods, and her rolling pin. "You're not using your wheel?"

"Nope. I'm not skilled enough to make sets of plates the same size and thickness on a moving wheel." After kneading the clay for a few moments on a fabric-covered work board, she used her rolling pin to press the clay disk into a slab between the two rods. "But when I know how I want my cow design to look, I'll throw the bowls and other serving pieces on the wheel."

When she had a slab slightly larger than her template, she rubbed it quickly with a rib tool to compress it and remove any air bubbles. "Now I'll make the spots, which won't be in the same places on any two plates."

"Just like no two cows have markings alike," Ezra observed.

Nodding, Vera plucked a small roller from a nearby can of tools. She used gentle pressure to create the irregular areas she would paint with black glaze. After she dipped a sponge into a bucket of water near the table, she smoothed the spots' edges.

"That is so cool," her companion murmured. "And now you need to cut around your template and then curve the edges up into a rim, right? So the food will stay on the plate?"

Vera chuckled, delighted with his question. "*You*

could make these plates, Ezra! You already understand the basic elements of forming them."

When she'd arranged the oval template and cut around it, she removed the clay scraps along the edges. "This plate needs to set for several minutes, so it'll be firm enough to work with. Shall we wait and see how we like it after I've formed the rim? Or cut out three more plates and make their spots now?"

"Go with it," Ezra replied immediately. "I can already see these plates white with the black spots, all shiny and smooth."

Vera glanced at the battery clock on her shelf. How was it already seven o'clock? "You have great faith in my ability," she said in a low voice.

"I do." Ezra's smile had an enticing curve to it. "I also have an idea how we can pass the time while we wait for your plates to firm up."

Her cheeks tingled. It was a new experience to have a young man hint at the pleasure he wanted to share with her. Vera focused more intently on the remaining three plates to keep from getting distracted, while Ezra remained quietly in his spot, leaning against the shed wall.

"And here's our fourth cow, ready to set up," she said as she surveyed the four ovals with their slightly indented spots. "These are going to be so much fun to finish—"

"How much time do we have, sweetie?" Ezra murmured. "It's twenty after."

Vera gently tested the edges of the first oval. "Maybe five minutes," she replied as she dipped her hands into the bucket of water. "If they set up too long, they'll crack when I press the rim."

"I'm about ready to crack," he whispered as he

slipped his arms around her. "Watching you work is a highly *inspiring* experience."

When Ezra's lips met hers, Vera tried to remain aware of the passing minutes but finally gave in to the wonderful sensations of his caress.

Is this what love feels like? Is Ezra the one I'm to marry?

She allowed her emotions free rein, daring to believe she might be falling for the man who held her captive with his kisses. When Vera finally eased away, she sucked in her breath.

"Seven forty-five!" she rasped, too exhilarated to be angry as she freed herself from Ezra's embrace. "But it's probably humid enough that the plates are still pliable."

"Pliable," he teased. "I like it that *you're* pliable, too, Vera. Soft in all the right places."

Those places tingled from his attention as Vera checked the plates. No one would know the difference if these dishes didn't turn out—they could be crumpled into balls, dampened, and returned to her clay supply.

It was probably best that she continue with them, however, because Uncle Harley or someone else might walk in on impassioned kisses they shouldn't witness— and she'd be in the same trouble Eddie and Fannie had found themselves in.

"Now for the fun part," she said softly. "I'll cover the first plate with this plastic wrap, put it on the foam pad, and then press my oval block into the center—because *jah*, we'd have a very messy dinner table if these plates were totally flat."

When the edges of the oval slab curved up around the

wooden block to form the rim, Ezra let out a laugh. "Whoa! You make that look so easy, Vera!"

She shrugged, carefully setting the formed plate on the worktable so she could continue with the other three. "Amanda was a *gut* teacher—and very generous about supplying me with all these tools. She also knew that I needed to make practical, useful pottery pieces so church leaders wouldn't crack down on me for wasting my time on artsy creations."

Ezra nodded. "My brother Raymond learned that lesson while he was making his wooden Christmas stars," he agreed. "Now that he's taken over the store in Coldstream—and Lizzie's expecting—I doubt he has much time for anything artistic."

As Vera smoothed the plates' edges with a wet sponge, she knew she would miss making her pottery if she were forbidden to continue—or didn't have time. Approaching voices made her turn toward the doorway as Ezra greeted their visitors.

"Fannie and Ed!" he called out jovially. "Come see what Vera's been making and tell us what you've been up to this evening—if you can talk about it, that is."

"Puh! Pottery's not the only thing happening in here," Vera's brother shot back.

"But we have news!" Fannie put in with a conspiratorial grin. "A little while ago we saw Maria running out of the lodge, crying, with Isaac chasing after her—"

"And they took off down the road on a pink motor scooter!" Eddie finished exuberantly. "And Isaac was driving!"

"Hmm. That was Lizzie's scooter," Ezra mused aloud. "Wonder what happened? Last I knew, Isaac preferred to gawk at Maria's, um, *attributes* while staying out of her clutches."

"Oh, she was clutching him, all right," Fannie said with a laugh. "Fast as Isaac was driving, Maria was hanging on for dear life."

As Vera carefully set the four plates on a clean section of shelf to dry, she had no trouble imagining the scene her brother and his fiancée had described. She couldn't help smiling at her work. She would fire the plates on Thursday, and her fingers itched to apply the white and black glazes sometime on Friday so she could fire the plates again on Saturday and complete them.

"Isaac and Maria have more in common than you might think," she said softly. "I suspect they're both frustrated and lonely—"

"And if they're exasperating one another, they're leaving the rest of us alone," Ezra finished. "Who's up for ice cream? We should celebrate Vera's new pottery design by driving into Forest Grove—my treat!"

While Fannie and Eddie admired her fresh plates, Vera smiled at Ezra. He was such a generous soul, and more attuned to her craft than she'd imagined. And when he blew her a kiss, she knew exactly what Ezra wanted—even more than ice cream.

Chapter 24

"May I have a word, Isaac?"

Isaac jumped, snatched from a racy fantasy involving Maria. It was Friday morning, and he'd lost count of all the daydreams he'd had about the buxom blonde who'd taken him to the moon and back a couple evenings ago.

"Um, did you say something, Dale?" he stammered. "I was so engrossed in arranging these cookies, I—I didn't notice you'd come up beside me."

The storekeeper's wry smile told Isaac his story hadn't been very convincing. "You've seemed a little preoccupied lately," Kraybill said in a low voice. "Is everything okay?"

"Oh, *jah—jah*, just fine. Um, why do you ask?"

Isaac kicked himself for using the conversational trick that flipped the focus onto the other person. Dale didn't shy away from asking spot-on, nosy questions.

Kraybill shrugged, glancing up at the clock. "We have a few minutes before Marlene arrives and the store opens. I was wondering how your scooter ride with Maria went Wednesday evening. She was awfully upset when she bolted from the table."

Isaac swallowed hard. He would not admit to sharing long, hot kisses inside Maria's home—and again in the storage shed behind the store, after they'd returned to Promise Lodge.

"I, um—I think I talked her down from the ledge," he said. "And I think I convinced her to reopen her bakery in Cloverdale."

Dale's eyebrows shot up. "*Gut* for you—and for Maria. She bakes fabulous pastries, but I suspect she needs guidance when it comes to managing her time and money."

"I agree. And I hope I haven't rushed in where any fool would know not to go."

Isaac sighed. He'd opened a whole new conversational can of worms. But on this Friday morning in early August, he was in over his head: ever since he'd held her and kissed her on Wednesday evening, he couldn't get Maria out of his mind. But he couldn't admit that to middle-aged, straitlaced Dale, of course.

Kraybill cleared his throat. "You kept your pants on, I hope."

"What the—*jah*, I did!" Isaac yelped. "But barely."

The storekeeper nodded, waiting him out.

Isaac sighed. "The scary part is that I offered to set up a computer system for her bakery, so she could run her business as efficiently as you do," he admitted. "And, well—Maria probably thinks that implies something more, um, ongoing."

Dale nodded. "You're probably right. Maria's the most emotionally needy person I know, and you've just thrown her a lifeline—"

"But I don't want it to turn into a noose!"

Kraybill's chuckle suggested he might've fallen into

the same sort of predicament when he was younger. He was still an attractive fellow, so Isaac could imagine that the girls must have pursued him when he'd been in his late teens and early twenties.

"I had the same fears when I fell for Irene earlier this year," Dale confessed. "I was a sworn bachelor, living my life exactly the way I wanted to, so bringing a woman—a *wife*—into the picture terrified me. I . . . I was afraid I couldn't keep her happy and interested in me for the long haul."

Isaac blinked. He wasn't about to ask if silvery-haired Dale was talking about sex—it wasn't any of his business. "But you got past that."

"I did. Best thing that ever happened to me, jumping in with both feet." The shopkeeper glanced away, maybe so his expression wouldn't reveal more than he intended. "Irene and I had more in common than we figured. We've been friends for years, yet we didn't really *know* each other.

"Which sounds ridiculous to you, I'm sure," Kraybill added with a laugh. "When I was your age, I never thought about anything beyond the next weekend, let alone how my life would play out when retirement was on the horizon."

Isaac bit back a grin. The upcoming weekend had indeed been on his mind, and he was hoping for another ride on that scooter—even if it was pink. He was also hoping Maria would move beyond the kissing stage, even as he knew she'd interpret such involvement as another step in a permanent direction.

"It was very considerate of you to insist on driving Wednesday night, and to offer Maria help setting up a computer program, Isaac," the storekeeper said as he briefly squeezed Isaac's shoulder. "A relationship with Miss Zehr will be anything but predictable, so be careful. Older women aren't necessarily wiser women."

Isaac laughed out loud. "I doubt anyone will ever call Maria *wise*."

"Ah, but she's figured out how to capture your imagination and attention," Dale pointed out. He waved to Marlene as she entered the store through the warehouse doors. "Don't ever underestimate the power of a woman, Isaac. Especially that blonde who's dancing through your fantasies right now."

Isaac blinked. Once again Kraybill had hit the bull's-eye.

As the storekeeper ambled down the aisle toward the checkout counter to speak with Marlene, Isaac quickly shelved the remaining packages of cookies. Somehow, he had to remain focused on his work for the rest of the day when all he really wanted was to make Maria laugh and hold him tight as they drove off on her scooter this evening.

When Isaac entered the lodge for supper, he paused to be sure his clean shirt was properly smoothed into his pants. A glance in the mirror of the antique dresser where Rosetta displayed her goat milk soaps told him his hair was reasonably presentable—

And Maria's reflection—she stood a short distance behind him in a fresh blue gingham dress—told him she knew he was primping. For her.

"Caught me," he muttered, unable to suppress a grin.

"*Jah*, I have," she agreed. "Hook, line, and sinker."

With a wink and a laugh Maria made light of what

she'd just said, but Dale's words came back to Isaac as he walked with her into the dining room.

Don't ever underestimate the power of a woman. Especially that blonde who's dancing through your fantasies right now.

"What do you say we take the scooter out after supper?" she asked in a low voice. "I'd like to stop by the Wickeys' and tell Truman I'm going to reopen the bakery in Cloverdale—unless you've changed your mind about helping me."

As he saw himself mirrored in her beautiful blue eyes, Isaac knew there would be no going back on what he'd offered her. If he was ever to escape the web Maria was swiftly, skillfully spinning around him, he'd have to cut himself free immediately—and the consequences would be loud, dramatic, and very ugly.

Isaac paused before answering, telling himself the suspense would keep this bold young woman wondering—and it would give him a momentary sense of control over the situation.

How ridiculous is that? Maria had me from the moment she held me on her scooter. We can only go forward from here.

But was he ready for all that this entanglement entailed? He'd never given marriage to Maria a serious thought—and he knew better than to say that word out loud.

"I—I'm sure Truman would appreciate knowing your intentions," he hedged.

Maria played along, her mischievous smile suggesting that she had the same evening activities in mind that he did. Isaac went through the motions of greeting Ezra, Eddie, and the Kuhns while the sisters set out a simple supper of cold sliced ham and chicken they'd fried earlier that morning. He spooned two or three different salads onto his plate, but he barely tasted them. He tried not to stare or stammer when Maria batted her eyes at him from across the table.

Grateful that Ezra and Eddie were engaged in a conversation with the Kuhns about the different cheeses they made, Isaac tried to eat his usual amount of supper. The last thing he wanted was to draw Beulah's or Ruby's attention—or to make them think their food didn't taste good. Just as he felt Maria's bare toe tapping his knee, the phone rang in the kitchen.

"I'll get it," Beulah said as she rose from her chair.

"And I'll fetch the ice cream sandwiches I made for our dessert," Ruby put in as she followed her sister.

When the Kuhns were gone, Ezra let out an exaggerated cough. "Are you two going to get a room, or do we have to watch this hanky-panky all night?" he asked as he elbowed Isaac.

"Ezra, that's no way to talk!" Maria pretended to be offended—apparently forgetting that she'd flirted just as outrageously with *him* not so long ago

"Don't even think about sneaking into the back of my wagon," Eddie warned playfully. "I'll be the first one to know if you—"

Beulah's appearance in the kitchen doorway hushed their playful banter. "The phone call's for you, Isaac," she said with a purposeful gaze.

Isaac's supper dropped into the well of his stomach. Who would be calling him? Surely Dale hadn't thought up another piece of advice. Hopefully Preacher Amos hadn't discovered another tidbit from his past to grill him about . . .

All the way to the back kitchen wall, his thoughts churned. When he picked up the dangling receiver, he paused before speaking into it. "*Jah*, this is Isaac."

A woman on the other end let out a long, shaky breath. "God is *gut*," she whispered. "Isaac, I was so relieved to get your letter—"

"Mamm?" Isaac swallowed hard, hoping to disguise the sudden emotion in his voice.

"—and when I realized you'd been at Promise Lodge all this time, I was so thankful that you'd had the sense to go where decent folks would look after you," she continued in a rush. "You can't imagine how many nights I've worried about you being safe—or how many times I've kicked myself for those things I said before you left."

"Well, you didn't say anything that wasn't true," Isaac admitted sadly. "I *had* stolen money from the auction accounts. I never intended to upset you or—"

"My word, listen to you, son." His mother paused, chuckling softly. "You sound like a different person altogether from the cocky young know-it-all who seemed so proud of his wrongdoing."

Isaac leaned against the wall with his back to the dining room, hoping his friends weren't eavesdropping from the table. He felt wretched for putting his mother through so much worry after he'd left home in such a huff. All his life, she'd been the one to stand up for him—the person who'd refused to believe her youngest boy could be as depraved as his brothers and his *dat* considered him.

"Well, a lot has happened since I got here," he murmured.

"Please, son, will you come home now?" his mother

pleaded. "I can convince your father that you've turned over a new leaf—"

"Mamm, I'm sorry, but I can never be the son Dat wants me to be," Isaac said ruefully. The words came to him from out of nowhere—or maybe straight from God. "Truth be told, I don't want to join the Amish church, and—and I seem to have a girlfriend now who's Mennonite. You know what he'll say about *that*."

His mother sucked in her breath. "My word, you've been busy at a lot of things besides working in the new bulk store."

"And we'll talk about everything sometime soon, I promise," he said. His thoughts whirled wildly as he wondered how he could make amends for the worry he'd caused her. "And you know what else I'll do, Mamm? I'm going to send you a—a check in the mail. So you'll see that I'm turning myself around by—by repaying what I stole from the auction account."

His mother was silent for a moment. "You should send that check to your father—"

"But I want you to know that your boy made *gut* on his word, Mamm. Dat won't see it that way. He'll continue to hold my past over my head," Isaac interrupted in a rush. "He might *speak* of forgiveness, but he'll never let me forget."

She sighed. She knew he was right.

"Well, returning the money will be a big step forward," his mother said. She sounded sad about Isaac's decision—about their family dynamics—but she was holding herself together for the sake of their conversation. "You're nineteen now, and you need to find a life that suits you. We've known for years that the auction company won't support another family . . . but I'm pleased to hear there's a chance you might marry someday, Isaac. That's more of a blessing to me than you know."

He nodded, swallowing the lump in his throat. Never had he imagined having such a heartfelt talk with his mother, considering the way things had been when he'd left home. "I'm glad you called, Mamm," he whispered. "I—I *have* changed. And I hope someday I can make you proud of me again. I'd better go now."

As he placed the receiver in the old wall phone's cradle, Isaac wondered what on earth had happened during the minutes he and his mother had talked. She'd responded to his letter—apologized for being so hard on him. Yet now, after a few weeks at Promise Lodge with folks who encouraged him, Isaac could look at the hard cold facts of his life in Coldstream and admit that he'd made a horrible mess for so many people there.

And he had no one to blame but himself.

He also felt strangely detached from his strict Amish upbringing as the bishop's son. And he felt *free*. He had declared himself to be someone different from the dutiful son his father had always tried to make him, and yet the ensuing damnation his *dat* preached had not struck him.

And rather than condemning his decision, Mamm had accepted it. Was that not a miracle?

Isaac took a few moments to compose himself, glancing over his shoulder toward the dining room. Eddie was in high humor, recounting a story about one of his painting jobs. Ruby was taking a big bite out of an ice cream sandwich made from two homemade cookies with at least an inch of ice cream between them. When she smiled at Isaac, his emotional load lightened.

It had taken something out of him, speaking so seriously to his mother—

Like an adult. Like a son who wants to be trusted.

—so when Ruby beckoned for him to join them, Isaac felt better all over.

"We saved you some of these fun ice cream sandwiches," she called out.

"But I've been eyeballing your share," Beulah teased. "Your time's running out, Isaac."

As he strode toward the table where his friends were sharing dessert, Isaac sensed that perhaps his time was *not* running out—that maybe he was on the verge of a whole new life filled with a sense of accomplishment. A sense of belonging.

He didn't have to be the outcast anymore. He had indeed reached the point of starting fresh in so many ways, despite the misdeeds he'd once bragged about.

Maria handed the platter across the table to Isaac as he sat down. The three remaining ice cream sandwiches had softened, so when he bit into one, the filling surged over the bottom chocolate chip cookie and onto his hand. He laughed as he lapped it up. He felt like a kid again—but a kid with a keener appreciation of this emotional high he was on.

The enthralled expression on Maria's face was a foretaste of what awaited him later in the evening. Was she the woman he wanted to spend his life with? With her, it would be all or nothing.

I'm asking for a buttload of drama and a constant

emotional rollercoaster ride. Is that what I really want for the long haul?

Isaac laughed at himself. Maria was in for a few surprises, too, when she found out why he'd come here and what he needed to overcome. Maybe she'd want nothing more to do with him when she knew the truth.

But then, maybe that meant they were perfectly suited to one another.

Chapter 25

As they walked across the lawn toward the scooter that was parked behind the bulk store, Isaac squeezed Maria's hand. "Before we take off, I need to ask Dale for a quick favor, sweetie. You can either look around in the store or wait for me out here, all right? Won't take but a minute."

Her expressive eyebrows rose. "Well, for *you*, Isaac, I suppose I could shop—"

"Great. I need to send my *mamm* something. That was her on the phone."

Maria's clear blue eyes widened, but she was polite enough not to ask questions as they entered the back warehouse door. It was a point in her favor, that she understood some things were too personal to talk about—especially when it involved a parent. As he hurried up the stairs, he felt her speculative gaze following him.

It was another point in Maria's favor that she didn't follow him upstairs to his apartment—not this time, anyway. As he yanked his duffel out from under his bed, Isaac knew he'd have no plausible explanation for the wad of big bills he was pulling out of a yellow plastic sack. After quickly assuring himself that all the money was there, he dashed off a note on the scratch pad in the kitchen.

This is the entire sum I stole from auction sales over the past several months, minus the thirty dollars I paid Dick Mercer to drive me to Promise Lodge. Please forgive me. Isaac.

He put the money and the note into the sack and tucked it under his arm before descending the stairs. Maria was studying Vera's pottery display. When she gazed up at him, Isaac's need for her became more urgent, but that would have to wait.

"I'll run this over to Dale's and be right back," he assured her. "If you find some things you want, put them in a shopping basket and I'll buy them for you."

He'd probably opened a new can of worms, offering to indulge Maria's whims—but he'd specified that anything she wanted would be *paid for*. No need for her to wonder if he helped himself to items from the store—at least not until he could tell her the whole truth about his sticky fingers.

Isaac loped across the lawn between the store and Dale's new home. Was he being a total idiot, asking his boss to take care of this favor? When Kraybill saw how much money was in his sack, would he think Isaac was too much of a thief ever to be trusted again?

He knocked on the door before his second thoughts left him holding the bag. Luckily, Dale answered—and seemed genuinely happy to see him.

"Isaac! I just saw you and Maria walking toward the scooter—"

"I, um, need to ask you a *huge* favor before we take off," Isaac interrupted.

Kraybill's eyes widened at the urgency in Isaac's voice. When he spotted the yellow sack, he opened the door wider. "Come on back to the office. What can I do for you, Isaac?"

On impulse, Isaac shut the small room's door after they'd both entered it. He didn't want Irene to know the nature of his favor—at least not while he was still in her home. If Dale told his wife what he'd done later, there was no way Isaac could stop him.

When Kraybill pulled over a straight-backed chair for him and then sat down at his desk, Isaac handed him the plastic sack. "Dale, could—could you please take this money and write out a check to my mother for it, and send it to her?" Isaac said in a rush. "It's a lot to ask, but I don't have a bank account. And I don't want to go all the way home to return this cash in person."

The storekeeper studied him closely. He unfolded the bag and held the stack of money for a moment before counting it with quick, practiced fingers.

"Twelve hundred twenty, by my count."

"*Jah.*" Isaac couldn't expect Dale to fulfill his favor without some sort of explanation—and he couldn't entrust such a transaction to anyone else. No one else had pegged him and his past sins the way Kraybill had. No one else had shown an inkling of understanding— or compassion—for his habit of stealing just because he was slick enough to get away with it.

"I, um, skimmed that from the accounts of the auction company my *dat* and older brothers run," Isaac admitted softly. "I've always had it in the back of my mind to run off someday—to get away from everything I don't like about my father. This money was going to help me start over."

Dale sat back in his chair, considering the story Isaac had told him. "And you want me to write the check to your mother?" he asked.

Isaac nodded. "She called me during dinner tonight. We . . . reached an understanding, and miraculously, she asked me to come home," he added in a quavering voice. "I told her to watch for this check in the mail, because if I send it to Dat, I'm pretty sure he won't tell her I repaid what I owe him. And I—I told her I couldn't come back and that I couldn't join the Amish church."

Dale's eyes widened. "That must've been quite a conversation."

"It was." Isaac felt intensely relieved that the man across the desk seemed to comprehend what had transpired. "Something about the sound of her voice—the fact that she'd called to check on me and was relieved that I was all right—"

He paused to regain control of his voice. "Well, I had to prove that I've truly changed, didn't I? This seems like the best way to do that—but on my terms."

Dale nodded. "I see where you're coming from, Isaac. And I applaud you for setting things right with your family's company as a gesture of restitution," he added. "I'll have that check in the mail tomorrow."

After Isaac jotted his *mamm*'s name and address on a piece of paper, Kraybill stood up and shook his hand. "I'm pleased you're doing this. You've made great progress since you've come here," he added. "You'll never be sorry that you came clean to your mother, Isaac."

A few minutes later as he crossed the lawn, Isaac felt as though his feet were floating above the ground. The roar of the scooter's engine made him laugh. Why wasn't he surprised that Maria had already donned her pink helmet and settled herself on the vehicle's seat?

When she approached him, swerving just in time to avoid hitting him, Isaac had a feeling it was going to be a wild, wonderful night.

Maria drove up the Wickeys' lane with a pounding heart. She'd avoided being alone with Isaac since they'd gone to Cloverdale Wednesday evening, and if he'd changed his mind about the offer he'd made her, she didn't know what she'd do. The idea that Isaac would set up a computer system and maintain it implied that he intended to stick around—to be with *her*. And his remarks about loving her longtime home had cemented the situation for her.

In her fertile, overactive imagination, she and Isaac were already married and living out their happily-ever-after.

In front of Truman and Rosetta's house, Maria shut down the engine. She paused to savor the sensation of Isaac's strong, slender arms around her—and to enjoy the way he'd allowed her to be in the driver's seat this evening. She removed her pink helmet and turned to him.

"You might as well come in with me, Isaac," she said with her most winsome smile. "You can help me answer Truman's questions."

One of Isaac's eyebrows rose slightly, but he nodded. By now he'd surely figured out what she was going to discuss with Truman—and he'd stuck with her. It seemed like a sign that they were meant to be together, but she wasn't going to celebrate until their new business agreement was official.

When Rosetta greeted them, Maria reminded herself that this woman who'd once accused her of being a relationship wrecker had nothing to hold over her anymore. Rosetta was getting very round with Truman's child and seemed extremely happy.

"I'd like to speak with Truman about the building in Cloverdale. *Please*," Maria added.

Rosetta motioned them in and led them toward the kitchen. "He's just finishing his supper," she said. "Had a long, complicated day with his landscaping business but iced tea and air conditioning have put him in a better mood. Can I pour you some tea—or cut you some chocolate pie?"

Maria decided to keep the focus on her announcement. "*Denki*, but we won't take up a lot of your time."

Rosetta's smile waxed speculative as she looked from Maria to Isaac. "Better things to do on a Friday night than talk to old married people, *jah*?" she teased. Her face took on a glow as she smiled at her husband, seated at the table. "You have company, Truman."

His brown hair was still drying after a shower, and Maria couldn't help thinking how lucky Rosetta was to have such a handsome husband.

"Maria and Isaac! What's up?"

Maria suddenly felt nervous, but she was doing the right thing, wasn't she? After all, Truman had been waiting for her answer about renting the building—and Isaac had told her more than once she should return to Cloverdale.

"I'm going to reopen the bakery!" she blurted out. "And Isaac's setting up a computer system, so I can keep better track of my income and inventory."

Truman's expressive brows rose as he set his fork on his plate. "Sounds like a promising idea—as long as you realize, Isaac, that Maria might need some ongoing assistance with her new technology."

Maria chuckled nervously. "*Jah*, when I told him I've been using an old adding machine and keeping paper receipts, he suggested I might do better with a setup like Dale has in his store."

Isaac looked away and was shifting his weight from one foot to the other, as though he might flee at any moment. Was he going to back out? After a few agonizing moments of silence, however, he cleared his throat.

"*Jah*, I've agreed to get a system going for her," Isaac confirmed, "and I'll stick around to help her with it. It seems the least I can do, after so many folks in Cloverdale have said they miss her bakery."

"Glad to hear it," Truman said, smiling at them.

"And—and I really appreciate the way you've gotten the building cleaned up already, Truman," Maria put in quickly. Fighting the urge to slip her hand into Isaac's, she wondered if everyone in the room could hear the joyful hammering of her heart. "Baking is what I do best—it's my purpose in life—and with Isaac assisting me, I won't have to go it alone anymore."

She gazed adoringly at Isaac as she continued. "I'm also going to take his advice and accept the Kuhns' offer to pay for my new appliances—something about a Coffee Can Fund they started a while back."

"*Gut* for you," Rosetta put in as she slipped into the chair beside Truman's. "All of us gals who run businesses at Promise Lodge have pledged a percentage of our profits toward that fund, for women who need a boost to get back on their feet. Of course, it would be nice if you told the Kuhns that you'll repay that money over time, so the cash will be available when someone else needs it."

Maria swallowed hard. She hadn't thought about anything beyond buying her new ovens—hadn't considered that the Coffee Can money might have strings attached.

"We can set up her new computer to remind her each week about returning some of that money," Isaac said. "That way, payback will be part of Maria's financial plan from the get-go."

Was it her imagination, or did he seem rather smug about holding her accountable?

"Anyway," Maria said, "I'll be in the building again as soon as it's ready. I—I feel very hopeful about this chance to start again!"

A few minutes later, when she and Isaac were outside and seated on the scooter, Maria glanced over her shoulder.

"You're not going to back out after you set up my new bookkeeping program, are you?" she demanded, trying to keep the fear out of her voice. "If I don't have you along for this ride, Isaac, I'll be right back where I—"

"I've told you I'll keep your business system going, Maria." His face was a few inches from hers as he slipped his arms around her waist. "I have *not* promised you any other sort of ongoing relationship—"

"We'll see about that."

Maria turned the key in the ignition and revved the engine. If he had to hold her tighter on the curves in the road, it would be best to keep driving for a while, wouldn't it? As she steered the pink scooter up the county highway toward Cloverdale, pushing her speed as much as she dared, Maria considered the various back roads, cornfields, and other potentially romantic places where they might stop.

After several minutes of flying along the blacktop, however, she knew the best place to take Isaac for a little chat that would help him see their future together the way *she* envisioned it. When they reached Cloverdale she slowed down, turning carefully into a narrow alley that ran behind the comfortable older homes she'd known all her life. She pulled up behind her house and killed the engine.

"I thought of something I need to do while we're in town," Maria said breezily. She removed her pink helmet and dismounted after Isaac did, smiling at his uncovered hair. It resembled a haystack caught in a windstorm, so she reached up to smooth it for him.

Isaac playfully grabbed her wrist. "I know what you're up to, Maria," he muttered. But he didn't sound the least bit irritated.

"I know you do," she said in a low voice. She gently disengaged his hold on her. "You want to kiss me, and I want to kiss you right back—but we should step inside first, *jah*?"

Maria started for the back door, but then turned to extend her hand.

Isaac gazed at her for several long moments, silent. His Adam's apple bobbed when he swallowed.

When he took her hand, Maria held on as though she never intended to let go, continuing toward the house. She smiled triumphantly.

Hook, line, and sinker.

Chapter 26

Late Saturday afternoon, Vera held her breath as she opened her kiln. The four Holstein dinner plates awaited her—too hot to handle with her bare hands, so she carefully removed them with her heat-proof gloves. When the plates rested safely on her worktable, she let out a laugh of pleasure as she gazed at the shiny white dishes with their random black spots.

"Somebody sounds pretty tickled," Ezra said as he came through the shed door.

"I'm glad you're the first to—oh, Ezra!" Vera exclaimed. "I liked Mrs. Stoughton's royal blue set with the red and yellow tulips, but this cow design just makes me *happy*!"

Ezra's smile lit up his handsome face. "See there? You went with your instinct and your plates came out looking as fabulous as you'd hoped. You must love it when that happens."

"Now I can't wait to make some bowls and salad plates," she said. "But first, I'll ask Christine if she'd be interested in having this set, and what other serving pieces she'd like. And if she doesn't want them, I'll display them in the store."

"I predict they won't be around long, sweetie," he said in a low voice. "Everyone who sees your work loves it."

The husky timbre of Ezra's voice made sparkly things happen in Vera's stomach. She gazed at the black-and-white dinner plates, wanting to suggest that the two of them do something together this evening—or would that be too suggestive, too forward?

"Ezra, I was wondering—"

"What if we went for a ride—maybe got some ice cream?" he said at the same time.

They laughed, releasing the momentary anxiety that had tied their tongues.

"It's a perfect night for ice cream," Vera said gratefully. "Just out of curiosity, have you seen Isaac around?"

Ezra gestured for her to precede him outside. The breeze felt refreshing after working in the enclosed shed. She smiled when she saw Ezra's rig waiting for them. It meant he'd intended to spend his time with her even before she'd tried to ask him.

"Last I knew, Isaac and Maria had gone to tell Truman she was reopening her Cloverdale bakery," he replied. "They seem to be keeping the roads hot on that pink motor scooter."

Vera allowed him to help her up to the seat of the open buggy. "Do you think they're a couple now?"

Ezra vaulted up on the driver's side and settled beside her, taking up the lines. "Let's just say Isaac's offered to help her with a new computer system, and Maria's acting over the moon in love with him. I can't tell you what a relief that is!"

Vera laughed out loud as the buggy started down the road. "The drama gets tiring, ain't so?" she asked. "I've not been around Maria much, but I'm glad she and Isaac have found each other. And it's nice of him to help her."

As the horse clip-clopped down the hill, heading for the county road, Ezra slipped his arm around her. "In some ways they're birds of a feather," he mused aloud. "And if they do their own squawking and flapping and feather-ruffling, that leaves us free to . . . explore our own quieter path. Together."

"I like the sound of that," Vera whispered.

Ezra's body tightened with need. Holding her as the buggy gently jostled them together only fueled the flame flickering inside him, and in Forest Grove, their ice cream wasn't nearly cold enough to settle his suggestive thoughts. It was a humid August evening, so lots of other customers crowded the outdoor tables—but when he noticed a little smear of ice cream on Vera's upper lip, he kissed her anyway.

Startled, Vera sucked in her breath. But—maybe because they hadn't seen anyone they knew—she kissed him back.

Ezra couldn't wait to be alone with her, under cover of the summer night. As he drove them back to Promise Lodge, the orange and magenta sunset lingered along the horizon and a welcome breeze rippled the trees. Somehow, he stayed aware of the cars on the state highway while occasionally easing his mouth over hers. His horse knew where to turn, or he might've missed the blacktop that ran alongside the Helmuths' nursery.

Moments later they passed beneath the arched Promise Lodge sign in the light of the full moon. Ezra steered the horse off the private road and into the shadow of Christine's barn. Vera's kisses became as feverish as his as they sat tightly entwined in each other's arms. All he could think about was slipping down from the rig and up into the hayloft above the barn's main floor. He didn't want to rush her, yet he suspected Vera wouldn't resist if he invited her to cuddle in the hay and—

"Hey, Sis! You and Overholt should get a room!"

Vera jumped away from him. Ezra glared at Ed—who, alongside Fannie, was walking in the shadows as though they, too, were caught up in summer love.

Had the young couple come out of Ed's tiny home?

"I could ask what you two have been up to," Ezra retorted.

"Oh, I don't have to ask." Vera's voice had an impatient edge to it. "It's a *gut* thing you and Fannie are tying the knot in a few weeks, *jah*? Nobody will speculate if your firstborn arrives sooner than the usual nine months."

When a wounded expression puckered Fannie's face, Vera sighed.

"I'm sorry," she muttered. "But Eddie, you've got no right to call us out for kissing in Ezra's rig. I saw you helping Fannie down from the back of your wagon, but I'll say no more."

Ezra took this as his cue to steer the horse back onto the private road. He'd often fantasized about showing Vera his tiny home—or the barn's hayloft—so it was time to step away from temptation.

"Sorry," he rasped as they rounded the curve. "I didn't mean for us to get caught—"

"If Eddie had kept his mouth shut, no one would be the wiser," she pointed out softly.

He smiled at her big-sisterly viewpoint. "Even so, we're passing Preacher Marlin's place, so I'll keep a respectable distance until we get to Harley's. I—I hope you don't think this kissing stuff has come on too fast—"

"Thinking is highly overrated, Ezra," Vera whispered. "Especially when I'm with you. But *jah*, we need to be careful. *Gut* night."

He'd barely brought the buggy to a halt before Vera nimbly slid down from the rig. Like a shadow she flitted through the dusk to disappear into the house.

Through the window Ezra saw Harley at the kitchen table, where the lamp was lit. He hoped Vera's uncle wouldn't quiz her about what they'd done this evening. Vera's open, guileless face probably didn't hide her fibs very well.

"*Gut* night, sweetie," he whispered. He drove back to his quiet little house on the lake, dreaming of the time when he wouldn't go home alone.

On Tuesday morning, Ezra headed over to the bulk store to buy a few bathroom supplies—but he was really checking on Isaac. For the second morning in a row Chupp hadn't come to the lodge for breakfast. Maria had been in such a foul mood that a dark cloud cloaked her like a veil—as it had when a sullen Isaac had eaten supper across the table from her. Ezra, the Kuhns, and Ed had known better than to question the two irritable blonds about the trouble that had come to their paradise.

The pounding of hammers and the *zap-zap-zap* of pneumatic nail guns made Ezra pause to observe the progress on Rosetta's new cabins. He waved at Preachers Amos and Eli, along with Bishop Monroe, who were attaching roof shingles to three of the structures. Lester Lehman was installing windows in the cabin nearest the lodge while Roman and Noah Schwartz were hanging its front door. The men of Promise Lodge were completing Rosetta's cabins, knowing that Ed and Fannie were eager to watch their new home take shape next, as their wedding date approached.

"I'll be there to help you in a bit," Ezra called out.

"Bring it on!" Roman shot back. "Nice to do work that doesn't involve sterilizing udders, tails swishing at flies, and cow muck!"

Chuckling, Ezra continued toward the bulk store's front door. Only a few cars were parked in the lot. He hoped he could speak quietly with Isaac without causing him any trouble with Dale—although the storekeeper probably knew that something had changed the euphoric state Isaac and Maria had shared earlier.

As he entered the store, Ezra paused to admire Vera's pottery display. She'd added some small items after Mrs. Stoughton had bought so many dishes: bright green parrot vases and exotic tiger-striped bowls boldly announced Vera's talent for creating unusual, eye-catching pieces.

Ezra spotted Isaac restocking baking supplies from a large, wheeled cart. The blond was so focused on his work—or so overwhelmed by his troubles—that he had no idea anyone was approaching him.

"We, um, missed you at breakfast," Ezra began in a low voice. "Are you okay, Isaac? You seem . . . upset."

Isaac scowled. "None of your beeswax, Overholt."

Stung by Chupp's bitterness, Ezra stepped back. "Okay, so you think I'm being nosy," he said gently. "But Ruby and Beulah are concerned, too. Last thing we heard—from Maria—you'd agreed to help run her bakery in—"

"Well, last *I* heard, I was a cruel, heartless traitor who'd promised to be her man forever—and then I backed out. End of story." Isaac exhaled loudly, obviously exasperated by Maria's accusations.

Ezra could certainly imagine the bright fantasies Maria had concocted from the moment she'd first clung to Isaac on the scooter. "Ah. Her fairy-tale expectations raced ahead of yours and you told her to slow down?" he ventured cautiously. "Or did you call it off altogether?"

Isaac raked his hair back from his face. His bloodshot eyes appeared haunted as he focused on Ezra. "I'm in over my head," he whispered miserably. "It's like I'm addicted to a drug that took me way up—"

He raised his hand high above his head.

"—and now I've crashed," he said as he smacked his hands together. His voice was a ragged whisper. "Trouble is, I don't think I could give Maria up even if I wanted to. I saw this coming, Ezra—*you* know what she's like—"

Ezra nodded.

"—but she's got a comfortable home, and it would be easy to get her bakery on its feet again," Isaac continued, shaking his head. "It could be a sweet life in Cloverdale, but emotionally, Maria's a hot mess. Physically, she's just . . . four-alarm *hot*. Even if I break away now, I'll have burn marks for the rest of my life."

Ezra secretly envied what Isaac was implying. But he didn't want to trade places.

"And yet, I suspect we'd be better off in Cloverdale." Isaac looked around to be sure no one else could overhear their conversation. "We're two maladjusted misfits—with so many strikes against us that Promise Lodge people don't really want us here, anyway. We don't match up with Rosetta's plan for happiness."

Ezra frowned. He couldn't imagine why Isaac would express such a harsh opinion of the compassionate folks who'd welcomed Chupp and himself to this community about a month ago.

"What makes you say that?" he asked softly. "Dale gave you a *gut* job here, even after he heard what you'd done in Coldstream—"

"See there?" Isaac challenged. "No matter how well I do, the folks I grew up with know exactly what sort of guy Isaac Chupp used to be. One slip, and I'll revert to being a hellion again, the way they see it."

Isaac's attitude startled Ezra. Maybe he was in a funk because Maria had dumped him—and because he'd lost control of his feelings for her.

Aha. That's the key—for any of us.

Ezra cleared his throat, noticing that Dale was coming from the back of the store.

"Maybe it's a control issue, Isaac," he suggested. "If you believe folks here have a bad opinion of you because of what you did before you came, take the bull by the horns. Apologize for the barns you burned and the way you treated Rosetta, Christine, and Deborah. Nobody can argue with that, Isaac.

"And truth be told," Ezra added quickly, "I think you're so overwhelmed by whatever Maria did to you this weekend, you're seeing everything through the panic glasses she's put on you. Don't get sucked into her moods! It'll all work out if you believe it will—if you act rationally and take the lead. *Gut* luck, buddy."

Ezra headed toward the toiletries, hoping Dale wouldn't chastise Isaac for chatting with him instead of working. For good measure, he approached the storekeeper to make conversation, giving Isaac time to pull himself together. Kraybill was excited about the six cabins that would soon be completed between his new house and the lodge. He was also interested in how Christine's dairy herd was doing now that new cows had been integrated with the survivors of the tornado.

As Ezra left the store with his toothpaste, soap, and an assortment of snacks, he hoped he'd helped Isaac sort out his troubled thoughts.

He couldn't help chuckling, though. Maria had sent poor Chupp into quite a tailspin. She'd made Isaac need her the way he needed air to breathe—and Ezra suspected Isaac had never been in such a vulnerable position. Chupp was accustomed to being in the black, putting *others* on the minus side of the emotional ledger.

Would the two volatile blonds strike a balance, or strike out?

Chapter 27

Maria stood staring out the window of her apartment. Surely Isaac's absence at breakfast meant that he really was abandoning her, even though she'd given him her body . . . her very soul. Now she felt sullied. Betrayed. She'd been so sure Isaac was the man she'd marry, or she wouldn't have surrendered to her shocking need for his touch.

"What am I supposed to do now?" she whispered as tears dribbled down her cheeks. "If I go back to Cloverdale, I'll be all by myself again. But I can't stay here. Not if I have to watch Isaac turn his back on me every day."

And it's such a beautiful back. Strong as steel with skin as soft as a baby's.

A knock at her door made her groan. She did *not* want company—

"Maria, we've got iced tea and fresh chocolate-chip cookies," Ruby said.

"And better yet, we've got a plan for helping you," Beulah put in.

Maria sighed. There was no escaping the Kuhns if they wanted to cure what ailed you.

"The longer you stew over Isaac, the more control you allow him to have over you," Beulah insisted.

"Truth be told, you could do better than to hitch up with *that* one," Ruby warned. "Can we chat, Maria? We'd feel bad if you did something foolish because you think Isaac's your only chance at happiness."

The aroma of melting chocolate eroded her willpower—along with the hint that the Kuhn sisters could dish on subjects Isaac had danced around this past weekend.

Wiping her eyes on her sleeve, Maria opened the door. She'd often considered Ruby and Beulah the world's worst busybodies, but they'd reached a gray-haired age of independence and a state of contentment she envied. They also baked the best cookies ever—even better than her own.

"All right, come join the pity party," she said. As the sisters entered, she snatched a cookie from Ruby's tray and jammed it into her mouth. Beulah, carrying three tumblers in the crook of her arm and a pitcher of tea, looked at Maria closely before crossing the room to set her refreshments on the coffee table.

As the warm chocolate, brown sugar, and walnuts worked their magic, Maria felt better. It was a temporary fix, but it was a step in the right direction.

"So, what's Isaac not telling me?" she asked as the Kuhns perched on her sofa. "No doubt in my mind he's been a bad, bad boy—"

"Which is why you adore him," Ruby pointed out. "Like a moth to a flame."

Maria's mouth snapped shut. Was she *that* transparent?

Beulah chuckled as she filled the glasses with iced

tea. When she and her sister had taken cookies, she said, "It's not our place to tattle on Isaac, dear. You'll have to hear his story from the horse's mouth, so to speak."

"He's been acting more like the other end of the horse," Maria muttered.

The three of them laughed, filling the apartment with a conspiratorial mirth that settled Maria's nerves. She sat down in the armchair closest to the cookies and took another one.

Beulah gazed steadily at Maria. "We've come to restate our offer of funding for your bakery appliances," she began. "After talking with all the gals who run businesses and contribute to the Coffee Can Fund—"

"And there are several," Ruby put in with a nod.

"—we believe you can succeed in Cloverdale, Maria. To put our money where our mouths are, we're offering you up to forty-five hundred dollars."

Maria's mouth dropped open so suddenly that a wad of chewed cookie nearly fell out. "But that's—who's paid into this fund that you've accumulated so much money?"

The sisters looked at each other, holding up their hands to count on their fingers.

"Rosetta kicks in from her rental income and soap sales," Ruby replied, "and Christine puts in a percentage of her milk income—"

"And their sister, Mattie, shares cash from her roadside vegetable stand," Beulah continued. "And Ruby and I contribute from our cheese sales."

"Besides that, we've gotten donations from Gloria Helmuth, who manages the apartments for Rosetta, as well as her *mamm*, Frances, who was grateful to have an apartment here after her husband, Bishop Floyd, passed away." Ruby was holding up seven fingers by now, smiling gently at Maria.

"Marlene Lehman and Sylvia Fisher, who also lived in the lodge before they married, felt compelled to turn their gratitude into cash, as well," Beulah put in. "Have I forgotten anyone, Ruby?"

"Promise Lodge Pies puts in a hefty percentage each month—because they sell a lot of pies," Ruby said. She laughed, waving her extended hands above her head. "If you count both Irene and Phoebe on that, I've run out of fingers and need to start on my toes!"

"Spare us that part. Please," Beulah said wryly.

Maria was speechless. It was embarrassing that the Kuhns had spoken to so many women about her needs— her failure to accumulate any savings. Yet they were all willing to contribute a sizable chunk of change to help her start over.

"I—I don't know what to say," she murmured. "Forty-five hundred dollars will buy—"

"We'll pay the money directly to the appliance dealers when you make your choices," Ruby clarified. "You might ask Rosetta how she found the new equipment for the kitchen downstairs. She bought it online after the tornado, you see, because the selection was so much wider than what any local appliance store could offer."

"And I—I'll pay it back in monthly installments!" Maria blurted out. "Isaac told me he could set up . . . but if he's not going to help me anymore . . ."

Ruby gently grasped Maria's hand. "Part of our point is to prove that you can do this *without* him," she said gently. "And you know what? Sally Swanson at our church in Cloverdale—the high school business teacher—has told us she'd be happy to help you with your computer system. She said you could pay her in pastries!"

"So, see?" Beulah chimed in happily. "You can do this, Maria. You have friends in two different towns who want you to be back in business again, supporting yourself—"

"Because nobody else makes apple fritters and Danish and sticky buns as *gut* as yours," Ruby declared. "And if you don't want to work by yourself, we'll scare up some part-time help for you. Where there's a woman there's a way, Maria."

"And when you've got a whole gaggle of women involved, watch out, world!"

Maria fell back against her chair, gazing at the two silver-haired sisters in their colorful paisley-print dresses. "After all the stupid things I've said and done, you still want to help me," she whispered.

"I say the same thing to Jesus every day," Ruby admitted. "What would any of us do without help from a power that's so much greater than we are alone?"

"That's why we're supposed to help folks who need it," Beulah said reverently. "We're to be the hands and feet of Jesus here on earth. So, what do you say, Maria? Will you give your bakery another shot?"

Maria paused. She felt abuzz with a new sense of hope and purpose. She could succeed without Isaac, couldn't she? She still longed to believe he could come to love her as much as she adored him, but meanwhile, she was being offered the fresh start she'd come here looking for.

"I'm gonna go for it," she said, thumping the arm of her chair. "I'm going to Rosetta's right now, to ask for her help picking my appliances! Well, after one more cookie!"

Chapter 28

When Isaac went downstairs Friday morning to begin work about an hour before the store opened, he stopped with his hand on the swinging warehouse door. Why did he hear voices? Not one, but two—and neither of them was Dale's. A burst of laughter revealed that a group of women had gathered, probably in the storekeeper's office.

And one of them was Maria.

He'd tried to avoid an emotional confrontation at meals the past couple of days—and Maria had ignored him, chatting with the Kuhns instead. But he had to pass Dale's office to load the men's straw hats that would go on sale today. Besides, Isaac's curiosity had gotten the better of him: why would a bunch of women be crammed into the tiny office this early in the morning?

He entered the warehouse but stayed in the shadow near the doorway. Through the office window, he saw Marlene seated at the computer while Maria stood behind her, with Rosetta and Christine on either side. The door was open, so he heard everything they were saying.

"We want you to have appliances that suit the way

you bake, Maria," Rosetta said, pointing to the computer monitor. "So, if this double oven works better for you than a range and oven combination like we all use at home, you should get it."

Maria pressed her lips into a line, a sure sign she was frustrated. "But that one costs more than what you're giving me from the Coffee Can Fund," she mumbled plaintively. "And I'll have to have a big fridge and a dishwasher to comply with health department codes, so . . . I'd forgotten how expensive commercial appliances are," she added with a sigh.

Isaac's heart went out to her. Maria was learning a hard lesson about business economics. He had no money to offer her, however—not that it would be a good idea—so he remained quiet rather than interrupting their online shopping session.

"Now that I'm seeing firsthand what your equipment will cost," Christine put in, "I'm wondering if our church district's aid fund could help you cover some expenses."

Maria's expression lit up for a few seconds and then fell flat. "But I'm not a member of the Amish church— and not really a resident of Promise Lodge," she pointed out sadly.

When Rosetta straightened to her full height, leaning backward to stretch her spine, she looked as though she'd swallowed a basketball. The blatant roundness of her expanding belly made Isaac's mouth drop open—

Please, God, don't let Maria be in the family way. I'm sorry I didn't keep my pants on, as Dale recommended. It won't happen again—

"The Mennonite Fellowship has an aid fund, too,"

Rosetta pointed out brightly. "You're a Cloverdale businesswoman, so why wouldn't our church contribute to your reopening, Maria?"

Once again Isaac witnessed Maria's sudden radiance, followed by her sigh. "Because I don't go to church anymore?" she answered. "Because I got too busy staying afloat by myself after Lizzie moved away?"

Rosetta slipped an arm around Maria's shoulders, her expression resolute. "Maria, dear, if we're to move forward with this effort, you need to leave your negativity behind and set your mind on *success*," she said. "You're surrounded by women who've overcome great loss and heartache—"

"And we wouldn't be doing well today if we'd told ourselves we were ruined," Christine added firmly. "You're either in or you're out, Maria. If you don't believe in yourself and the help we're offering you, we'll save our time and effort."

Isaac almost applauded, hearing the two sisters say they'd help Maria only if she helped herself. But the women's words were also a stark reminder that the loss and heartache Rosetta and Christine had suffered in the past had been *his fault*.

As he observed the animated expressions the three women from Coldstream wore while they awaited Maria's decision, Isaac suddenly realized that Rosetta and Christine didn't need his apology. They had moved beyond their burned-down barns and Willis Hershberger's death to live among people who did indeed forgive and forget. They had founded Promise Lodge as a church district where courtesy was common, and where folks would receive respect rather than recrimination.

Isn't that why I left Coldstream, too? To escape Dat's threats of damnation and his inability to encourage and support the members of his congregation . . . or his family?

Isaac pondered the wisdom he'd just received, as though the God he'd dodged all his life had whispered in his ear—and he'd chosen to listen this time. It stood to reason that if he didn't apologize and receive the forgiveness Rosetta and Christine—and everyone else at Promise Lodge—was so generous with, he would remain an outsider. The eternal misfit.

Haven't I had enough of that? If I stop believing that admitting guilt—or accepting help—makes me appear weak, maybe my entire life will change. What have I got to lose? And if I come clean to Maria and keep my promise to help her—

"Isaac! *Gut* morning!"

"Getting your day off to an early start, *jah*?"

Isaac blinked. He'd been so lost in his thoughts he hadn't realized that the women had emerged from Dale's office. Rosetta stood before him, as did Christine—who carried a box of something white with black splotches. Behind them, Marlene and Maria watched him, too, their brows arched with curiosity.

Before he lost his nerve, Isaac jumped in feet first, hoping God was more in control of this tricky situation than he was.

"I—I couldn't help hearing the way you helped Maria select her new appliances—offering suggestions for how she might come up with more cash, and I—"

Isaac's mind went blank. When he met Rosetta's gaze,

however, he felt the unmistakable flow of her goodwill, like a jolt of power that energized his intentions.

"Rosetta—Christine," he stammered, "when I was in your barns with my friends, drinking and smoking, I—I had no idea that the lanterns were kicked over as we ran off when Deborah caught us, or that our burning cigarettes might've—but I'm really sorry about the fires and about Willis getting killed when that burning beam trapped him and—"

He stopped to gasp for breath, desperate to get this apology right the first time. "You women are *amazing*," he blurted out. "This place you started from an abandoned church camp is so different from Coldstream—and you were so *right* to come here. And, well—I hope you can forgive me. And I'm glad I've come here, too."

The sisters glanced at one another briefly before Christine stepped forward. As she slung an arm around him from one side, Rosetta grabbed him from the other. They looked like they might cry.

"Listen to you!" Rosetta crowed softly. "Can this be the same belligerent Isaac Chupp who thought he could do no wrong?"

"And who showed no remorse or concern for others?" Christine chimed in. "Bless you, Isaac, you've made my day—my entire year! I accept your apology."

"And so do I," Rosetta said as she beamed at him. "It's similar to that Bible verse about seeing through the glass darkly but later coming face-to-face—with who you are, and with what you know now that you couldn't grasp earlier."

She held his gaze with a pride in her eyes Isaac had rarely seen in his lifetime.

"You've seen a light that your *dat* hasn't allowed into his heart, I'm sorry to say," Rosetta whispered. "*Gut* for you, Isaac."

"Amen to that," Marlene put in.

"*Jah*, that's true," Christine said with a shake of her head. "But with God's help, we can all move on. We've been blessed because we followed God's call to do something new and different with the gifts He's given us.

"And speaking of gifts," she continued, tapping the box she held against her hip, "I'm adding these cute cow dishes to Vera's display! She offered them to me— and I've ordered a whole set of them—so we'll put these finished plates out for customers to see."

"I predict we won't have them by the end of the day." As Marlene pushed the door open, she flashed Isaac a knowing smile. "You came in here to fetch those hats we're putting on sale, *jah*?"

Isaac chuckled. "I did. And I'd better hustle if I'm to have them out before Dale gets here."

As he watched Christine, Rosetta, and Marlene enter the main room of the store, he rode an incredible wave of relief. The apologies he'd been sidestepping for so long were behind him! He no longer had to wait for the right moment or the right words, fearing he'd say exactly the wrong things.

Isaac exhaled. Even breathing seemed easier now.

When he turned, however, Maria stood watching him. Her blue eyes were wide with a curiosity that overrode her resentment toward him.

"You really did burn down a barn, and—and Christine's husband died in the fire?" she whispered.

"Two barns," Isaac clarified ruefully. "The one on

Willis Hershberger's farm—where Christine, Phoebe, and Laura lived—and the barn on the Bender place, where Rosetta lived until after their parents passed. That's where Deborah Peterscheim—Deborah Schwartz now—caught us guys drinking and smoking."

"Oh, my. No wonder Beulah didn't want to tell me what you'd done."

Maria looked away, considering what she knew about him now—perhaps deciding she wanted nothing more to do with him. She could be demanding and emotionally erratic, but she'd opened herself to him—had made herself vulnerable even as she'd led him into irresistible temptation. And deep down, Isaac really liked Maria.

He just didn't love her. Yet.

"My offer to set up your computer system is still open, if—if you want it," he said quietly. "I can't commit to your fairy-tale ending, Maria, because it's too soon for that. But I'll be your friend."

For a painfully long time, Maria remained silent.

Isaac glanced at the clock above the door. "Well, I've got hats to put out. Talk to you later."

As he loaded the first large cardboard carton onto a dolly, Isaac felt torn. Part of him wanted to kiss Maria until they lost their minds—yet he wondered if she was giving him the silent treatment to manipulate him. He sincerely hoped she hadn't written him off now that she knew why he'd eluded her questions about his family and his past.

Isaac wheeled the box toward the double doors, lowering the dolly so he could prop them open. Maria stepped out of his way—but as he rolled his load into the store, she placed her hand on his arm.

"Be my friend, Isaac," she whispered, holding his gaze with her wide blue eyes. "When I reopen my bakery, I'll need all the help I can get. You know that better than anybody, right?"

Once again relief—and a deep sense of joy—flowed through him. "*Jah*, I guess I do."

Chapter 29

Saturday evening felt ripe with promise. As Ezra strolled up the hill after supper to meet Vera, his mind skipped happily from one scenario to another.

Maybe it was because Ed and Fannie were committed, and Isaac and Maria had roared off to Cloverdale on the scooter: Ezra felt the need to state his case. He didn't want to rush into a miserable marriage from which they could escape only when one of them died, but he needed to know if Vera was on the same page he was, romantically.

It was one thing to love kissing. It was another thing entirely to sign up for a lifetime of responsibilities that wore on every couple unless they loved each other for a *lot* of reasons.

As he reached the Kurtz property, the sound of singing drew him to the shed. It was a treat to watch Vera in her heat-proof gloves, removing several putty-colored oval plates from her kiln. Ezra allowed her time to set them on the worktable before he greeted her.

"I can hear your happiness," he said from the doorway. "And it looks like someone has ordered a set of your Holstein dishes, *jah*?"

Vera beamed at him. When she nudged her turquoise glasses into place, the habitual gesture endeared her to him even more.

"Christine took the first four plates to the bulk store, because she wants twelve place settings for herself!" she said. "You were right, Ezra. A customer who saw my display yesterday has also ordered a set, so I'm off and running with black-and-white dinnerware."

"Happy to hear it!" Ezra gazed at her, admiring the turquoise dress that accentuated her glasses and her trim figure. "You look so pretty, Vera. I—I hope you'd still like to take a walk this evening?"

His compliment made her blush and look away. "And I hope I'm more than just a pretty face to you, Ezra."

His heart stood still. It finally seemed right to say what had been on his heart for days. "We haven't known each other all that long, sweetie, but—but I was wondering if I could court you. I'm ready to take that step if you are."

Vera's expression filled him with intense joy. She quickly peeled off her gloves and checked to be sure her kiln was turned off. "Oh, but I've been hoping you'd ask, Ezra! And I'm so relieved that Isaac has lost interest—"

"He and Maria took off for Cloverdale after supper. He's helping her reopen her bakery," he put in with a chuckle. "I suspect their trip will be more pleasure than business, though. At supper, your brother asked the Kuhns for a fire extinguisher, in case we needed to douse the lovebirds."

Vera rolled her eyes as she stepped outside with him. "Leave it to Eddie to point out behavior he and Fannie are just as obvious about."

"But they're deliriously happy, ain't so?" When they'd strolled beyond the buildings on the Kurtz property, heading toward Harley's sheep pasture, Ezra stopped beneath a big maple tree. "So, we're courting, are we, Vera? That would make *me* deliriously—"

"Stop talking and kiss me," she teased. "You know what they say—*happy wife, happy life.*"

Ezra's pulse raced. He surged with need. Who could've imagined that shy, quiet Vera would make such a provocative statement? He kissed her firmly, holding her close as they leaned against the tree. He hoped he could live up to the challenge of her stirring words. In his mind Ezra knew they needed time—weeks, at least—before publicly declaring their intentions to marry, yet his body was caught up in the present moment.

And Vera was matching him kiss for fevered kiss.

When they broke apart to continue their walk, Ezra knew they'd soon be in trouble if they remained so visible. "What if we disappeared for a while?" he asked softly. "I know a place that's nice and private."

"All right," she whispered as she grasped his hand. "But—but we need to be careful, Ezra."

"*Jah*, we do."

He felt anything but careful as he steered Vera behind other trees and outbuildings to kiss her along the way. Her touch, her kisses, made him crazy with yearning as they gradually approached Christine's barn. With Isaac and Maria in Cloverdale and Ed and Fannie pursuing their own activities, Ezra figured they had all evening to explore the affection they both craved.

From the barn door, he looked around. No one was in sight. The August sunset was still an hour away before the evening dimmed to dusk. The few cows that weren't out in the feedlot watched them with curious brown eyes as they walked along the manure-free path near the wall and clambered up the ladder to the loft.

Stacks of rectangular hay bales awaited them—and behind the front wall of bales, Ezra had created a small hideaway. He'd noticed a broken bale earlier, and it had inspired him to spread hay on the loft floor. Anticipating this rendezvous, he'd also brought an extra quilt he'd found in the tiny home.

When Vera saw the secret nest he'd prepared, she grinned. "Is this where you bring *all* your girlfriends, Ezra?"

He chuckled, taking her into his arms. "*Jah*, here you are, sweetie. My one and only."

Their first kiss sent jolts of longing through him. They soon progressed from sitting on a bale to rolling on the lumpy quilt. Vera's glasses, *kapp,* and apron soon came off, and Ezra's shirt and suspenders did, too. They toed off their shoes and socks, losing them in the loose, sweet-smelling hay as they lost themselves in lush kisses.

All the important body parts are still covered. We're doing fine—staying safe.

Ezra's hand ventured to Vera's waist as she lay alongside him, encouraging him with her soulful gaze. Her fingers found a sensitive spot on his bare back, and he let out a moan of excruciating need.

Then he froze. He covered Vera's mouth with his hand, listening. Her eyes widened as she, too, heard the voices in the barn below.

"Christine, I hear a lot of rustling around. I'm going to make sure a family of raccoons isn't making a home in your hayloft."

With a whimper, Vera rolled away from him, groping for her apron and *kapp*. As each rung of the wooden ladder creaked with the bishop's weight, Ezra's mind scrambled to concoct a story—but of course, any viewer would know exactly what had been going on.

He barely had his arms in his shirt when Monroe Burkholder peered around the stacked bales.

The bishop's brown eyes took in their state of partial undress. When he spoke, his voice remained calm.

"A word to the wise," he said softly. "You've both joined the church, so if you believe God has led you to each other—and you don't want to embarrass your families with a shotgun wedding—maybe you should marry sooner rather than later. I'll be happy to begin your premarital counseling whenever you're ready."

As he turned to go, Vera muffled a sob.

Bishop Monroe stopped, smiling gently at her. "Desire's not a bad thing, you know—God created it. But if you don't think a long-term relationship will work out," he added, raising an eyebrow, "back away from this temptation *now*. Lust is a bug that keeps on feasting as long as a meal's available. You two deserve love and happiness rather than lifelong disappointment after the fire burns out."

As the bishop's footsteps crossed the loft, Vera began to cry in earnest.

Ezra grasped her trembling hand. "He's not calling us out for a confession in front of the congregation, sweetie. He's telling it like it is," he whispered.

"*Jah*, but you can bet we'll be the subject of his sermon tomorrow—even if he doesn't mention us by name," she shot back in a tortured voice. Vera stood up, frantically brushing the loose hay from her dress. "Now

I understand why Marlin insisted that Eddie and Fannie weren't to spend time alone together—"

"But now that they're engaged—*committed*—he's relaxed his stance," Ezra reminded her. When he'd buttoned and tucked in his shirt, he gazed steadily at Vera. She was sweet and gentle and concerned about their reputation, because she cared about the things that mattered most.

He suddenly knew beyond a doubt that he loved this pretty young woman. Vera would make a fine wife, and he could offer her a solid, stable future—if she would still have him, after this humiliating episode with the bishop. When they were dressed again, he gently pulled a strand of hay from the soft brown hair beneath her *kapp*.

"Let's go," Ezra suggested, reaching for her hand. "We can talk outside—in case the bishop and Christine are waiting to see if we stay up here."

Nodding, Vera wiped her eyes on her sleeve. Ezra descended the ladder first, so he could help her down the last few rungs, shaken as she was.

Sure enough, the Burkholders had lingered in the corral to look at some of the newer cows. They returned Ezra's wave as he walked Vera toward Rainbow Lake. Awkward conversation with the adults who'd caught them in a compromising position was the last thing either of them wanted.

As they approached the shoreline, where the water lapped gently, Ezra pondered his options. They were holding hands but walking with a visible space between them—a space he hoped wouldn't become permanent.

"This incident with the bishop won't come between us, will it, Vera?"

"It was so embarrassing," she said with a whimper. "And if this gets around, it'll be humiliating to—"

"I suspect we're not the first couple—or the last—at Promise Lodge to get caught," Ezra pointed out. "What we did wasn't wrong, Vera. We just went against the rules that unmarried Amish are to follow.

"And I—I love you so much for being with me tonight," he added, still grasping her hand as they strolled along the edge of the lake. "I'm even more determined to be the best husband ever, now that we're courting. We still *are*, *jah*?"

When Vera stopped walking, gazing at him with her misery-filled, pink-rimmed eyes, Ezra's heart dropped into a bottomless abyss.

"I need to think about it," she rasped. "I'm sorry."

When she stepped toward the road, Ezra sensed he should let her go home without making a scene. It was the hardest thing, to watch Vera's stride widen until she was nearly running up the hill away from him. But if their marriage was to work, she had to be as certain about her feelings and intentions as he was.

As Ezra lay in his tiny home's built-in bed that night, he fervently hoped God would hear his prayer that Vera's fears would not multiply until she could focus on nothing else. She was sensitive that way.

God, if You could convince Bishop Monroe to preach on something other than sin and sex tomorrow, maybe we can convince Vera to love me the way I truly love her. I'd be eternally grateful.

Chapter 30

As Isaac sat on the pew bench in the lodge Sunday morning, he reminded himself that he was there so he wouldn't spend another long day alone. Because Maria wanted to chat with the business teacher in Cloverdale, she'd gone to the Mennonite service with the Kuhns and the Wickeys. He figured on enduring church, eating the common meal, and then waiting for her to return.

Meanwhile, his mind wandered back to her house on Maple, where he'd entered Miss Zehr's domain as though in a trance, knowing she would effortlessly make him see things her way. It was humbling, the way she took control of him.

But so, so satisfying.

The most amazing part, however, had been when she'd driven them to the drugstore in Forest Grove—where no one knew them—and had bought a box of protection before they'd driven to Cloverdale.

I want you, Isaac, but I don't want a baby.

If that wasn't love, it at least demonstrated a sense of responsibility he could appreciate—and respect.

"'He hath shewed thee, O man, what is good; and

what doth the LORD require of thee, but to do justly, and to love mercy, and to walk humbly with thy God?'" Preacher Marlin read from the large King James Bible. "Let us listen to the Lord's wisdom as He leads us to become the best followers we can be."

Stifling a yawn, Isaac settled in for the three-hour service. Ezra, on his right, seemed unusually withdrawn. To his left, Eddie was gazing steadily toward the women's side of the congregation, probably flirting with Fannie.

As Preacher Amos rose to address them, Isaac's thoughts were already in Cloverdale. He'd listened to Troyer's sermons most of his life—until the preacher had sent shock waves through the Coldstream district by joining the three Bender sisters when they'd bought a deserted church camp. Amos wasn't demonstrative as he spoke, but he usually made a relevant point—if you stayed awake to listen for it.

"We understand the concepts of doing justice and loving mercy—often interpreted as showing kindness to those around us," Preacher Amos began. "But what does it mean to walk humbly with God? Do we listen for His voice and allow Him to guide our everyday lives? Or do we insist on having our own way?"

Sounds like Maria. Having her way with me.

Isaac stifled a chuckle, hoping his friends didn't suspect his inappropriate thoughts.

"Do we allow those around us to express their desires and opinions, and to help us when we need it?" Troyer continued earnestly. "Or are we closed to all voices except our own?"

Preacher Amos paused so folks could ponder his

questions. A few of the men in front of Isaac shifted on the benches, as though the preacher had struck a nerve.

"If so, that's *arrogance*, my friends," Troyer insisted. "And it's a slippery slope that keeps us sliding farther away from the faithful life our Lord would have us live."

Arrogance. Isaac scowled, recalling how irritated he'd felt when Ezra had described him that way a while back.

Yet something in the preacher's message compelled him to pay closer attention. Amos was giving examples of arrogant behavior, and Isaac realized he could've been describing Bishop Obadiah Chupp—right down to the way he sneered at someone he considered beneath him and told them God would punish them because they didn't agree with his opinion.

"And the ultimate form of arrogance can be announcing that God is on your side of an argument," Preacher Amos warned. "How can any of us presume to know that?"

Isaac was wide-awake now, thrumming with the recollections of his father's one-sided mindset. His hypocritical self-righteousness. Claiming that he was channeling God's opinions had been one of his *dat*'s ways to control folks he felt were straying from the One True Path—which, of course, was the path that favored Obadiah Chupp.

I always resented Dat's holier-than-thou attitude. But wasn't I acting the same way when I shoved Deborah into that ditch because she called the police? I believed she was dead wrong and that I could do *no wrong . . . so maybe the apple hasn't fallen far from the tree.*

As he sat up straighter, the air rushed from his lungs. At that very moment, sisters Christine Burkholder and Mattie Troyer looked right at him, as though they'd seen the proverbial light bulb flashing on above his head. And what kind of miracle was it that Deborah also met his gaze as she bounced her toddler on her knee— and she was *smiling* at him?

Do I look different because Troyer's sermon sank in?

Isaac's mouth went dry. He felt lightheaded. Were the ladies' encouraging expressions a figment of his imagination? Or was God whispering in his ear through Preacher Amos's sermon, urging him to wipe the slate totally clean?

It was all he could do to stay on the pew bench during the remaining hymns, prayers, and Preacher Eli's meandering sermon. When Bishop Monroe pronounced the benediction, Isaac was ready to bolt—but folks listened to a few announcements before anyone moved.

"We have a *lot* of blessed events to look forward to!" the bishop said with sparkling brown eyes. "God is truly showing us a fabulous future in the form of first babies for Phoebe and Allen Troyer, Gloria and Cyrus Helmuth, and Marlene and Lester Lehman!"

Somebody whooped and the congregation burst into excited applause. As the burly bishop held up his hand, his smile widened. "Oh, but there's more—and we don't want to leave anyone out!" he exclaimed. "Once again, the double twin families of Sam and Simon Helmuth are carrying at the same time, and Barb and Bernice couldn't be happier. Deborah and Noah Schwartz—as well as Mary Kate and Roman—are also expecting second children. Let's break for lunch and congratulate them all!"

"We need to be careful, Chupp," Eddie teased beneath the loud chatter that filled the meeting room. "Must be something in the water."

"Speak for yourself," Isaac retorted, urging Eddie into the aisle ahead of him. Talk of impending births wasn't nearly as compelling as his need to speak with Deborah.

"You must have a really hot date," Brubaker teased as they stepped into the stream of men heading for the door.

"Something like that."

Peering eagerly ahead, Isaac slipped into every gap in the dispersing crowd. When he stepped out into the sunshine, he shaded his eyes as he sought out the young mother he urgently needed to speak to. The women were carrying covered bowls and pans of food to the tables set up in the shade, congratulating the expectant mothers among them. Deborah was handing her little girl over to her husband.

Isaac saw that Deborah's waistline had indeed thickened beneath her apron. When he caught up to her, he realized that he had no idea what he was going to say— but it was too late to back down.

Deborah smiled at him again, reminding him what an amazing, resilient young woman she was. "It was *gut* to see you in church this morning, Isaac," she said as he walked alongside her. "You seemed totally engrossed in Preacher Amos's sermon—"

"Because he was talking about *me*," he blurted. He motioned her to step aside, so their conversation wouldn't be so public. "I realized that I wasn't so different from

Dat—which isn't a compliment. I've been so arrogant. So blind to other people's feelings and—rude and brutal and—"

Her mouth formed a surprised O as her hand fluttered to her stomach. What a beautiful young woman she was—and how wise Noah had been to marry her, even after Isaac had sullied her reputation a couple of years ago.

"Deborah, I'm sorry about the way I treated you the night of the Bender fire and—and I'm sorry about that day I tried to trap you in the cabin you were painting. I hope you'll accept my apology," he said in a rush. "You were doing what you felt was right—because I was wrong. And I'm sorry your *dat* and mine also treated you as though you'd done something even worse than I'd done. You didn't deserve any of that grief we heaped on you."

She blinked rapidly, fighting sudden tears. "I—well, this is quite a surprise—"

"Please say you'll forgive me," Isaac whispered. "I'm glad you've moved beyond those dark days in Coldstream and that you've got a nice family now—"

"And it's growing," she whispered with a delighted smile. "I'm at the mercy of my moods these days, Isaac, but I let go of my anguish about that night long ago— for my own *gut.* Consider yourself forgiven. We can say we honored today's Scripture about doing justice, loving mercy, and walking humbly with God, *jah*?"

Isaac gazed at her, shaking his head in wonder. "*Denki* for making this moment so much easier than it might've been," he said softly. "I hope all goes well with your new baby."

As he started toward the serving line, Isaac felt so

much lighter in his soul. He hadn't anticipated making his final apology today. Now that it was behind him, however, he realized that Dale, Ezra, and the others who'd counseled him had been right: saying *I'm sorry* had truly set him free.

When Isaac saw the tight expression on Overholt's face, however, he sensed that his friend wasn't feeling nearly as lighthearted as he was.

Which is odd, considering that Vera is heading his way.

The reflection in her mirror as she'd dressed for church had told Vera she looked as exhausted as she felt, but after a sleepless night she'd reached a conclusion. It was only fair to share it with Ezra because all during church, he'd appeared as unsettled as she was.

After she set her bowl of pistachio pudding salad on the long serving table, she let the other women finish preparing the common meal. She wouldn't be able to eat a bite until she'd talked with him.

His handsome face, tight-lipped and shadowed beneath his eyes, stilled as he watched her approach. Ezra stood separate from the other men, as though he felt far removed from their jovial mood as they congratulated the expectant fathers.

"Ezra, is this a *gut* time to talk?" Vera asked softly.

"Do you have *gut* things to say?" he shot back. He looked away, pained. "Sorry. That wasn't fair."

She sighed. She hadn't made things easier by running off last night, had she?

"After a long heart-to-heart with Aunt Minerva, and

a lot of soul searching," Vera began hesitantly, "I—I believe I overreacted last night. And I'm sorry, Ezra."

His dark brows rose. His eyes shone with a more hopeful light. "I'm listening."

She stepped closer to him. It was impressive, the power she wielded over Ezra's emotions. But she couldn't make a habit of manipulating him with her moods if they were to have an honest relationship.

"I hurt your feelings after our, um, incident with the bishop, when you were being so careful to protect mine," Vera said with a sigh. "I hope we can still be a courting—but careful—couple?"

Ezra's dear face softened, yet he cleared his throat. "Was that Minerva's idea or yours?"

Her confidence faltered. But Vera reminded herself what was at stake. "It's mine," she said, detesting the quaver in her voice. "I encouraged your affection last night—didn't exactly shove you away—so you have reason to question my intentions—"

Vera suddenly found herself in Ezra's embrace, pressed firmly against his broad chest before he released her.

"Sorry, everybody can see us," he said, glancing at the folks who were lining up at the serving tables. "But *jah*, I want us to still be courting because I want *you*, Vera. Being caught by the bishop last night was only a bump in the road, sweetie. Not a dead end."

Her breath left her in a rush. "Oh, thank *gut*ness! You're so much braver than I am, Ezra. I spent way too much time worrying—"

He gently grasped her shoulder. "I love you, Vera,"

he whispered. "Nobody gets everything right all the time, ain't so?"

A tear escaped her eye, yet the sun had never shone brighter, had it? "I love you, too, Ezra. I'm ready to take our instruction from the bishop and get married anytime you are," Vera continued in a rush.

Ezra's eyes widened. "Me, too, but we need to arrange for a few practical things, like where we'll live and—"

"We can get by in your tiny home for a while, *jah*?" Vera blurted out. "It'll be a tight squeeze, maybe—but we seem to do all right without much space between us."

He glanced away, but not before she caught his secretive grin. "Oh, I've imagined *that* situation a time or two," he admitted. "Christine and the bishop would probably let us stay at their place a while, but I want to provide you a real house, Vera. A *home*, where we can raise our family."

Vera nodded. "It's what I want, too, Ezra. We have another option—Aunt Minerva and Uncle Harley have a lot of empty bedrooms. Before Marlin married Frances and moved into her house with Fannie and Lowell, they all lived in the house next to the barrel factory. My aunt wanted us to know we'd be welcome there."

Ezra nodded. "So we won't be homeless."

Vera laughed. She felt light and airy as her world settled back into place with Ezra beside her. She'd worried that he might not be so ready to kiss and make up— yet another fear in the night that hadn't come true.

"Shall we speak to Bishop Monroe? I'm ready if you are, Ezra. Really, I am!"

His face lit up as he grasped her hands. "So, you'll marry me? No more doubts or second thoughts?"

Vera's soul swelled with intense happiness. "I'm yours, Ezra."

His breath escaped him. "Well, then—let's tell the bishop and eat lunch. And we should probably call our parents, *jah*?"

Chapter 31

The following Friday morning, Isaac found a note under his apartment door.

Let's talk before the store opens. Dale

It was a simple message, but Isaac kept reading things into it. Was Kraybill dissatisfied with his work? Was he curious about the progress on Maria's bakery?

Or had he figured out that Isaac's days at the Promise Lodge bulk store were numbered?

Isaac kept an open mind and a straight face as he entered Dale's office after breakfast. Maria had hinted that she'd be ready to roar off to Cloverdale as soon as he could leave the store that afternoon. She'd suggested skipping supper at the lodge in favor of enjoying private time and a meal at her place.

When Maria spoke, Isaac listened. And his imagination ran wild. He reminded himself to concentrate on whatever the shopkeeper had invited him to discuss.

"Happy Friday, Isaac," Dale said from behind his desk. "Hard to believe it's already the seventeenth of August. And at least for a while today, it'll be just us guys manning the store. Marlene's having a run of morning sickness."

Isaac nodded, slipping onto the straight-back chair. "If you count Rosetta and Minerva, I've tallied up nine gals carrying babies, after Bishop Monroe called out names Sunday at church. Ed Brubaker thinks there's something in the water."

Dale laughed out loud. "Seems to me it's more the natural cause-and-effect of so many folks getting married these past several months. But don't look for a similar announcement from Irene and me."

Isaac chuckled politely. He looked around at the shelved ledgers and the computer monitor, where Dale was working on an order. He had plenty to say, but he let Kraybill talk first.

"I heard a fine piece of news yesterday, and I want to congratulate you, Isaac." Dale leaned his elbows on his desk, smiling. "Deborah Schwartz told me you two had settled your differences after Amos's sermon moved you to apologize. Happy to hear it."

Isaac blinked. He hadn't expected to be called into the office about that, yet he was pleased Deborah had told his boss about last Sunday's conversation.

"Troyer was talking about arrogance," he recalled. "I had a flash of understanding about how I'd grown up a lot like Dat even though I've always despised his 'my way or the highway' mindset. So, I cleared the slate."

"And you've apologized to all three ladies well ahead of the September fifth deadline we discussed at your interview," the storekeeper remarked with a nod. "That's commendable, Isaac. And considering how well you've done around the store, I think it's time for a pay raise. Let's consider your probationary period over, shall we?"

Isaac swallowed hard. Should he lay it all out, about his plans to go to Cloverdale?

Kraybill studied him for a moment. "Meanwhile, it's also gratifying to hear that Maria's been working with Rosetta and one of the other gals who attends our Mennonite Fellowship—Sally Swanson, a business teacher," he continued. "Maria says the new appliances are to be delivered next week. And because the school's phasing out some old computers, Sally's donating one to the bakery and will set up a new bookkeeping system for Maria."

Isaac heard the imaginary whizzzzz of a fishing line being cast. What was Dale trying to catch?

"*Jah*, Sally seemed eager for the bakery to reopen when we saw her a while back. Nice folks there in Cloverdale."

Kraybill's gaze held steady. "I was pleased to hear about all this help Maria's getting," he said, "but I had to wonder why *your* name wasn't mentioned, Isaac. I was under the impression that you were going to manage her business. Have you and Miss Zehr parted ways?"

It was all Isaac could do to keep a straight face. Considering how affectionate they became the moment Promise Lodge was in the scooter's rearview mirror, *parted* wasn't a word that described them these days.

But what was he supposed to think about Maria keeping his name out of her conversations? Was she avoiding personal questions from her church friends? Trying not to feed the rumor mill at Promise Lodge?

Considering all the things Dale Kraybill knew about

him—and all the times he'd helped Isaac despite his checkered past—Isaac decided to lay his cards on the table. It was only right.

"Truth be told, I'll be moving to Cloverdale soon," he confessed. "Maria and I are expanding the bakery to include a light lunch menu in addition to her usual pastries and breads."

Dale's eyes widened, but his gaze remained calm. "That's a great idea. Cloverdale has very few places to eat lunch. Any idea when you'll reopen?"

Isaac nodded. "Week after next, most likely—when we've got the menu finalized and all the new equipment is in place," he replied. "Shall we consider this my two-weeks' notice? I—I'm sorry to leave you shorthanded again, especially with Marlene not feeling well—"

Kraybill shrugged. "Once I saw the way you and Maria were getting on, I had no illusions about keeping you here to run the store after I retired," he admitted. "She'll do much better, having you as a business partner—although I'm sure there's a lot going on behind the scenes, *jah*? None of my business, but I'll ask anyway: when's the wedding?"

A laugh escaped him. Isaac had figured Dale would broach that subject—and once again, he figured he should be honest. Word got around in small towns like Cloverdale, no matter how discreet he and Maria thought they were being.

"Considering our family situations," he began cautiously, "we're starting our instruction and premarital counseling sessions with Zachary Miller, and we'll have a no-fuss wedding ceremony—just the two of us, with witnesses. It suits us both not to deal with all the meal arrangements and the guest lists and—"

"Why do I suspect you haven't told your parents about this?"

Isaac coughed nervously. "I figure if Maria and I are already married when the folks find out about it, there's nothing they can do, ain't so?"

Even to his own ears, it sounded as though the belligerent former Isaac Chupp had returned. He wasn't surprised that Kraybill focused on his clasped hands for a moment, considering what he wanted to say next.

"You're certain in your heart of hearts that Maria's the woman you want to spend the rest of your life with?" he asked softly. "You might be jumping out of the proverbial frying pan and into the fire, committing to her so quickly, Isaac."

"What are we supposed to do? Live at her house without being married?" he shot back. "We've both done some wild and crazy things—broken a lot of rules—but we're drawing a more acceptable line here. I've told Miller I'll bunk in the back of the bakery until we're married, and I intend to honor that promise."

Dale's expression said he knew exactly what was going on between Isaac and Maria, but he didn't press that point. "And you won't at least invite your *mamm* and Maria's sister to your wedding? They'll be hurt, you know."

"Mamm won't come without Dat. And Dat wouldn't stoop to attend a wedding he considered unacceptable to God." Isaac sighed. He hadn't really thought about these matters, but it didn't take him long to reach his conclusions. "He'll already be ranting because I've jumped the fence. I'm pretty sure that even if my mother wanted to come, he wouldn't *allow* her to."

The storekeeper thought for a moment before looking at Isaac again. "I haven't gotten wind of this in Cloverdale, so I'm guessing no one else knows?"

"We decided most of this within the past couple of days—and I hope you won't spread it around," Isaac added quickly. "We want to do this our way, without everyone fussing about how we should have a big dinner and—"

Isaac shrugged, entreating Dale to understand his unique situation. "I know the Kuhns would be happy to cook for us, but hanging around all day while guests eat and chitchat doesn't appeal to either one of us," he insisted. "We have trouble waiting at the supper table for everyone to finish, as it is. Can't sit still. Nervous energy."

Dale's laughter echoed in his small office. "Is *that* what you call it?"

Kraybill seemed to realize that nothing he could say was going to change Isaac's mind, so he stood up. "Let me be the first to congratulate you and wish you all the best," he said, extending his hand. "You'll be hard to replace, Isaac, but if anyone's to keep Maria focused on running a profitable business, you're the man for the job. Let me know how I can help."

The warm, sincere strength of Dale's handshake and words touched Isaac deeply. "*Denki* for saying that," he murmured. "It means a lot."

As they entered the store with wheeled carts of fresh inventory, Isaac was relieved that Dale would be restocking hardware items in the back of the store. It gave him a chance to plan his strategy while he worked.

It would be startling news to Maria that they were beginning their instruction and having a very small Mennonite wedding ceremony.

Another minor detail: they hadn't actually decided to get married. *Jah*, Maria was seeking her happily-ever-after in the form of a husband, but he'd evaded her hints that they should tie the knot. Kissing her silly was always his best tactic when she got too serious.

When Dale had described Maria's setup help without mentioning his name, however, Isaac had figured turnabout was fair play. He'd pulled those wedding details out of thin air, as though he and Maria had already agreed on them!

As he reviewed what he'd said to Dale, however, it sounded like the practical way to marry the beautiful, erratic, unpredictable blonde to whom he'd become physically addicted. Maria would laugh in his face when he mentioned bunking in the bakery rather than living with her until they were married—but who would check on that? If he showed up for work at Dale's store for the next two weeks—and slept in his apartment each night—no one would be the wiser about what went on when he was in Cloverdale.

As he opened the store, Isaac hoped he could keep his story straight while he spent the evening with Maria. And he hoped she'd be so excited about his ideas that she wouldn't realize he'd taken control of their future.

Chapter 32

Vera sat on the lodge's front porch swing Saturday morning, telling herself not to be nervous about meeting Ezra's parents. Ezra was holding her hand, moving the swing a little faster than usual—which told Vera that he, too, was more anxious than he would admit.

"They're just ordinary, everyday dairy farmers—except for my artsy younger brother, Raymond," Ezra remarked. "They'll think you're the nicest thing since the invention of pie, Vera. Just be your wonderful self."

For the umpteenth time, she pushed up her glasses with her knuckle. They were watching for Dick Mercer's van, and it felt as if time was standing still.

"Wish I could've met Raymond and Lizzie at the Kraybills' wedding," Vera said softly. "But I left right after the ceremony to keep Aunt Minerva company."

"That's another reason my family will love you, sweetie. You *care* about people," Ezra said earnestly. "So, when you see my *mamm* in her wheelchair, you'll realize she needs nobody's pity. That chair's her throne, and she rules the roost!"

Vera laughed. "It's *gut* that the new cabins are finished

so your parents can stay in them. No stairs to mess with."

"*Jah*, not that stairs are a problem for Raymond. He's been maneuvering Mamm's chair for so long, it comes as second nature to him—which is one reason he's always been her favorite," Ezra pointed out. "If Raymond and Lizzie had stayed here at Promise Lodge, our mother wouldn't have let on, but she'd have missed her best boy something awful."

"Well, life always works itself out—"

"And there they are!" As a white van turned in from the county blacktop, Ezra sprang up from the swing and waved, his face alight with excitement.

Even with his new position in Christine's dairy—and even with lots of former Coldstream folks for neighbors—Ezra had missed being at home with his family. His deep green eyes shone with a special light as he extended his hand to Vera. He had more spring in his step as they descended the steps.

The moment the van stopped, Ezra opened the door behind the driver. "Mamm, Dat, you're here! It's so *gut* to see you!"

Without waiting for anyone to get the wheelchair out, Ezra scooped his mother from the back seat and held her to his chest as though she weighed no more than a child. And Mrs. Overholt, bless her, was clutching her boy as though she couldn't let go of him. The mother-and-son reunion radiated such love that Vera herself was awash in it.

The younger couple in the back seat slid out the other door and within moments they came over, rolling the wheelchair.

"Hey there, I'm Raymond—and you must be the

Vera my brother can't stop talking about," said the fellow with the red-framed glasses and a dark, untamed beard. He held Vera's gaze, taking in her turquoise frames with an approving nod. "And this is my wife, Lizzie—"

"Maria's sister—but don't hold that against me!" the young blonde said with a laugh. As she placed a hand on her protruding belly, it was clear she didn't have much longer to wait.

"And that fellow taking our luggage out of the car is our *dat*, Ervin," Raymond continued the introductions.

Vera nodded shyly at the stocky gentleman who was studying her closely. He was an older version of Ezra, a vision of what her husband would look like several years down the road.

"And this," Ezra said as he gently lowered his mother into her chair, "is the best *mamm* in the whole world. And Mamm, I know you're going to love Vera—almost as much as I do."

Vera's cheeks caught fire at the mention of his affection for her—and in front of the parents she was seeing for the first time! But that said something about the close-knit nature of the Overholt family, didn't it?

As she approached the woman in the wheelchair, she forgot to be nervous. Ezra's *mamm* glowed with an inner joy no hardship could conquer—and she'd surely known difficulties in her day. She wasn't sure how long Mrs. Overholt had been confined to her chair, but Vera couldn't imagine keeping track of five sons had been easy—unless she possessed inner powers to corral six males and keep them moving in the right directions.

"Vera, it's an absolute delight to meet you, dear," she said with shining green eyes that resembled her son's.

"Please call me Alma, or Mamm, whichever you prefer. 'Mrs. Overholt' sounds way too formal for this wild bunch I claim as my family."

The driver closed the van's hatchback with a *whump* and waved at them. "See you folks tomorrow afternoon. Enjoy your stay!"

"*Jah, denki* for driving us, Dick," Ezra's *dat* responded. Everyone stepped closer to the lodge as the white vehicle turned and drove back onto the private road.

Lizzie leaned closer. "She really loves it if you call her Mamm," she whispered. "It was an easy choice for me, since my mother's been gone a while, but things might be different for you, Vera. Just sayin'."

Ezra's mother chuckled. "I suspect you girls will come to be *gut* friends," she put in as she observed them. "The other boys' wives are quite a lot older."

"And those sons are running the dairy while you're visiting us?" Vera asked, focusing on Ervin. He was still watching her—and maybe feeling left out of the conversation. "Ezra's lucky to be working with Roman Schwartz, or neither of them would get much time off."

Ervin smiled slightly. "One of these days I'll let the three of them take it over. Rumor has it my name's being tossed into the ring for the preacher position that's opened—"

"*Jah*, when Amos Troyer and Eli Peterscheim left," Alma said with a shake of her head, "things took a turn for the worse in our district, I'm afraid."

"—because if the lot falls to me," Ezra's *dat* continued grimly, "I'll not have much time to devote to the family business."

Vera nodded sympathetically. Men who were chosen

by the falling of the lot—a slip of paper that fluttered from one of the hymnals the bishop had placed on a table—sacrificed a great deal to become a leader of their congregation.

"Hey there, you Overholts are looking mighty serious!" a familiar male voice called out.

"Have you already decided you don't like Promise Lodge?" his wife put in with a laugh.

Alma's face lit up like a summer's day. "Speak of the devil, there's Amos and Mattie now! Oh, but it's *gut* to see you, old friends!"

"Who're you calling *old*?" Preacher Amos teased as he approached at a trot. With a jovial slap to Ervin's back, he shook the man's hand—and Ezra's *dat* let out a laugh that brought him out of his somber mood.

Mattie slung her arm around Alma's shoulders and the two of them hugged as though they were long-lost sisters. She smiled at Lizzie then, assessing her protruding profile.

"Won't be long for you, young lady!" she exclaimed. "And Raymond, we've heard wonderful-*gut* things about how you've brought the Coldstream store at least into the twentieth century, if not the twenty-first!"

Raymond laughed modestly. "Considering how far back some of the inventory went when Lizzie and I took it over, we've made progress, *jah*."

"And you'll be pleased to know that your wooden star plaque still hangs in the meeting room," Mattie said, pointing behind them. "As slowly as we Amish tend to change things, you'll be our inspiration for years to come!"

Vera glanced at the slender young man in the red glasses, intrigued. The first time she'd attended service in the lodge, she'd been amazed to see a signboard sporting a flashy star embellished with gold paint, tiny shards of broken glass, and glitter.

Star of wonder, star of night . . . guide us to Thy holy light.

"You can't argue with the message, no matter what season it is," Preacher Amos put in, smiling at Raymond. "We were blessed to have you amongst us during that short time you worked for Dale and sold your signs in his store. But I'm sure your parents are ecstatic that you and Lizzie found your intended life in Coldstream."

"Amen to that!" Alma crowed.

Mattie smiled at the Overholts as though it were old home week. "If you're ready for some lemonade and goodies to tide us over until lunch, Christine has everything ready at her place—and here come Rosetta and Truman in the truck! I called them as soon as I saw Dick's van, figuring we more mature folks could ride up the hill while you kids walk. Unless you'd like to ride, Lizzie?"

Lizzie waved her off. "I sat in the van long enough, *denki*. Need to stretch my legs."

Once again Ezra gently scooped his mother up and waited for Truman's white pickup to stop on the lawn near the lodge. Raymond folded the wheelchair and put it in the back of the truck while Ezra slid Alma into the back seat—as though the brothers had been seamlessly seeing to their *mamm*'s needs their entire lives. When the Troyers and Ezra's parents were situated, Truman drove up the hill toward the bishop's house.

"The parents have been looking forward to this moment for a long time," Raymond said as the four of them watched the truck approach the curve in the road.

"When the Bender sisters and Amos left Coldstream, Mamm and Dat were concerned about so many other folks leaving that there wouldn't be a church district anymore. Now that Preacher Ivan Ropp—who replaced Preacher Eli—has found greener pastures, it seems their prediction is coming true."

"That discussion will probably keep them busy most of the afternoon," Lizzie said with a chuckle. "It'll be fine by me if we don't even head up to Christine's for a while—"

"Especially because we've heard about your cool pottery, Vera."

Raymond, although a married man about to become a father, had an endearingly nerdy appearance that Vera had liked the moment she'd seen him. With his uncombed black hair and unruly beard, he was clearly another artistically inclined person who struggled to fit the conservative, conforming mold of the Old Order—especially in a district where a strict bishop forbade creating art for its own sake.

"How about if we take our time walking up the hill? It's getting hot," Vera pointed out, thinking of Lizzie's condition. "I'll show you some of my pieces and the set of Holstein dishes I'm making for Christine—inspired by Ezra and the herd!"

Raymond and Lizzie laughed out loud as they clasped hands and began to walk. "Mamm would go crazy for new dishes that look like our cows!" Raymond said. "Let me pay you a deposit, and we'll give them to her for Christmas."

"She never asks for anything," Lizzie chimed in, "so *jah*, Mamm would be really tickled that you made them for her, Vera."

Vera smiled at Ezra as they all started up the hill. Already she felt comfortable with his parents and the youngest Overholts, so the weekend's visit was off to a promising start.

"I'll be happy to make them," she said. "I've already gotten so many orders, I might not have time to take up teaching this fall—and school's to start in a couple of weeks!"

"And somehow, you'll need to make time for me," Ezra teased. "We need to set our wedding date to allow for all the fine, fun things coming our way, sweetie."

"Take it from us," Lizzie said in a conspiratorial tone. "Sooner is better than later."

Chapter 33

Maria's eyes widened when she saw Isaac entering the church with Dale and Irene. He was dressed in his Sunday black trousers with his white shirt neatly tucked under his suspenders—which meant he was more Plainly dressed than many of the Mennonite men attending. With his blond hair neatly combed and a beguiling smile on his face, he was the handsomest young man she'd ever seen.

And he was *her* young man.

As she came down the center aisle to greet him and the Kraybills, Maria was glad she'd chosen one of the better dresses she'd left in her Cloverdale closet. After Isaac had driven the scooter back to Promise Lodge, she'd spent Saturday night at home. She wanted some time in the bakery Sunday afternoon, to get ready for her appliance delivery Monday morning. It had given her a night in her childhood bed—alone—to ponder the reopening of her business and the details of working with a partner . . . who would soon be her constant companion and associate in all the most important, permanent ways.

Maria just needed to get Isaac on *her* schedule.

She dazzled him with her best smile and held out her hands. "Look who's here! It's so *gut* to see you, Isaac— oh, and you, too, Irene and Dale," she added quickly.

The newlyweds chuckled. When Isaac gripped her fingers, he looked ready to kiss her into oblivion.

"It's time I became part of the Cloverdale community, *jah*?" he asked in a silky voice. "Folks need to know who I am when I restock the bakery cases or serve them lunch."

"We were tickled that he wanted to come today," Irene put in as the four of them chose a pew in the center of the sanctuary. "He's been attending church at the lodge but today's a visiting Sunday—"

"So instead of sleeping in, I've come to be with you, Maria," Isaac put in.

It felt different to be settling on the pew beside a man who would spark all manner of curious questions from other folks after the service. Moments later the Kuhn sisters sidestepped into the row from the other direction, followed by Truman and a very round Rosetta. Their four faces were alight with pleased surprise.

"What a joy to join you in church, Isaac," Beulah said as she briefly clasped his arm.

"Great way to start our week, in the presence of the Lord and the cutest couple we know," Ruby quipped as she grinned at them.

Truman and Rosetta nodded and waved as they sat down at the other end of the pew.

Maria told herself that this sort of conversation ought to become the norm. She should get active in church life again because it would bring members of the congregation into her bakery. Of course, God wanted her to pay attention to *Him*, but it was difficult to think about religion when Isaac's thigh lightly touched hers.

Zachary Miller walked to the front and welcomed everyone. When he spotted Isaac, he said, "Do we have any guests this morning?"

The minister focused on Maria, expecting her to introduce Isaac—but caught off guard, she hesitated. Isaac, however, stood up and looked all around at the congregation.

"I'm Isaac Chupp," he said without a hint of hesitation. "Maria Zehr and I plan to reopen the bakery soon—and we're engaged!"

The congregation murmured approvingly as he sat down. Maria was delighted that Isaac had taken care of the introduction, yet a mental red flag sprang up. Time and again she'd tried to coax a proposal from the man who'd become the center of her world, and he'd always distracted her with mind-boggling kisses.

In her daydreams, Isaac dropped to one chivalrous knee and brought her to tears of joy with his eloquent proposal. But she was diverted from her disappointment in his matter-of-fact announcement by the realization that at long last she was going to be married. Her thoughts lingered lovingly on all the special moments of their ceremony and the reception meal—a banquet topped off by at least three splendid cakes, which she would bake and decorate to perfection. It would be a storybook event, and Maria intended to play Queen for the Day as hundreds of guests wished her well and told her what a beautiful bride she was.

"We'll talk later," she whispered near his ear. But she slipped her hand into the crook of his elbow as though her dreams were coming true at last.

The service went by in a blur. Maria was aware of standing, sitting, and singing in all the usual places, but her mind was aglow with wedding fantasies. Thankfully, Isaac didn't want to linger for chitchat any more than she did. As he quickly maneuvered them through the crowd, Maria smiled sweetly and nodded at her church friends as she followed behind him.

When they were outside, she didn't challenge him about his engagement announcement. Maria wasn't surprised to hear Beulah calling out behind them as folks left the church building.

"We hope you kids will join all of us old folks for lunch—"

"Our treat!" Ruby said with a laugh.

"—and while we're in town, we'd also like to see your bakery!" Beulah finished enthusiastically. "We've walked past it, but it would be nice to see how it's come together inside."

"I'd like to see it, too," Irene chimed in. "It's always closed on Sundays when we're in town."

Before she could think of an excuse, Maria and Isaac were surrounded by their eager friends—folks who'd supported her with encouragement as well as cash. Between the Coffee Can Fund and Truman's building insurance allowance, these kind people had literally put her back in business. The bakery was only half a block away, so Maria had no reason to refuse their request.

"I'll get the spare key around back and meet you at the front door," she said, waving them toward Main Street. Her keys were in her purse, but she needed a moment with Isaac—so she grabbed his hand. "*You're* coming with me, Mr. Chupp."

Maria hoped she'd sounded demure rather than

demanding. Isaac smiled as though he planned to sneak a kiss or two before they reached the main room of the store—and she allowed him to. When she'd let them into the back storeroom, however, she arched her eyebrow.

"And when do you intend to make *gut* on your *announcement*, my love?"

Isaac snatched the key from her fingers, smiling like the cat that ate the canary. "All in *gut* time," he hedged before entering the main room of the bakery.

He waved at the friends who awaited them out front, as though it was perfectly natural for him to let them in. Isaac's proprietary air perturbed Maria—but then, within the next two weeks he'd be helping her run the shop . . . and more if she had her way.

And Isaac knew how much better everything went when Maria got her way.

The Kraybills, Kuhns, and Wickeys came in and gazed around the freshly painted bakery.

"Love these happy yellow walls!"

"Oh, look at those glass-top tables and cute metal chairs!"

"Ah, the workmen have installed the glass cases and front counter since I was last here," Truman noted as he stepped behind them to assess the workmanship.

"That's a fabulous stainless-steel sink—so deep and roomy," Irene said as she followed her son into the work area. "Wish we had one like that for Promise Lodge Pies."

Maria refrained from reminding Irene that she and Phoebe could have installed any kind of sink they'd wanted after the tornado—when they'd refurbished *her* little building. Instead, she rode the waves of praise as the four women complimented the way she'd arranged her workspace. She was picturing the ovens and refrigerators that would soon fill the gaps along the walls, and she could practically smell the cinnamon, sugar, and fresh coffee that would entice customers into her store again.

"Isaac, we have an extra bunk bed at our place," Truman remarked as he gazed into the storeroom. "Would you like it? It should fit along that south wall."

All talk stopped. As Maria felt her friends' curious gazes, the heat rising from beneath her collar formed a red shield that blocked everyone from her vision except Isaac.

What was going on with him? First, he'd shown up at church without telling her, and then he'd said they were engaged. And he'd apparently spoken to Truman—but not to *her*—about a bed in the back room? Were their guests thinking they wanted a place for quick, urgent encounters during the business day?

"You folks go ahead and enjoy your lunch," Maria said tersely, gesturing toward the door. "My fiancé and I have some business to discuss."

As their bewildered visitors left, Isaac heard Maria noisily rummaging through a drawer of utensils. Was she looking for a knife?

He'd really stepped in it. Should've realized that Kraybill would share the tidbits about his wedding plans with Irene, and that she'd pass along his suggestion about the bed to Truman, whose home still contained most of the furniture he'd grown up with.

"So, you've talked to everyone except me about this *bed*?" Maria demanded shrilly. "And you've already spoken to Zachary about us getting married—"

"Well, no," Isaac put in softly. "He didn't know who I was this morning, remember?"

"—and you thought I'd go along with this engagement idea, even though you've dodged the issue every time I've mentioned it?" She sliced the air with a long metal spatula as though it were a sword instead of a tool to spread frosting or batter. "What else have you told Truman? What else are you trying to pull over on me, Isaac?"

He had the wisdom not to rise to her angry bait. And he sensed it would be better to confess the sins of omission he'd committed rather than stringing Maria along, hoping she wouldn't find too many loopholes in his story. The devil was in the details—and Maria resembled a fallen angel with a weapon—and a vendetta that stretched from here to eternity.

Isaac took two chairs down from the new café tables and placed them on the shining vinyl floor. He was trying to recall all the details he'd created for Dale on Friday morning—because who knew how much the storekeeper had shared with Irene?

"Can we sit down and discuss this like rational adults?" he suggested. "If we make each other angry—"

"Oh, I'm way past angry, Isaac!"

"—we'll say things we regret."

"No, *you're* going to regret whatever you've told Truman and—"

"It was Dale I spoke with, actually," Isaac put in, stepping behind one of the chairs as Maria approached.

"When I told him I'd be helping you run the bakery and adding the lunch shift we talked about—and I gave him my two weeks' notice at the bulk store—he asked when the wedding was."

Maria pointed the spatula at him. "And what did you say? Have you taken it upon yourself to set the date, too?"

Isaac sighed. "No, I sidestepped that by telling him we'd soon take our premarital instruction from Miller," he replied in a voice that wavered slightly. "And—to make it look more honorable—I said I'd bunk in the storeroom until after the wedding."

Maria stepped toward him, glaring incredulously. "And where did *that* idea come from?"

"I, um, made stuff up as I went along," he admitted. "Trying to make the right impression—"

"Impression? The Kuhns and Rosetta and Irene probably thought you wanted a bed to *fool around* in when we weren't serving customers!" she blurted out. Her fist went to her hip as she leaned toward him. "What else did you tell Dale? You might as well come clean, because I can ask him to repeat whatever delusional ideas you shared with him."

When her metal spatula met his chest, Isaac realized that she could do a lot of physical damage with her weapon, even if it had a blunt, rounded tip. He realized now that he'd been astoundingly stupid to share plans with Dale as though Maria had helped make them. He'd also been foolish to assume she would go along with them.

With a heavy sigh, Isaac came clean. "I told him we

were starting our instruction to join the Mennonite faith—"

"Wrong!" Maria interrupted brusquely. "I was baptized years ago."

"—along with premarital counseling, and that because of our family situations," he said, holding her gaze, "we'd decided to have a wedding with just the two of us and witnesses rather than a big to-do where we had to sit around chatting with dinner guests all day—"

"What planet did you fall off?" the blonde shrieked, waving her hands in exasperation. "Have you ever known a bride who didn't want a big dinner with all her friends—"

"And who would we invite, Maria?" Isaac countered. He was tired of her tirade. She wasn't thinking before she lashed out. "You have only a sister. None of my family would come because I've shamed them by joining you Mennonites.

"Besides, you *despise* sitting around the dinner table talking!" he continued, fighting fire with fire. "And why do you think our wedding would only be about *you*? Don't I count for anything? I'm helping you keep your business afloat, after all."

It was the wrong thing to say. Maria's eyebrows shot up and she grabbed the front placket of his white shirt, still brandishing her spatula.

"Let's not forget who drives this whole situation," she whispered vehemently. "Because if I walk away, do *you* know how to bake, Isaac?"

His mouth clapped shut and he knew to leave it that way.

"And you suggested these asinine ideas to Dale *why?*" Maria demanded.

Isaac had to stop and think about that. He replayed Friday morning's calm, unruffled conversation with the storekeeper and finally recalled the remark that had started him thinking so creatively, on the fly.

"Dale said something about you getting help from the women at Promise Lodge, as well as from Sally the business teacher—but that you hadn't mentioned my name, or how I planned to save your bacon," he recalled softly. "I guess I was just getting a word in edgewise, man to man. Dale didn't think any of my ideas were far-fetched or—"

"Of course, he didn't! Dale's a conservative middle-aged *guy*—"

"And what do you have against *guys*, Maria?" Isaac challenged. "We seem to come in handy when you want something, or when you're caught up in a crying jag, or when you can't stand to be alone. Am I just a convenience to you?"

Maria scowled, gearing up for another attack. Rather than listen to her, Isaac crossed his arms.

"If I can't be more than your Mr. Fix-It when things go wrong—a toy for you to wind up when you're bored and lonely—maybe I'm the one who should walk away."

He swallowed hard, but he meant every word he'd said. "I'm a man, Maria, and I'm looking for a woman who loves me for who I am, faults and all," he said. "I need a wife who cares as much about my happiness as she does her own—a woman who at least *listens* before she spouts off at me. If you know of anybody like that, send her my way, will you?"

As he walked out the front door, Isaac feared he was

leaving a sweet dream—and a comfortable future—
behind him.

Or was he? Had he been so blinded by desire that
he'd not seen what his future with Maria would really
hold? Why would he want to endure more brutal argu-
ments and Maria's self-centered habits for the rest of
his life?

On a hunch, Isaac went to the pizza place up the
street—because he had to go somewhere hotheaded
Maria wouldn't be. Sure enough, a waiter was setting
two very large, very cheesy pizzas in front of his friends
from Promise Lodge.

When Dale spotted him in the doorway, he waved
Isaac over. "Come have some lunch," he said as Truman
grabbed an extra chair from another table.

Isaac gratefully took his seat. His expression probably told the Kuhns, the Wickeys, and the Kraybills exactly why he'd shown up—without Maria—and they
were kind enough not to quiz him about it.

Rosetta grabbed a plate and some utensils from the
unoccupied table behind her and set them in front of
him. "Looks like your business meeting's over, *jah*?"
she asked gently. She picked up a big slice of sausage
pizza, with hot, melty cheese dangling from the tip, and
laid it on his plate.

The aromas of onions, sausage, and warm mozzarella
eased Isaac's pain. As he looked at the friendly, familiar
faces around the table he realized just how far he'd
come since he'd arrived at Promise Lodge looking for a
job—any job—that would get him away from home.

"I suspect this whole business with Maria is over,"
he said, shaking his head. "I've been a fool to fall for
such a childish, hotheaded, selfish—"

Chuckling, Truman grasped Isaac's shoulder. "We've all done it, Isaac. Women have their ways of reeling us in before we realize we've been caught—hook, line, and sinker."

"I've heard that phrase before." Isaac sighed. Seemed a lot of fishing had been going on.

"Not to be nasty, understand," Rosetta put in softly, "but there was a time all those descriptions you just pinned on Maria also applied to, um, another person we know."

Isaac blinked. His slice of pizza remained in front of his mouth as he considered this.

"Could be you and Maria are too much alike," Beulah suggested.

"Opposites attract and likes repel," Ruby added sympathetically. "Not too late to change your mind about her."

"And you still have a job if you want to stay on at the store," Dale said. "I'd be delighted to keep you on, Isaac."

As he sank his teeth into the fabulous pizza, Isaac felt extremely grateful and blessed. He had options. And he had folks who cared about him—and who'd give him a ride back to Promise Lodge.

He also had time to reconsider his feelings about Maria and her dreams—not to mention his own dreams.

Not a bad place to be. I've done a lot worse.

Chapter 34

As Ezra sat down at the long table with his heaped plate, he felt over-the-top ecstatic. For this visiting Sunday, the Bender sisters and other women from Coldstream had organized a potluck for everyone at Promise Lodge in honor of his parents' visit, and happy chatter was one of the finest dishes being served. Long tables had been set up in the shade of the large trees on the lodge's front lawn, and everyone talked and laughed together—a scene that had rarely taken place in Coldstream.

Maybe common meals there ended quickly because folks didn't want to socialize after Bishop Obadiah's sermons about sin and damnation—the consequences of not submitting to his vision of the straight and narrow Amish path.

A burst of laughter made Ezra set aside his regrettable memories, however. His mother beamed as longtime friends greeted her. Dat—who'd spent time in deep discussion with Preachers Amos, Eli, Marlin, and Bishop Monroe—appeared more relaxed about the role he would assume if the paper "lot" fluttered out of the hymnal he chose next Sunday.

"It doesn't get any better than this, kids," Ezra said as he sat down beside Vera.

Across the table, his younger brother chuckled. "*Jah*, it does," Raymond countered, grinning at Lizzie beside him. "I had no idea what *happy* really meant before I signed on with this bubbly, unpredictable wife of mine. And who knew how distinguished and mature I'd look when I grew a beard?"

The four of them laughed—something they'd done a lot over the past couple of days. Ezra wasn't surprised that Raymond had allowed his untended fringe of facial hair to go its own way. With the hair on his head and face standing on end, he resembled a surprised black-haired lion wearing red glasses.

"What did your folks say when you told them you and Ezra are getting married the same day as Eddie and Fannie?" Lizzie asked Vera. "Seems like a great plan, considering your family and friends from Bloomingdale will already be here, *jah*?"

Vera's cheeks flushed prettily. She reached for Ezra's hand under the table. "I'm going to call them later today and give them our news," she replied. "They met Ezra a few weeks ago, when they helped my brother win Preacher Marlin's approval to marry his daughter. They won't be surprised that we're also tying the knot earlier than they'd expected."

"It makes sense to have the wedding before school starts, too," Ezra added as he forked up a bite of potato salad. "We'll have a few days to, um, get to *know* each other better—"

"And Aunt Minerva says the older boys won't be as likely to tease me about having a boyfriend," Vera put in. "Fannie's brother, Lowell, and Lavern Peterscheim are of an age where they love that sort of talk."

"It's unusual that Promise Lodge allows married women to be teachers," Raymond remarked as he split a dinner roll.

"They don't have a lot of choice," Ezra pointed out. "Minerva Kurtz took the job when she moved here because the unmarried girls were still in school themselves."

"Well, Gloria Helmuth was single then," Vera said, "but folks agreed that the education of their scholars would be in much better hands if Minerva did the teaching."

Ezra chuckled. He'd only seen Gloria after Sunday services at the common meal—knew that in addition to helping at the Helmuth Nursery, she managed lodge apartment rentals for Rosetta, and was also the scribe for Promise Lodge's column in *The Budget* newspaper. But Roman's tales about boy-crazy, desperate Gloria Lehman had entertained them for hours as they'd been milking.

Ezra cut his slice of ham, delighted that his family had encouraged his marriage despite only meeting Vera yesterday. He was even more excited because Vera had suggested holding the ceremony when the Brubaker family would be here for Ed's wedding.

His life was falling into place very quickly now. Bishop Monroe had agreed to accelerate their premarital counseling, and he believed they had a solid basis for a satisfying life together. His parents had offered to put money toward a house, as a wedding gift—and Vera thought her family would contribute, as well, because they'd done that for Ed and Fannie.

We're living in the sweet spot. And it'll only get better.

The rumble of tires on gravel made him look up. The Kraybills were pulling in, after church and Sunday dinner in Cloverdale, and Truman's pickup was behind them. When the two vehicles stopped a short distance from the picnic tables, Ezra wasn't surprised to see Rosetta and the Kuhns hurry from the truck, waving and calling out as they joined their friends.

He had not expected Isaac to get out of the Kraybills' back seat. One look at the slender blond's forlorn expression told Ezra that Chupp's bubble had burst—and that Maria had most likely held the pin that popped it.

Raymond pushed back from the table. "Let's flag Isaac down before he disappears," he said to Ezra. "Mamm has told me again and again that she needs to speak to him."

"*Jah*, she mentioned that to me, as well," Ezra agreed as he, too, rose from his chair. "Excuse us, ladies. We're on a mission."

Isaac was in no mood to socialize. But escaping to his apartment to lick his wounds seemed out of the question, considering all the people gathered at tables beneath the trees—who seemed to be watching *him*.

What's the occasion? When did everyone decide to have a big picnic and—

"Hey, Isaac! Wait up!"

"You've got a special visitor, buddy!"

Isaac sighed—although the sheer outrageousness of Raymond Overholt's beard made him forget his troubles for a moment. Ezra's brother resembled a shaggy black bear with a bad case of bed head. Isaac couldn't imagine his *dat* allowing Coldstream's new storekeeper to remain so unkempt—and so noticeable, considering that Amish folks weren't supposed to draw attention to themselves. The artsy red glasses had always been an issue for his conservative father; surely Raymond had added more fuel to that fire.

"You're looking very *married* these days, Overholt," Isaac teased when the brothers had stopped a few feet away.

Raymond laughed. "Lizzie thinks I'll be trimming my beard once the baby grabs hold of it," he said jovially. "Meanwhile, we enjoy getting a rise out of the bishop, if you know what I mean."

"Doesn't take much." Isaac scanned the faces in the large crowd. "I can't think that you're my special visitor—"

"Our *mamm* wants to talk to you," Ezra put in.

"She has some news from your mother, Isaac," Raymond added quickly.

Isaac's heart skipped a beat. Once again, he regretted leaving his mother in order to attain his freedom. "Has something happened? Is she sick or—"

"Mamm just needs to speak with you before we leave this afternoon. Dick Mercer's to pick us up around six."

Ordinarily, the thought of chatting with an older woman would've been the lowest priority on his list, but Alma Overholt was his mother's close friend—and she didn't have many. Isaac suspected the women of the Coldstream district kept their distance because Bertha Chupp was married to the powerful, outspoken leader whose attention they preferred not to attract.

Because of her wheelchair, however, Alma seemed

to roll under Bishop Obadiah's radar—maybe because he perceived her as physically weak, an object of pity.

When Isaac spotted her metal chair at the end of a table, she was already focused on him, as though by her will alone she could compel him to come over. Alma waved, and he returned her greeting.

"I'll see you guys later, maybe," he said. "*Gut* luck with that baby, Raymond."

As he strode across the lawn, Isaac wondered what he'd say to Mrs. Overholt—especially if his mother was involved. He should've known, however, that Alma was never at a loss for words. And when she turned from the table and threw open her arms, gazing at him with her shining eyes, a stampede of Bishop Monroe's Clydesdales couldn't have chased him away.

"Alma, it's *gut* to see you," he said as he leaned low to return her embrace. He hadn't anticipated the surge of affection and longing he felt, almost as though his own mother was hugging him for dear life. Alma's arms were powerful from wheeling herself around the house, so Isaac was held captive for several seconds.

"Shall we take a walk?" she suggested. "With all these folks kicking up so much hoopla, I want to be sure you—and you alone—hear me, dear. Your *mamm* has asked me to pass some things along while I was here."

With a nod to Ervin and the other folks seated nearby, Isaac grasped the handles of the wheelchair. He pushed Alma's chair past the front of the large, rustic lodge, toward the row of six new cabins.

"Our cabin made a nice guesthouse," Alma remarked cheerfully. "But then, everything here at Promise Lodge seems to be designed for happiness."

Isaac smiled. "That's mostly Rosetta's doing, you know."

"I have no doubt." She gestured for him to go between the last two little buildings. "We've got a small concrete patio with a couple of chairs behind our cabin. Let's talk there, so you can sit down, Isaac."

When they were situated in the shade of the only tree in this area that had survived the tornado, Isaac lowered himself to the plastic lawn chair. His thoughts were racing. What could his *mamm* possibly want to share that was so urgent?

When Alma inhaled deeply, focusing her serene green eyes on him, Isaac held his breath. She had an undeniable presence about her that her age and physical condition would never diminish.

"First of all, Isaac, your mother is so happy for you. Glad that you've gone your own way and landed a *gut* job," she said in a voice gone husky with emotion. "She was so excited about that big check you sent that she showed it to me before she gave it to your *dat*. We had to agree that miracles happen at Promise Lodge. Bertha believes you'd never have repaid what you took, had you stayed at home."

A lump rose into Isaac's throat. "She's probably right," he whispered, although he wasn't proud of his admission. "How is she, Alma? I—I think about her a lot."

Alma's thin-lipped smile and resigned shrug told a sad story. "Bertha's quieter these days. She seems a bit depressed and keeps things to herself—"

"Because Dat limits her activities away from home now? Watches her like a hawk?" Isaac had feared his father would feel slighted because he'd sent the check to his mother rather than to him, and that he'd take his anger out on Mamm.

She nodded, glancing away. "Bertha told me later that he snatched that check from her hand without a word. Since you've been gone, he refuses to say your name or speak of you, as though you no longer exist."

"I'm not surprised. And I'm sorry, for Mamm's sake."

Alma gazed at him sadly. "There's not much light in her life these days, except that you have found a job and a place to be amongst *gut* people who encourage you— folks she knows and trusts." She brightened a bit. "And she says you have a girlfriend!"

Isaac exhaled loudly. "I'm not so sure about that right now. The only thing you can predict about Maria— Lizzie Overholt's sister—is that she's unpredictable."

With a gentle laugh, Alma reached for his hand. "Your *mamm* sends you her love and encouragement, Isaac. Your *dat* has forbidden her to write or call you, or you'd have heard from her, you know."

"He's written me off as his son."

This revelation came as no huge surprise, yet it carried an emotional wallop. Isaac had spent most of his life at odds with his father, but he'd never considered the possibility of no longer having a family—because if his *dat* had declared him nonexistent and not welcome in the Chupp household, his brothers would go along with it.

It took a moment to untangle his injured feelings, at least enough to continue talking to Alma. But Isaac reminded himself that as bad as he felt, his mother was dealing with a much more negative situation every moment of every day.

"I wish I could snatch her away and bring her here," he whispered bitterly.

Alma nodded, squeezing his fingers to show her support. "That would only make things harder for Bertha when your father came to take her back to Coldstream. She's his wife. Your *dat*—and other Amish husbands—believe she belongs to him and must submit to his will and opinion."

"Which is one reason I *cannot* become Amish," Isaac spat. "The Old Order I've grown up in values punishment—shunning—far more than forgiveness. The Promise Lodge district is totally different," he clarified, "but I'm carrying too much baggage from my past to commit to the Amish faith. If Maria and I get our act together again, I'll become Mennonite so our marriage can be sanctioned by her church. If we don't—"

Isaac shrugged, not wanting to think about that possibility just yet. "We'll see."

Alma nodded, searching his face as though memorizing details she would pass along to his mother. Isaac knew it would take him a while to process all she'd told him, but he was extremely grateful that she'd sought him out.

"Tell Mamm I—I send her my love," he whispered. "And I'll do my best. And I'll get word to her now and again, in ways that Dat won't find out about."

"I'll do that, dear. You could write to her and send the letters to me," she added in a pensive tone. "Bertha and I still see each other fairly often."

Once again Alma gazed at him. "I'm so glad I got to talk to you," she said softly. "You're a different young man—changed for the better since the last time I saw you. I wish you all the best, Isaac."

As he wheeled Alma back to the picnic, Isaac's mind reeled with unforeseen sensations and sentiments. He parked her at the end of her table, kissed her wrinkled cheek, and walked away after sharing a quick, minimal conversation with Ezra and Raymond.

As he hurried away, Rosetta called out behind him. "How about some pie, Isaac? Or homemade ice cream? Come and join us!"

Come and join us.

Even as he shook his head and waved at her, Isaac was reminded of that old hymn about grace that was amazing—and being lost and then found. At long last he'd found himself, and the folks at Promise Lodge valued him as a member of their community. Even though Maria had rejected him, it was a sweet revelation to know that he was no longer alone.

He walked quickly across the lawn and ascended the stairs to his solitary apartment. He had a lot to think about.

Chapter 35

On Tuesday afternoon, Maria watched in awe as the appliance guys uncrated her new ovens and installed them. When the big stainless-steel refrigerator hummed to life, she applauded gleefully. She gazed at the new heavy-duty floor mixer she would use for bread dough, as well as the stand mixer on the back counter that would handle smaller jobs like frosting.

"Any questions?" the taller of the two installers asked as his assistant picked up the flattened cardboard crates and packing materials. "If you run into trouble, give us a call at that number on the side of your oven."

"I think I'm all set," Maria replied. "I need to look at the owner's manuals—"

"And don't forget to go online and register these items so their warranties will be valid," the short, blocky fellow put in. "You've invested a chunk of change in remodeling your business, so be sure everything's covered in case you have problems."

Maria watched them lower the large back door of their truck and drive off. She promptly tossed the owner's manuals into an empty drawer. Then she gazed at her kitchen for several minutes, looking at the shiny knobs, electronic screens, and digital timers.

Everything was so much newer and cleaner than what she'd lost in the fire. Maria felt like a princess in a fairy tale, living in a castle at long last. And with a computerized cash register and a laptop to be her management system—compliments of the school—her business had truly entered a new era.

She spotted a postcard on the floor. It was the registration form for the new ovens, so she took her seat at the laptop. After Sally had given her a crash course on running the register and the computer yesterday afternoon, Maria felt confident she could find the website and enter the model and serial numbers. How hard could that be?

As she painstakingly entered each letter and dot of the website, Maria wished she'd taken a typing class in school. After three corrections, she was sure she had it right, so she pushed the Return key.

Nothing happened.

Scowling, Maria deleted her original entry and started again. Sally had made this process look so easy! Maria had watched her agile fingers fly over the keys, nodding as the business teacher pointed out step-by-step ways to reach the places she needed to go online—

"Phooey!" Maria cried out when her second attempt failed. "This isn't the way it's supposed to—Isaac, why aren't you here doing your job?"

Silence. Except for the hum of the fridge, the bakery was so quiet that she missed the steady *click-click-click* of the battery clock that had burned in the fire. A little colored ball was spinning on her computer screen.

Maria shoved the wheeled stool backward as she stood up, suddenly too frustrated—too devastated—to try again. She had no clue how to run that computer! And she was too proud to call Sally at the school and ask for help, because it would never end—she would never understand the ins and outs of digital business.

"Why was I so stupid, going along with Isaac's idea about getting a computer—and about him being my business partner?" she wailed as tears rushed down her cheeks. "Why did I fall for him, anyway? And why did I believe everything he told me? It was the dumbest thing I've ever done!"

She yelled for a few more minutes, filling the bakery with her anger and desperation. But when she ran out of breath, collapsing on the wheeled stool, Maria realized she hadn't finished chastising herself.

No, the dumbest thing I've ever done was to let him drive the scooter back to Promise Lodge Saturday night. Now I'm stuck here without any way to get around.

And I can't open my bakery.

Maria locked up and stalked home via the alley so no one would see she was crying. Once inside the house, she went to the fridge and grabbed the first thing she saw—leftover pizza she'd shared with Isaac—and jammed a slice into her mouth. It had oozed cheese and been delicious when they had eaten it together, but now the cold crust and fillings were tasteless.

Which pretty much described her life without Isaac, didn't it? But after all the confidence—and cash—the women of Promise Lodge had invested in her, she could not spend the day bewailing her failure.

What would Ruby do? If Rosetta were here, what

would she suggest? In her mind, Maria heard Beulah telling her to get her act together—to be smart about it instead of losing herself in another pity party.

But eventually Isaac's handsome face came to mind. He was smiling, assuring her that together they could make the bakery not only successful but solvent. Why had she gotten so upset about his wedding plans that she'd driven him away without even considering his ideas?

Of course, he walked out! What man in his right mind would tolerate being prodded with a spatula? He probably rode home with the Kraybills, and he's working at Dale's store today. I'm sure he's put our fight behind him.

And he's convinced I'll never grow up.

With a sigh, Maria picked up her phone. As the number for the bulk store rang, she had no idea what she'd say if Dale answered—knew better than to interrupt Isaac while he was working—

"Kraybill's Bulk Store. How can I help you?"

Oh, Isaac, please can you forget all those idiotic things I did—

"*Jah*, hello? You've reached the bulk store at Promise Lodge—"

"Isaac, I—I need you," Maria blurted. "Please, can we talk? My computer quit and . . ."

Silence. After several moments, she wondered if he'd set aside the receiver and gone on about his work.

"We'll *talk*," he finally muttered. "But it'll have to wait until after the store closes." *Click.*

* * *

As Isaac reached the city limits of Cloverdale that evening, he slowed the scooter to a legal speed. Determined not to fall for Maria's curves and come-ons, he drove past the bakery. Through the big front windows, he saw her working in the kitchen.

He parked behind the building and went in the back door. Reviewing the stipulations he'd rehearsed in case she widened her eyes and spoke in her take-me voice, he stopped in the storeroom.

Maria was arranging bins of flour and commercial-sized boxes of other baking ingredients on the shelves above the back worktable. The new appliances glimmered in their places. From all outward appearances, she could open the bakery tomorrow if she chose to.

But Isaac knew better.

When she looked up at him, he nodded. Went straight to the laptop. "You probably hit a wrong key after you typed something," he suggested when the spinning ball came up. "Did Sally tell you to shut down and try again after a couple minutes?"

"Probably. I dunno," she admitted.

"Did she tell you all the school's files had been deleted?" he asked as he clicked a couple of boxes and flipped the power switch. "Were all the online caches emptied? Do you have the right programs installed to run *your* business, instead of whatever textbook businesses her students might have been learning with?"

Maria's confused frown was all the answer he needed.

"She showed me how to—Sally made it look so easy and I didn't want to seem stupid," she said forlornly, "so I . . . didn't tell her I've never worked on a computer before. *Denki* for coming, Isaac. I'm sorry I'm such an idiot. About so many things."

Rather than fall for the familiar whine in her voice, he sat down on the stool. Within a few minutes he'd confirmed that Ms. Swanson had done everything necessary to get a basic workable system ready for the bakery. When he swiveled to face Maria, he reminded himself to stick to business. It didn't help that she had a smudge of flour on her adorable nose.

"You're not an idiot, Maria," he began. "You could run this place again with your adding machine and receipt pads. Shall we discuss what else you've done that wasn't so smart?"

She scowled as though she might protest his brusque remark, but she paused before she spoke.

"I, um, shouldn't have attacked you with that spatula," she began. "I'm sorry."

Isaac fought a smile. "All right. And I shouldn't have spoken to Dale about wedding plans—or declared we were engaged—without discussing those matters with you first."

Maria's shoulders relaxed. "Some of the things you mentioned—like maybe getting married sooner, just the two of us—weren't such bad ideas," she admitted softly. "I guess the idea of having a bed in the storeroom got me off to a bad start."

"It's an unusual place to sleep," Isaac agreed. "But I was thinking of you, Maria. In a small town like Cloverdale, it's *your* reputation that would be toast if I lived with you, because you're the woman. I wanted the minister to believe we had honorable intentions."

"Oh."

Her delectable lips formed an O, but somehow Isaac

kept his seat. If he caved now and hugged her close, their serious discussion would be forgotten.

"I can also understand why you've envisioned a wedding like the ones you've attended at Promise Lodge, with lots of people and a big dinner," Isaac said. "And Zachary performed the Kraybills' ceremony at the lodge, so he'd probably do that for us, too."

Maria's lips curved slowly. "But if we did our counseling and got married soon after that, with just the minister and witnesses, we wouldn't have to do all that planning and *waiting*," she pointed out. "Trouble is, we'll need Social Security cards and photo ID's. And Amish don't believe in Social Security, right?"

Isaac was pleased that she'd thought of that issue. "Amish folks don't collect benefits, but because we often work for English employers—or just need a Social Security number to get by in an English world—I've got a card," he replied. "I also have a driver's license. I think it expires in September or October—"

"Then we'd better get married before that!" Maria blurted out.

Isaac smiled. He admired her enthusiasm—especially because Maria was including him in her future again.

"I'll use it after I became a Mennonite, *jah*?" he reminded her. "So, I should renew it anyway. And if *I* have anything to say about it, we'll be driving something better than a pink motor scooter."

Maria burst out laughing. She rushed toward him, flinging her arms around Isaac's neck. As he inhaled her light perfume and savored the way her body fit so enticingly against his, he dared to hope that today's rational conversation would be the first of many.

After they shared a long kiss, Isaac stood up, easing her away so they could talk some more. "Shall we decide what we want to do about our wedding, Maria? Will you marry me even though I suspect we'll fight now and then?"

It wasn't much of a proposal. Isaac wished he'd been more romantic during this special moment.

"Will you marry *me*? Even though my mouth races ahead of my brain?" Maria shot back.

Her earnest expression and heartfelt self-assessment touched Isaac deeply. Life with this woman would never be dull, even if he'd feel exasperated by Maria's tendency to speak first and think later.

"I will if you will," he whispered.

She blinked, but then realized that he'd answered her. "Oh, Isaac—I will, too! The past couple of days without you have been—well, I don't want to *ever* go through such a tough time again, not knowing if you love me enough to keep me around."

Isaac hugged her close. It didn't really matter that the most important conversation of their lives had been held in a bakery where dozens of folks might've looked in and seen them. He now believed that he and Maria stood a decent chance at a happily-ever-after—and it would be so much more satisfying than the fairy tale of her dreams.

Chapter 36

Vera's stomach fluttered as Bishop Monroe stood up to begin the wedding sermon.

Within minutes she and Fannie Kurtz, seated together on the front pew, would have new surnames and the husbands to go with them. The days leading up to August thirtieth had sped by in a flurry of planning. Yesterday, they'd welcomed the entire Brubaker and Overholt families to Promise Lodge, finding places for everyone to stay at the cabins or in friends' homes.

On the men's side of the meeting room, she caught Ezra's boyish grin as he shifted on the pew beside Eddie. He looked so handsome in the new black trousers and vest he'd gotten for the wedding, along with a shirt so white it seemed to radiate its own light in the lodge's meeting room. His appreciative gaze told Vera he liked her wedding dress of deep teal, a few shades darker than Fannie's dress. When the bishop cleared his throat, however, she faced forward to focus on his message.

"As we prepare to join Fannie with Ed and Vera with Ezra in marriage, let's reconsider the attributes Preacher Marlin read to us from the Bible, otherwise known as the fruits of the Spirit—the blessings the Holy Spirit grants us when we follow our Father God and His Son, Jesus Christ," Bishop Monroe said to the large crowd. "We don't often preach about these gifts at weddings, but why not? As these young couples begin their lives together it seems relevant to reflect upon them."

When the bishop smiled at the four of them, Vera felt enveloped by a sense of holiness. In the short time she'd known Monroe Burkholder, she'd come to understand that his love, faith, and strength were every bit as large and powerful as he was. What a blessing they all shared, that this man of God had come to live at Promise Lodge.

"As I often do, I'm going to replace some of the King James terminology with more modern words, so we don't miss out on this passage's meaning for our lives today," he said. "So, the fruit of the Holy Spirit refers to love, joy, peace, patience, kindness, generosity, faithfulness, gentleness, and self-control.

"These nine gifts don't just drop into our laps, however," Bishop Monroe continued as he gazed at the large crowd. "God wants us to work at them so we've invested ourselves and won't take them for granted— much like a *gut* earthly parent knows that free gifts often become forgotten gifts."

Vera noticed many of the men across the room nodding in agreement.

"A pertinent example of that is the way the Brubakers, Overholts, and Kurtzes have agreed to provide new houses for their children," the bishop said with a nod toward those parents, "with the understanding that Eddie will be doing the painting and finishing work while Ezra puts down money for clearing the lots. These young men will also be working alongside our local carpenters while

Vera, Fannie, and our other women provide lunches for them."

Bishop Monroe's face took on a glow that might have been from the morning sun, but Vera believed it was his own inner radiance.

"It delights me, the way folks here at Promise Lodge have always worked together as a community of faith—because our kindness, generosity, and love for one another translate into the joy of watching our young people take on their adult responsibilities. Our gentleness and patience when someone confesses a mistake bring the peace of forgiveness that passes all understanding.

"And if you've been keeping track," the bishop said with a chuckle, "you'll realize that I've just named eight of the nine fruits of the spirit that are so evident amongst us. The toughest one—for these young couples as well as older folks—is self-control. We humans want what we want when we want it. That's why it's so hard to rein in our physical and emotional desires so we can lead lives God would be pleased with."

Vera's eyes widened as she shared a fearful glance with Fannie.

Please, please, God, don't let Bishop Monroe preach about catching Ezra and me in the loft. And let's leave Fannie and Eddie out of it, too!

Vera's cheeks burned with embarrassment she was sure everyone in the room would interpret as guilt. She noticed Ezra and Eddie shifting nervously on their bench, as well. She was so caught up in her concerns that several moments and sentences went by before she let her shoulders relax.

Bless him, the bishop had kept the secrets about their

lack of self-control. Soon he was motioning for the four of them to come forward and stand before him. Vera was relieved that Bishop Monroe led her and Ezra in their vows first, so she could get her heart rate back to normal while Fannie and Eddie repeated the same age-old promises.

Next thing she knew, Ezra was kissing her. The meeting room rang with wild applause and cheering.

"I love you, Mrs. Overholt," her new husband whispered. "And I'm glad the stressful part's behind us."

"Amen to that," Vera said with a laugh. "I love you, too, Mr. Overholt. But I won't often call you that because it brings your *dat* to mind—not that there's anything wrong with him!"

"Fine by me," Ezra shot back. "And I promise I'll never confuse you with my mother!"

As they accepted the congratulations of their friends and family members, Vera knew the joy of this special day would be with her forever. Her only regret was that Aunt Minerva was home alone, resting so her baby would grow inside her for a few more months.

When she and Ezra had filled their plates at the steam tables, Vera peered into the kitchen. The Kuhn sisters were taking pans of brisket in barbecue sauce from the oven, as well as more hash brown casserole.

"When you get a free moment," Vera called back to them, "could you please make up a plate for Aunt Minerva? I don't want her to wait all afternoon for her dinner."

Ruby laughed as she picked up a picnic basket stashed behind the worktable. "It's ready when you are, sweetie."

"We figured you'd do that," Beulah put in, "because you're just that thoughtful and kind, Vera."

Ezra, who stood right behind her, said, "What if we put some foil on our plates and take that basket to Minerva right now? We can let Ed and Fannie entertain the crowd for a while, ain't so?"

Vera stepped into the kitchen, beaming. "See why I married this guy?" she crowed. "Who else would give up a place at the *eck* table to eat with the bride's aunt?"

"It's the sign of a perfect match," Beulah agreed as she tore off pieces of foil.

Ruby flashed them a thumbs-up. "And it's all *gut*. Give our best to Minerva."

Chapter 37

September sixth was the most terrifying day of Isaac's life, yet the most exhilarating. As he stood in the front of the Mennonite Fellowship's sanctuary with Zachary Miller and Maria, awaiting their witnesses, he felt the momentary urge to excuse himself to the restroom and escape.

But when Maria grasped his hands, gazing at him with her shining blue eyes, he knew he'd gone past the point of no return.

"Here we are," she whispered giddily, although her voice quavered with a touch of nervousness. "It's the day I've waited for most of my life, and because of you, Isaac, it's even better than I'd dreamed it would be."

He wanted to give a disclaimer—to tell her they would have some bumpy roads and disagreements, and that they were destined to disappoint each other from time to time. Maria would still throw pity parties and he would do things his own way because he thought he was more rational than she.

But this isn't the time or the place. I want to look back fifty years from now and recall the joy on Maria's beautiful face as we tied the knot.

The squeak of the metal entry doors alerted them to the arrival of the Kraybills and the Kuhns. They'd invited these folks, as well as Truman and Rosetta, to witness their ceremony—because where would they be without them?

Maria had asked Beulah and Ruby to attend so they wouldn't cook up a big feast or prepare a daylong celebration, because Isaac and Maria had agreed they wanted simplicity. And privacy. They were only taking off today before the bakery would be open again tomorrow.

"And there's the happy couple!" Ruby called out as she and her sister approached the front of the sanctuary in colorful floral-print dresses.

"Congratulations on your big day, Isaac and Maria!" Beulah put in. "I'll admit there were times I believed you'd not make it to the altar."

"And we'd have been disappointed if you hadn't asked us to come, as well," Dale put in as he shook hands with Isaac and the minister.

Irene slung her arms around Isaac and Maria, beaming at them. "*Jah*, we've had our questionable moments, ain't so?" she said with a chuckle. "But it's all worked out the way God intended. And the Cloverdale bakery has taken on a new life—"

"And everyone in town is delighted about that," Zachary added with a laugh. "I can attest that the chicken salad sandwiches, the cheesecakes, and the apple fritters are fabulous, because my waistbands seem to be shrinking." He glanced at his watch. "We're waiting for the Wickeys, right?"

"I hope Rosetta's not had a complication with the baby," Maria said with a concerned frown. "She's gotten really big, and her due date is still several weeks away."

"They'll be here," Beulah assured them kindly. "Truman and Rosetta are the most dependable folks I know. If they weren't going to make it, they'd have called us."

"*Jah*, Rosetta said she wouldn't miss this wedding for anything," Ruby put in with a nod.

Was it his imagination, or did the Kuhns and the Kraybills exchange a knowing glance? Isaac chalked this impression up to being antsy, wanting to get the exchange of vows behind him. Ezra and Ed had admitted that their minds had gone completely blank during the ceremony. They'd nearly lost the power to speak when Bishop Monroe had led them in their vows.

For a few minutes, Isaac and Maria sat awkwardly on the edge of the front pew, too uptight to join the conversation the Kraybills and the Kuhns were having with Zachary. The wedding should have started at ten o'clock and it was a quarter past. At what point would they decide to move on without—

The squeak of the front door made everyone look back. Truman and Rosetta entered with smiles and waves as they bustled inside, while—

Isaac froze. His mouth dropped open. He squinted to be sure he wasn't hallucinating.

"Mamm!" He shot down the center aisle, grateful that the Wickeys stepped aside so he didn't barrel into them. "How did you know—how did you come here without—"

When her arms closed around him, Isaac felt her trembling. Tears streamed down her dear, wrinkled face, but Isaac had never seen her look so incredibly happy. Mamm had lost weight since he'd left home. The dark circles beneath her eyes were more pronounced, but her eyes shone as she gazed at him. She was wearing the same black dress and pleated *kapp* she'd worn to church, weddings, and funerals for years, as befitted a bishop's wife.

Why hadn't Dat figured out she was up to something and prevented her from leaving the house?

"'Behold, I show you a mystery,'" his mother said with a chuckle. It was a Bible passage she'd quoted whenever she'd kept a secret from her sons. "All that matters is that we're together, and you're getting married, Isaac! It's a miracle! Plenty of time for revelations after the ceremony."

Somehow, he made it back to the front of the sanctuary with his arm around her and without crying, although he blinked rapidly, and his throat was tight. After he introduced his *mamm* to Maria, the minister, and the others, everyone relaxed. The six witnesses and Mamm sat in the front pews on either side of the aisle, and Zachary Miller began to speak.

Isaac was glad he and Maria had insisted on keeping the ceremony short and sweet, because the minister's opening remarks flew right past him.

Mamm has come all the way from Coldstream—somehow without Dat knowing—to see me get married. What kind of love is this, that she took such a risk to attend today?

"'Place me like a seal over your heart, like a seal on your arm,'" Miller was reading from his black notebook.

As the minister continued, Isaac recalled that the passage from the Song of Solomon had come from a newer translation he and Maria had found online. The verses about love being as strong as death—and burning like a blazing flame that even rivers couldn't quench—

had reminded them of their physical attraction as well
as the love that was deepening with each passing day.

When Maria glanced at him—and winked—Isaac
knew she wanted to be out of church and on to the
earthier joys of married life, just as he did.

He was glad Maria repeated her vows first. He was
even happier that he somehow got through his part of
the ceremony without mangling the phrases he was
required to say.

"Isaac and Maria, I pronounce you husband and
wife."

Without waiting for the usual prompt, Isaac embraced his sweet Maria and they kissed for several
shameless, blissful moments, oblivious to the folks
looking on from the pews. By the time they came up for
air, their witnesses had positioned themselves along
one side of the aisle in a receiving line.

One last formality and we're outta here.

Isaac held his mother again, delighted that she embraced Maria as though sincerely delighted with her
new daughter-in-law. As they hugged and thanked all
the folks who'd helped them reach this pinnacle moment,
Isaac was thinking of what to say to excuse the two of
them. It was time to dash down the street to the house.
Beulah was the last in line, so after they'd said all the
polite things—

"I know what you kids are thinking," Beulah teased
as she held him fast. She wrapped her arm around
Maria, too, while Ruby joined the huddle across from
her sister, preventing their exit.

"*Jah*, you've figured on having your own private
celebration," the younger Kuhn put in playfully, "but

there'll be plenty of time for that. Consider yourselves kidnapped!"

"I'll bring the truck to the door," Truman said. "Bertha, you and the newlyweds can ride with us."

"Off we go!" Beulah crowed. "You can join us in Dale's car, Zachary. You've earned a nice dinner, same as these kids have. They just *think* they don't want a Promise Lodge wedding celebration!"

Although some nice food and a small white cake awaited them at her house, Maria saw no graceful way to refuse the Kuhns' hospitality. It seemed best to let Isaac's mother sit between them in the back seat—and at least she would learn more about the Chupp family dynamics during the ride from Cloverdale. Because Isaac had told her how difficult his *dat* was, she hadn't pressed him to meet his parents and siblings.

The way Bertha Chupp held both their hands, gazing raptly at her son as she spoke, told Maria that this woman endured a great deal of continuous stress in her home.

"If it hadn't been for Alma Overholt telling me about your wedding day, I wouldn't have been here," she began in a tight voice. "Thank the *Gut* Lord you mentioned it to her when they were at Ezra's wedding. And we owe our thanks to Truman and Rosetta for going all the way to Coldstream to fetch me this morning."

Bertha inhaled deeply, as though she got short of breath imagining how things might have turned out differently. "I think God arranged for your *dat* and brothers to be at a big livestock auction all day. That made it easier for me to get away."

Maria blinked. Was this woman a prisoner in her

own home? Was Isaac's *dat* as controlling as Bertha made him out to be?

Isaac, however, wore a frown. "But what happens if Dat comes home and you're not there? Is it wise for you to spend the afternoon at a big dinner—"

"What's he going to do—kick me out?" Bertha countered boldly. "I watched my older sons get married and I refuse to snub you, Isaac.

"Besides," she added with a chuckle, "I've heard so many folks rave about the wedding meals those Kuhn ladies prepare. Why would I want to miss out on *that*?"

"And you'll get to visit with a lot of your friends from Coldstream," Rosetta pointed out from the front seat.

Truman nodded, catching Bertha's eye in the rearview mirror. "We'll take you back anytime you're ready," he assured her. "And we'll be happy to help with any explaining you might have to do if Obadiah's waiting for you. You've done nothing wrong, Bertha."

"*Denki* for understanding," Isaac's *mamm* murmured. "We'll cross that bridge when we come to it—and meanwhile, I want to get better acquainted with *you*, Maria."

Before they'd talked very long, the arched metal entry sign to Promise Lodge came into view. As soon as the truck passed beneath it, Maria's heart rose into her throat. Truman rolled down the windows, grinning.

A loud cheer arose from the crowd that lined both sides of the private road to greet them. All the folks she knew—and some she'd barely met—had given up their day's activities to spend the afternoon with her and Isaac. The redheaded Helmuth twins from the nursery, Sam and Simon, and their twin wives, Barbara and Bernice—who bounced toddlers on their hips—

were waving and applauding. Gloria and Cyrus Helmuth were there, too, as were his brother Jonathan and Laura, standing alongside Laura's sister, Phoebe, and her husband, Allen Troyer.

Maria could barely take it all in. Folks were applauding, laughing with the delight of the big surprise they were all a part of.

"Isaac and Maria, congratulations!" Ezra called out from beside Vera, Eddie, and Fannie. Preacher Marlin and his wife, Frances, waved excitedly alongside Harley. The next section of road was flanked by the Peterscheims, the Schwartzes, and Preacher Amos and Mattie.

"Let's hear it for another set of newlyweds!" Bishop Monroe declared, and another round of applause thundered around the truck. Christine waved both her hands, and beside her, Marlene and Lester Lehman did the same, as did Marlene's brother, Mose, and his tiny wife, Sylvia.

Lo and behold, a huge brown Clydesdale was coming down the road from the direction of the bishop's pasture, ridden by Lavern Peterscheim and Lowell Kurtz, who worked with the Burkholder horses every day.

"My word, that's the biggest horse I've ever seen!" Bertha exclaimed, wide-eyed. "And those two boys are riding it with just a training bridle. It's a long way to the ground if they fall."

As though to prove their mastery, Lavern steered the horse over to the side of the road to form the end of the receiving line. With wide grins, the two boys slid to the ground beside the Clydesdale as it stood perfectly still.

Isaac laughed. "Well, *that's* something we didn't see at Ezra or Ed's wedding!"

"These folks must think you two are pretty special," Bertha remarked.

When the crowd on the left parted, Truman drove the truck slowly toward the lodge. "We do," he agreed. "We've all seen the amazing way these kids have turned their lives around—"

"And we wouldn't have felt right letting them slip away to Cloverdale without a going-away party," Rosetta put in. "We're very proud of them, Bertha. And I'm so glad you could join us for their big day."

"Happy to be here," Isaac's *mamm* said in a voice choked with emotion. As she looked through the windshield, however, her expression brightened.

"My word, would you look at this lodge building! And that nice row of cabins, and the big garden plots we've passed," she said excitedly. "No wonder you Bender sisters wanted to come here and start over. From what I've seen so far, you've created your own little slice of paradise—and you've had lots of other folks come to join you."

"Our plans for happiness have succeeded beyond our wildest dreams," Rosetta agreed wistfully. "We've been blessed recently with several weddings and new homes for our young couples—and so many of us are carrying babies now that Bishop Monroe has declared we'll soon build a schoolhouse!"

The man in question had been striding alongside the truck, and when it stopped, he opened both doors on the passenger side.

"I understand the newlyweds have brought along another guest of honor," Bishop Monroe said, steadying Rosetta as she slid down from the truck's front seat.

"Mrs. Chupp, it's a special pleasure to welcome you to Promise Lodge for today's wedding meal."

Maria quickly stepped down and out of the way so the tall, sturdy bishop could reach in to help Isaac's mother.

Bertha paused with her legs over the edge of the seat, studying him as he enveloped her small, mottled hands with his larger ones. "Bless you," she murmured, holding his gaze. "I understand now why folks have so many fine things to say about you, Bishop."

Monroe Burkholder bowed slightly—or maybe he was just leaning in to assist Isaac's *mamm*. Either way, Maria stood in awe of his gracious tone as he spoke to the wife of a man who'd stirred up so much negativity for the residents who'd left the Coldstream district— and within his own family.

A loud racket immediately changed the mood. Ruby came out onto the lodge's porch, banging a metal spoon against the bottom of a cooking pot.

"Let's eat our dinner while it's nice and hot!" she called out to the crowd coming in from the road. "Many thanks to you ladies who kept an eye on the food so Beulah and I could attend the wedding!"

Ruby gestured for Maria, Bertha, and Isaac to enter first. And once they'd passed through the lobby they stopped to stare.

The dining room had been transformed into a scene from a fairy tale.

Maria clasped her hands, gazing at the beautiful tables set with a multitude of pastel tablecloths, the best white china, and sparkling glasses. Across the back wall hung a huge banner that said BEST WISHES, MARIA AND ISAAC!

The usual *eck* table for the wedding party was in the back corner, raised on a dais. And on the sideboard sat three tall wedding cakes! One was bridal white edged in glittery frosting, and one was the chocolate cake that had become a Promise Lodge wedding tradition. The third cake was three tiers, frosted a deep raspberry at the bottom and gradually lightening to a pale pink at the top—reminiscent of her apartment's paint scheme the first time she'd lived here.

"Oh, my," Maria whispered, blinking back tears. "Oh, Ruby, you shouldn't have—"

"But we did!" the woman in the flashy floral dress countered gleefully. "You surely know by now that Beulah and I will do things *our* way if it means more time to enjoy our friends and a lot of *gut* food."

"We couldn't ruin the surprise by asking what you kids wanted," Beulah put in from the steam table. "So, we cooked up a hodgepodge of various dishes everyone likes."

"Hodgepodge?" Bertha challenged. "This is a feast like I've never seen! Not the usual chicken and stuffing with creamed celery folks traditionally serve. And look at all those pies! And cookie platters. And three different cakes."

She turned to her son, shaking her head in wonder. "Isaac, I might never go home! What a fine life it would be, to live in one of the apartments upstairs and eat the Kuhns' cooking every day."

Maria pressed her lips together, determined not to cry. She had lived the life Bertha had just described— twice—and it was finally sinking in, just how well she'd been welcomed and cared for despite the many disruptions she'd caused. It was humbling to realize what a debt of gratitude she owed the Kuhns, Rosetta and her sisters, and all the other folks who'd put up with her hissy fits and erratic behavior.

And it's a miracle that they—and Isaac—love me anyway.

"Shall we fill our plates, sweetie?" her husband asked as he gently took her elbow. "A lot of folks are waiting for us to go first."

Maria had been too antsy to eat breakfast, so she was famished—and she had no idea what Isaac might've scratched up for his morning meal in the bakery's back room. As she spooned slivered ham in barbecue sauce onto a homemade roll and added large servings of macaroni salad and slaw alongside it, she reminded herself that if she took such large portions her plate wasn't going to hold everything that looked and smelled so delicious. She chose a fried chicken leg anyway, along with items from the relish tray and helpings of fresh fruit salad and baked beans.

"This is insane," she whispered to Bertha, who was coming along behind her. "I can't possibly eat this much—"

"Puh!" her new mother-in-law teased. "We'll see who gets up first to fetch pie and cookies. I'm not missing out on *any* of this wonderful-*gut* food!"

As the three of them sat down in the center places at the raised table, Maria was pleased that Ezra and Vera took their seats to Isaac's right. It was a total surprise when Raymond and a very round, waddling Lizzie slipped through the kitchen to take the seats to her left.

As Maria embraced her little sister, she whispered, "I should've invited you two to the wedding, but we were determined to—"

"It's just as well," Lizzie admitted. "I can't ride any distance these days without stopping to pee. Better to come here than to go all the way to Cloverdale."

As the younger Overholts went to fill their plates, Bertha protested about sitting between the bride and groom. But Isaac silenced her.

"I'll be with Maria for years, Mamm," he said as he forked up some steaming green beans, "but how often will we get to sit with *you*? Besides, you already have friends coming up to see you—as befits the guest of honor."

Maria nodded, chewing a mouthful of her delectable ham sandwich. For the next several minutes she could only snatch a bite here and there because after Preacher Amos and Mattie had congratulated the three of them, Preacher Eli and Alma Peterscheim did the same. Then Roman Schwartz introduced his wife, Mary Kate, and toddler David to Bertha, and Roman's brother, Noah, came up with Deborah and little Sarah. The families from Coldstream seemed genuinely delighted to see Isaac's *mamm* . . . maybe because his contentious *dat* wasn't with her.

As these friends inquired about Isaac's many older siblings and their families, Maria realized that the small, wrinkled woman beside her had raised a houseful of children while dealing with the higher expectations—and agitation—that came with being the unpopular Bishop Obadiah's wife. Isaac's mother had also dealt with her husband's frustrations when the three Bender sisters and Amos had broken away from the Coldstream district and had been followed by so many other families these past few years.

Bertha's busy, encumbered years of turmoil suddenly made Maria's routine seem like child's play.

Compared to Isaac's mamm, I've had nothing to be upset about. Yet I've fussed and fumed about every little situation that didn't go my way.

Maria blinked. She hadn't expected to have such serious thoughts on her wedding day, yet she realized that this major life event might bring her even more unanticipated wisdom. Who knew how often she and Isaac would get to visit with his mother?

When the well-wishers who'd lived in Coldstream had greeted Bertha, Maria leaned closer to her. She *liked* Isaac's mother, who showed spunk and an inner strength most women hadn't had to develop.

"If you were going to give me any advice about dealing with the ups and downs of marriage," she said softly, "what would it be? Not that Isaac isn't a wonderful man—"

"Oh, trust me, dear, you'll have times when you don't like him much, even though you're crazy for him right now."

Bertha laid her fork aside to take Maria's hand. Her skin felt papery but there was no mistaking the grip she'd developed after years of managing her household.

"I couldn't get through my day without God's word— because He won't argue with everything I say, like some men I could mention," she began pensively. "I start in the morning with the Twenty-Third Psalm, which reminds me the Lord's my shepherd and that I have everything I need. By the time I've gotten through the noon meal, I remind myself of that verse in Philippians about how 'I can do all things through Christ who strengthens me'."

Bertha paused, gazing out over the folks who were being seated at the long tables in front of them. "And at night, after a long day," she said with a sigh, "it's the verse in the first chapter of John about how God's light shines in the darkness, and the darkness can't overcome it. Or the verse in Psalms about how weeping might fill the night, but joy comes in the morning."

She shook her head. "Not very uplifting advice for a new bride—and when I was your age, I was too busy wiping noses and butts to think about such things," Bertha added with a rueful chuckle. "But as the years pass, you come up with ways to work around whatever life dumps at your doorstep."

Isaac's mother focused intently on Maria for several seconds. A smile eased over her careworn face. "After meeting you and witnessing how my Isaac has turned himself around, however," she said softly, "I can add some verses about grace and hope and thanksgiving to my day. *Denki* for that, Maria. You're a lifesaver."

Maria's eyes widened. The only lifesavers she'd known were round candies with a hole in the center.

"And you're amazing, Mamm," Maria murmured. "May I call you that? I—I lost my mother years ago."

The name had felt perfectly natural coming out. Maria was delighted to see the shine returning to Bertha's eyes as she nodded.

When Isaac rose from his seat and came to stand behind her, Maria gazed up at him with a new under-standing. It seemed marriage would require more effort than she'd envisioned in her fairy-tale fantasies—

But didn't this day turn out exactly the way I wanted it? With a big party and happy people in a room specially decorated for Isaac and me—and with three *cakes?*

Her new husband leaned down to whisper in her ear, to speak beneath the happy chatter that filled the dining room. "You were right, sweetie," he admitted. "A wedding day calls for a big celebration with all the trimmings—as only the Kuhn sisters can do it. I hope we can always remember how our dreams came true today and celebrate our love every day of our lives."

"Words to live by," Maria agreed.

And as Isaac kissed her, their hopes soared even higher.

Epilogue

Wisps of snow blew past as Vera gazed out the birthing center's waiting room window. The doctor had instructed Aunt Minerva to come a couple of days ago to ensure the baby's safe delivery, and at last, in a room down the hall, she was in the final stages of labor.

Uncle Harley had been such a bundle of nerves that the mother-to-be had quietly asked Vera to come with them—and because Fannie enjoyed helping Vera in the lodge's schoolroom, she was with the scholars now. Vera had spent the two nights in a cozy guest room while Uncle Harley had bunked in Aunt Minerva's room—although she doubted either of them had rested much.

Uncle Harley, poor man, looked haggard and exhausted. He was pacing again, grimacing each time his wife cried out. Vera found Aunt Minerva's painful outbursts unnerving as well, but she focused on the miracle taking place. She prayed that the birth was going as it was supposed to, and that mother and child would be healthy.

Around eleven—just as the sunshine pierced the

wintry gloom outdoors—they heard a tiny wail that blossomed into a birth announcement.

"Your baby has a fine set of lungs!" Vera said with a laugh. "Mark this date—November second!"

Harley turned toward the hall, listening closely. As it dawned on him that Minerva's birthing struggle was finally behind her, his face eased into a smile. "By golly, she did it! She made it through this time and—and—"

A stalwart woman in aqua scrubs and a plastic cap over her hair entered the waiting room. "Mr. Kurtz, congratulations! You have a son!" she said, beaming at him. "If you'll give us a few minutes to clean everybody up, you can have a look at him. He's a little fellow, but he and Minerva are doing just fine."

"Oh, but that's *gut* news," Vera said as she rose from her chair. "I'll freshen up a bit while you go in first, Uncle Harley. You've waited a long time for this moment."

In her room, she smoothed her hair and used the bathroom, allowing time for the new father to get acquainted with his boy. When her excitement got the best of her, however, she peered into Aunt Minerva's room—and saw that her uncle was standing about five feet away from the bed, peering anxiously at the baby in his wife's arms.

"You won't drop him, Harley," Aunt Minerva insisted tiredly. "After all the lambs you've delivered, this little bundle shouldn't be a challenge."

When Vera caught sight of the tiny, wrinkled face resting on Aunt Minerva's shoulder, her breath escaped her in a grateful sigh. "Oh, would you look at this boy," she whispered.

"Would you like to hold him, Vera? Show your uncle how it's done?"

Holding her breath, Vera approached the bed. Aunt Minerva's auburn hair was in a braid trailing down her shoulder. She was wearing a clean hospital gown, propped up in the reclining bed. She looked pale and worn out, but deliriously happy as she lifted her blanketed son.

"Meet Joseph," she said. "We decided a while back that we'd name a boy after my *dat*—your grandfather."

"Joseph," Vera whispered, in awe as she slipped her arm beneath him and held his sweet, warm weight against her. "*Jah*, you're no bigger than a minute, but right now you're the whole world. Come and see your *dat*. He's shy."

Uncle Harley gazed wide-eyed at his son but made no move to hold him. "How do you do that? You make it look so easy," he admitted sheepishly.

Vera shifted the baby higher on her arm, giving her uncle a better view of Joseph's puckered little face. "When you're the oldest child and you're a girl, this goes with the territory," she explained. "Why don't you sit in the recliner with him, and I'll call Marlin and Frances to tell them he's here? He's being very quiet and nice right now."

Harley, a stocky man, filled the recliner when he sat—and Vera didn't give him time to get jittery again. She slipped the baby into his arms and stepped away.

"Can I bring you anything after I call?" Vera asked as she turned in the doorway.

Aunt Minerva had slipped off to sleep. Uncle Harley was gingerly holding his son—and by the time she'd reached her room next door, Joseph was starting to fuss.

She dialed the number for Marlin's phone shanty and waited for the answering machine's prompt. "Your new grandson has arrived," Vera said happily. "His name is Joseph, and I'm thinking either Fannie or I should stay on as a mother's helper for a while because, well— Uncle Harley's very nervous and Aunt Minerva's exhausted.

"But it's all *gut*," she added quickly. "They've got their little miracle. He's the answer to a lot of prayers."

As Rosetta checked into the birthing center, her pains were getting progressively sharper and deeper—which was exhilarating but terrifying. She was trying not to let Truman know just how badly they hurt, but once he slipped out to use the restroom, she cried out full-force.

Dr. Blanchard grasped her hand, smiling kindly. "No turkey dinner for you tomorrow, dear," she said. "Let's see how you're doing, shall we?"

Rosetta laughed wryly. "Puh! Looks like I've swallowed the turkey whole, ain't so? You've told me all's well with the baby to this point, so I'm putting this delivery in God's hands and yours."

"That's the best attitude you could have, and I'll give God the best assist I can," the doctor said. "The baby you take home will be so much more satisfying than anything you could've put on the table this year."

Rosetta did her best to keep this positive attitude in mind as the daylight passed into the most miserable night she'd ever spent. When Christine and Mattie slipped into the room to be with her and Truman, a part of her mind was able to relax even as her labor became more intense.

"Almost there, dear. Stay with me now, so when I tell you to push hard, you can."

Christine wiped her face with a cool washcloth while Mattie leaned close to whisper in her ear.

"Play along, all right, little sister? Imagine you're at Promise Lodge, and the room is full of all your friends and family," she said in a low, mesmerizing tone. "And when you feel you can't possibly push one more time, turn it over to the biggest, strongest fellow you know—"

"That would be Monroe," Rosetta rasped as the pressure in her abdomen surged with the next pain.

"So let Monroe push for you," Christine joined in, speaking on Rosetta's other side. "And if it helps, imagine one of his Clydesdales pulling the baby out while Monroe is pushing—"

"And everyone else is cheering you and Monroe and that horse to do your very best," Mattie continued more urgently. "And before you know it—"

"Oh! *Oh!*" The images in Rosetta's mind suddenly grabbed hold. With a wild sense of release the baby left her body. A few moments later she heard a dainty little hiccup that escalated into a steady wail.

"Good job, Rosetta!" the doctor crowed. "We'll check this little lady over and clean her up so you and Truman and your sisters can see who we're most thankful for this year."

Rosetta burst into tears, yet she'd never felt so elated. Truman was hugging her, and her sisters were grabbing her hands. As exhaustion hit her like a truckload of bricks, all she really wanted was to sleep uninterrupted for days—

But the blanketed bundle the doctor placed in Rosetta's arms gave her another heady, giddy shot of adrenaline. Dr. Blanchard excused herself to give the family some time with their newest member.

"Look at you," she whispered as tiny hands began to wave and little feet kicked against the blanket. "You surely must be the grace of God come down from heaven—"

"And wouldn't that be the perfect name for her?" Truman said in an awestruck voice. "Grace. Grace Wickey."

"Grace Irene," Rosetta proposed, loving the sound of it immediately.

"It's perfect," Mattie said as she looked on adoringly.

"Oh, but she's precious," Christine whispered. "Proof that our faith has paid off and that God is *gut*—"

"All the time," Mattie, Rosetta, and Truman chimed in.

When Christine opened her arms, Rosetta watched a cryptic smile flicker on her sister's lips as she handed the baby to her. Maybe Christine was thinking ahead to the day when she'd be holding Phoebe's and Laura's babies—her first grandchildren. Or maybe her older sister was wistful because she hadn't been able to have any more children.

"Well, you and Truman have your little miracle at last," Christine said in a voice that shimmered with emotion, "but I'm going to do you one better. I waited to be sure all was well with you and little Grace before I told you this—"

Rosetta and Mattie exchanged a wide-eyed gaze.

"—but Monroe and I have just learned that I'm carrying a child."

Rosetta sucked in her breath, her exhaustion forgotten. "But after Laura was born, your doctor told you—"

Christine burst into giddy laughter as she held

Grace close. "It seems the *Gut* Lord—and Monroe— had a different opinion! Needless to say, we're over the moon—and *jah*, we're also over the hill—"

"No, you're not! I know plenty of *mamms* who've had babies in their forties," Mattie crowed as she hugged Christine fiercely. "Oh, but this is fabulous news!"

"And after all the years Monroe went childless— because his first wife kept miscarrying—" Truman put in excitedly. "It's a wonder he hasn't exploded with the news or blurted it out before you were ready to share it."

"We just confirmed it with Dr. Blanchard a couple of days ago," Christine clarified. "She's going to keep close watch over me, so we're in *gut* hands. I'm due around the end of June, and I'm thinking the power of your prayers will work wonders for me, just as they did for Rosetta and Minerva."

"Not only *our* prayers," Mattie put in resolutely, "but the best wishes—the unshakable confidence—of every- one at Promise Lodge will be with you all the way. How can you lose, Christine?"

Christine nodded, blinking back tears. "I have to say it, sisters—when we sold our farms and bought that deserted campground, it was the best decision we *ever* made."

"Amen to that," Truman agreed.

Rosetta sighed wearily but with a deep sense of joy. "We'll keep on planning for happiness, long into the next generations," she declared. "Our faith hasn't failed us yet."

From the Promise Lodge Kitchen

Where do you get the best food ever? At potlucks! Women always bring their tastiest dishes and desserts, so this recipe section features great food that Beulah, Ruby, Vera, and the other Promise Lodge ladies have prepared in this story . . . which means that *I* have made these recipes and shared them with friends before I included them! As always, I lean toward ingredients already in my pantry, and—like most Amish cooks—I sometimes start with convenience foods rather than doing everything totally from scratch.

These recipes are also posted on my website, www.CharlotteHubbard.com. If you don't find a recipe you want, please e-mail me via my website to request it—or to let me know how you liked it!

—*Charlotte*

Dilly Potato Salad

I've never been a fan of potato salad with goopy dressing, so this recipe with chopped slices of dill pickle is now my go-to recipe! Rather than boiling the potatoes, I prefer to bake them directly on the oven rack, let them cool, and then peel them.

1½ pounds red potatoes, baked or boiled, then
  peeled and cubed
2 hard-boiled eggs, diced
¾ cup dill pickle slices, drained and finely chopped
½ cup celery, diced
4 green onions, thinly sliced
½ cup mayonnaise
½ cup sour cream or plain Greek yogurt
1 tsp. Dijon or yellow mustard
2 T. pickle juice
2 T. fresh lemon juice or cider vinegar
2 tsp. dried dillweed
Salt and pepper to taste

Either bake or boil the potatoes until firm but not overdone—timing on this depends on the size of the potatoes. Let cool, peel, and then cut into bite-sized cubes. (If you like the peel, leave it on.)

In a large bowl, combine the potato cubes, diced eggs, pickles, celery, and onions. In a smaller bowl, mix the remaining ingredients and then pour this dressing over the potato mixture. Mix well and place in a serving bowl. Cover and chill for a few hours or overnight. Serves 4-6.

No-Bake Peanut Butter Chocolate Bars

A luscious pan of bars without heating up the kitchen! These disappear fast!

- 1½ sticks melted butter
- 1 cup coarsely chopped dry roasted peanuts
- 1 7-inch sleeve of round, buttery crackers, crushed into coarse crumbs
- 1½ cups powdered sugar
- 1 cup crunchy peanut butter
- ¼ cup smooth peanut butter
- 1 10–12 oz. bag semisweet chocolate chips

In a medium bowl, combine the melted butter, peanuts, crackers, powdered sugar, and crunchy peanut butter. Spread on the bottom of an ungreased 9"x13" pan. In another bowl, melt the chocolate chips and creamy peanut butter (double boiler, or microwave in 1-minute intervals) and stir until smooth. Pour this topping over the peanut butter/cracker mixture, spreading to cover it evenly. Chill 15 minutes and cut into squares (if you wait too long, the topping will crack!). Freezes well, or store with waxed paper between layers.

Kitchen Hint: Put the crackers in a sealable quart bag and crush with a rolling pin.

Easy Fudge

Chocolate candy doesn't get any faster or easier! Amish folks would melt the chocolate and condensed milk in a double boiler, but a microwave works well, too.

> 2 12-oz. bags semisweet chocolate chips (4 cups)
> 1 14-oz. can sweetened condensed milk
> 2 T. water
> 2 tsp. vanilla
> 1½ cups chopped walnuts (optional)

Line a 9"x9" pan with waxed paper; set aside. On the stove: Melt the chocolate chips, milk, and water in a double boiler over boiling water, stirring until completely blended. In a microwave: Use a large microwave-safe bowl to melt the chips, milk, and water, and cook on High one minute at a time, stirring after each interval, until melted and blended. Add the vanilla and nuts, if desired, and pour into the lined pan. Chill about 20 minutes before cutting into squares. Store in an air-tight container with waxed paper between layers.

Kitchen Hint: For thinner pieces, use a larger pan.

Ruby's Best Chocolate Chip Cookies

The secret to these cookies is to remove them from the oven while they're puffy and underdone, so they firm up on the baking sheet. These freeze well, so you can always have some on hand!

2½ cups packed brown sugar
1½ cups butter-flavored vegetable shortening
¼ cup milk
2 T. vanilla
2 eggs
3½ cups flour
2 tsp. salt
1½ tsp. baking soda
2 10–12 oz. bags of semisweet chocolate chips

Preheat oven to 350° F. Cover cookie sheets with parchment paper. Cream the brown sugar, shortening, milk, and vanilla until light and fluffy. Beat in the eggs. Combine the flour, salt, and soda, and gradually mix into the batter until blended. Stir in the chocolate chips. Drop the dough by rounded tablespoons onto the prepared cookie sheets and bake about 8-9 minutes, or until just lightly browned—don't overbake! Remove from oven and allow cookies to sink and set on the cookie sheet before removing to a rack to cool completely. Makes about 6 dozen.

Kitchen Hint: You can replace one bag of the chocolate chips with either peanut butter or butterscotch chips.

Pistachio Pudding Salad

Here's a throwback to the era when we made a lot of "salads" that were really desserts! Always a hit at a potluck gathering.

    1 3.4-oz. box instant pistachio pudding
    1 20-oz. can crushed pineapple with juice
    1 8-oz. tub of whipped topping, thawed
    2 cups miniature marshmallows
    ¾ cup coarsely chopped pecans (optional)

In a large bowl, combine the pudding mix and the pineapple, stirring until the pudding is dissolved. Add the whipped topping, then fold in the marshmallows and pecans, if using them. Pour into a serving bowl. Cover and chill 3-4 hours or overnight.

Kitchen Hint: For more fun and flavor, use multicolored fruit-flavored mini marshmallows!

Turn the page
for more novels in the heartwarming
Promise Lodge series.

Family Gatherings at Promise Lodge

Charlotte Hubbard

With two spring weddings to celebrate, friends and family are reunited at the Amish community of Promise Lodge, where nothing—and no one—can derail an unexpected new love when it's part of a glorious plan . . .

In the year since he lost his wife in a tragic accident, Lester Lehman has found healing and purpose—helping construct Dale Kraybill's new bulk store, enjoying the Kuhn sisters' hearty meals, and settling into a tiny, built-for-one lakeside house. Falling in love again is surely not on Lester's mind. Yet despite his firm "no," two available ladies have set their *kapps* on the handsome widower—in a boisterous rivalry that weaves mayhem among the wedding festivities . . .

A welcome escape comes from a fresh-faced newcomer. Marlene Fisher disarms Lester with her witty quips on his romantic predicament, while her sparkling eyes inspire surprising thoughts of a shared future. But the heartbreak that brought Marlene to Promise Lodge runs deep, and the pretty *maidel* believes she's not meant to marry. In a season of vows to love and honor, Scripture holds the key to building their happiness together: love is kind, and above all . . . *patient*.

Hidden Away at Promise Lodge

Charlotte Hubbard

There are no secrets among Missouri's Amish community of Promise Lodge, as they share their joys, burdens, and blessings. But two visitors with a hidden agenda bring some surprising revelations— and unexpected saving graces . . .

When Karen Mercer and Andi Swann come to Promise Lodge for a week's stay, the Kuhn sisters quickly detect the guests are not Plain folk, despite their *kapps* and homemade dresses. Entranced by the idyllic Amish lifestyle they've read about in romance novels, the visitors have gone undercover to revisit the place that was once the church camp where they spent happy summers. They mean no harm— but when the truth is uncovered, their deception has an intriguing impact on the faithful, hardworking community . . .

Meanwhile, amid bustling preparations for a spring wedding, a shy horse trainer is encouraged to share his colorful world with a newcomer awaiting a miracle . . . while the widowed baker of luscious Promise Lodge Pies sees a longtime friendship in a romantic new light. And in the wake of a destructive storm, Karen and Andi's insider knowledge of the grounds may offer the safe passage they all need to renew and rebuild—stronger than ever . . .